HOT PURSUIT

JENNIFER BERNARD

PROLOGUE

THE KNIGHT BROTHERS ALWAYS DID THINGS THEIR OWN WAY. Honoring their father's passing with a pre-dawn plunge into the creek behind their property made complete sense to them.

It was the only time the old man had ever seemed happy—fishing in the stream with his army buddies when they came through Jupiter Point. Robert Knight had been a respected figure in town and a strict disciplinarian with his family. Sitting around a stuffy room with a bunch of other people who love-hated the man held no appeal. His children would honor him in their own damn way.

Will Knight, as the oldest of the four brothers, went first. From their favorite spot on the flat rocks above the gully, he dove through the ghostly morning mist into the rippling water. Ice closed over his head, a violent shock to his system.

Just like murder was.

He broke the surface, gasping. *Murder.* Dad had been murdered. And no one knew who had done it. But *someone* must know. That was the thought that kept him up at night. *Someone* knew.

"Still alive down there?" Tobias called to him, softer than he normally would because of the early morning hush of the surrounding woods.

"Give me a minute, don't know yet." Half panting, half laughing, he kicked his feet against the current to stay in place. "Come on, you wusses. Am I the only one man enough to take the plunge?"

"Nothing manly about hypothermia," Ben said. He was crouched on the rock, ready to tip over into a dive. "Something important might get frostbite."

Aiden, the youngest brother, still only eight, laughed like a drunken hyena. His spiky blond hair and wide eyes made Will's heart ache. What was going to happen to Aiden?

Their father had been found dead six weeks ago. Will had stepped out of his Constitutional Law class to receive the news in a phone call from Tobias, the second oldest brother. After delivering that bombshell, Tobias had added, "Mom's a mess. How soon can you get here?"

Will had immediately flown home from his law school in Arizona. The police had quickly determined Dad's death to be murder. Shortly after that, Mom had left, saying she needed some time to deal with the situation. Their sixteen-year old sister Cassie had insisted on going with her.

A mess. The whole situation was a mess. A godawful, gut-wrenching mess.

Tobias cannonballed into the creek. Tobias was a big guy, the strongest of them all, and he made a gigantic splash that nearly swamped Will. When he surfaced, water streamed off his dark hair as he gave a wild "whoop."

He paddled over to Will, who was busy spitting water out of his mouth. "I got news," he said.

"What, that you're a jackass?" Will swiped a bit of river debris off his neck. "I've known that for twenty years."

"You say jackass, I say badass." Tobias smirked as he treaded water.

On a normal day, Will might continue the back and forth. It was what they did, as Knight brothers. But today wasn't normal, no matter how much they tried to pretend. Everything was changing. Will felt it in the current swirling at his feet, the mist hovering in the air. "Okay, badass, what's your news?"

"I'm joining up. Saw the recruiter yesterday. Army, like Dad. I figure, I don't know. It's the best place for me right now."

Will's stomach dropped. He didn't want Tobias to leave, but his brother was right. He'd always been the wildest, the angriest of them all. He was a force to be reckoned with, the one most likely to clash with Dad. If Tobias didn't get a handle on his volcanic emotions, he might head down a bad path, and fast.

"Good move," he finally said.

"What is?" Ben's head popped up near them, sleek as a honey badger's. While Will and Tobias had been talking, he'd slipped into the water. Probably while making some kind of funny face to amuse Aiden. He was eighteen, soon to graduate high school, a mixture of bravado and vulnerability.

"Tobias has boot camp in his future. Better practice your 'Sir, yes sir', bro."

Ben blinked water out of his eyes. "Shut the fuck up."

Will frowned at him, surprised by his rattled tone. "What's wrong?"

"This friend of Dad's called me up, he runs an Air Force ROTC program at State. He thinks I should join. I could be a pilot."

Ben had been obsessed with flying since he was a kid. Will couldn't imagine anything more perfect for him than the Air Force.

"But I told him I wasn't sure. I should stick around here. What if Mom doesn't come back, what about the investigation, what about—"

"No," Will interrupted firmly. "Do it. Go. It's what Dad would want. Mom too, if she could get her head clear."

His two brothers stared at him.

"I got this. I'm not going back to law school. I need to be here. For whatever happens. For everything you said. The police investigation, Cassie, Mom—"

From the bank of the creek, Aiden whistled and waved at them. When they looked in his direction, he performed a goofy little dance before launching himself off the rock. He was still airborne when Will finished his sentence. "For Aiden."

Their youngest brother hit the water with a splash like an exclamation point. Or like a clash of cymbals, separating before and after.

It would be eleven years before all four Knight brothers found themselves in the same place at the same time again. Jupiter Point. Home. Where all the same questions still burned.

1

THE JUPITER POINT SHERIFF'S PRESS CONFERENCE WAS JUST GETTING underway when Merry Warren claimed her spot at the front of the small pack of reporters. As a workaholic and multi-tasking maniac, she'd been working on three other things during the drive from town. Between a phone interview, prepping questions for the sheriff, and breakfast in the form of coffee-from-a-cupholder, it was a miracle she'd made it in time.

She pulled out her little reporter's notebook. At the lectern set up outside the public safety compound, Sheriff Perez was reading a statement about a recent arson spree in the campgrounds and wilderness areas near Jupiter Point.

"Did I miss anything?" she whispered to a camera operator from one of the local cable channels.

"I'm missing my pillow, that's all I know." He yawned hugely, as if he couldn't possibly be more bored.

For Merry, any chance of boredom vanished when her gaze landed on the man standing just behind the sheriff.

Deputy Will Knight.

The tall deputy's hands were clasped behind his back, his

stance relaxed, but every line of his broad-shouldered, long-legged body warned, "don't mess with me."

Under his deputy's baseball cap, his cool gray eyes met hers. He showed no reaction to the sight of her, not even the irritation she normally got from him. Which was totally mutual. Deputy Slow-Mo, as she'd nicknamed him, was the most frustrating law enforcement officer she'd worked with in her three years in Jupiter Point. He ought to have "no comment" tattooed on his forehead. Even getting that "no comment" took forever; sometimes she thought he dragged the process out just to mess with her.

She screwed up her nose at him. Childish, she knew. But Will Knight had a way of bringing out the brat in her. He stared impassively back. He could have been one of the royal guards at Buckingham Palace for all the reaction he showed.

Sheriff Perez was finally reaching the end of his prepared statement. Since she already had a hard copy of it, she didn't bother taking notes.

Instead, she indulged herself with one more moment of tweaking Will Knight. She made another ridiculous face at him, twisting her features and lifting her upper lip in a snarl.

Was that a smile denting one corner of his firmly etched mouth? His eyes flicked away from her, as if he was trying to keep from laughing. Yes! Mr. Cool and Confident wasn't quite as oblivious as it seemed at first.

"Ms. Warren, did you have a question?" The sheriff's abrupt shift from reading his statement to addressing her directly made her jump.

"Oh. Yes, sir. I absolutely do have a question." She scrambled for her mental list of questions. One of her best assets as a reporter was her crystal-clear memory. She still wrote everything down, just to be safe, but she rarely forgot anything. "I'm sure readers of the *Mercury News-Gazette* will want to know if there's any risk of this arsonist striking inside the town itself."

"That hasn't been his pattern so far."

"'His'? Are you saying the arsonist is male?"

Sheriff Perez shuffled the papers on his podium. "We can't say that definitively, but most arsonists are male. We're working with a very specific profile on this one."

"Does it seem strange that, with such a specific profile, you don't have any suspects yet?"

Perez shot her a weary look. No other reporter ever asked as many follow-up questions as she did. "We're getting there, Ms. Warren. I have my best deputy on the case." He tilted his head toward Will. "He has a ninety-eight percent arrest rate. I'm sure we'll have a suspect soon."

He looked hopefully at the other reporters in the gaggle, but no one else stepped in with a question. So Merry waved her hand again.

"Is there a chance this is more than an arson spree and that's why you haven't been able to track down a suspect?"

"How about I let the deputy in charge take this one?" Sheriff Perez beckoned Will to the podium.

Will stepped to the microphone with as much wariness as if it were a snake. The TV reporter behind her gave a low, "mmm," as he arranged his long body behind the podium. Merry knew just how she felt. Will Knight was one long, tall drink of water.

Possibly spiked with valium for that extra dose of Slow-Mo.

"Can you repeat the fantasy...uh," he coughed, "I mean, question?"

Merry lifted her chin. She'd been following this particular story for a while and had a theory. No good-looking sheriff's deputy was going to mock it out of her. "My question is, since the profile doesn't seem to be resulting in a plethora of likely suspects, is there a chance you're working from an incorrect theory on the case? That it's not a typical arson spree but something different?"

"Such as? I'm all ears. Nothing we like better than having the press take care of business for us."

"Well, I'm wondering if you've considered the possibility that the fires might be related to the recent uptick in opioid arrests near Jupiter Point?"

"Absolutely." Will nodded soberly. "We've also looked into potential ties to the increase in unicorn spottings in the Sierras."

A titter ran through the crowd. Sheriff Perez, just beyond Will's shoulder, beamed. Merry's face heated.

Oh, that Will Knight, he was going to pay for this. It was one thing to deny, another to mock. And Will, with his dry, deadpan, slowpoke manner, knew how to slip the knife in.

No problem. Merry came from the mean streets of Brooklyn and could take care of herself. "Very thorough, thank you. Meanwhile, do you have anything to say to the tax-paying families in Jupiter Point who are wondering why a serial arsonist has been at large for more than six months?"

Will's calm gray gaze sparked with annoyance. *A-ha.* There was the irritation Will Knight usually showed around her. She'd take irritated over impassive any day.

"The families of Jupiter Point know we're working to keep them safe. And the *Mercury News-Gazette* can do its part by urging everyone to keep their eyes open for anything suspicious, especially if they're out hiking, fishing, or camping. Now if that's it for questions, we'll wrap things up here and get back to work."

Merry raised her hand again. "One more. Who's going to be in charge while Sheriff Perez is on his honeymoon? Congratulations, by the way, Sheriff."

Sheriff Perez shook his head with a laugh and leaned back toward the mic. "How'd that news get out?"

"You know I never reveal my sources." She gave him an impish smile. "But we're all really happy for you." She clapped for him, the other media members joining in. As a reporter, it paid to be on good terms with the law enforcement community. That meant that her life would become a lot more difficult if Will Knight filled in for the sheriff. He was the only one she hadn't managed to charm. He was un-charm-able, that was why. Rigid, stick-up-his-ass, arrogant—

"Deputy Knight will be in charge," the sheriff announced. "I'll be gone for two weeks, starting next month, and you'll get to make *his* life miserable for a while."

Will smiled—arrogantly.

Oh joy.

As Merry stalked toward her car after the briefing broke up, she heard footfalls behind her. Those long strides told her it was Will even before she spun around to face him.

"Are you following me? Because I just remembered another question," she said as he came to a halt before her. "Why are you such a jackass?"

"The unicorn crack went too far, huh?" He tipped back his baseball cap with a half-smile. "Sorry about that."

She gaped at him. When did Will Knight ever apologize? She didn't *want* him to. They were adversaries. That electric current that always hummed between them proved it. "Take that back."

He looked confused. "Which part?"

"The nice part. It doesn't fit. Unless..." She frowned at him. "You want something, don't you?"

"Maybe. How about a coffee?"

She jingled her car keys between her fingers. Her nerves were jumping. It felt as if he was standing unusually close to her, though she could see perfectly well that he wasn't. "Why?"

"For caffeinating. Every reporter I know drinks coffee. Don't tell me you're the one exception."

He rested his hands on his hips. Damn, he wore that uniform better than any man had a right to. She was already late for about five other things, but if he was going to give her a hot story tip... "I don't really have time for coffee. I have to race back to town for an interview and I have a deadline."

"I'll make it quick. It doesn't have to be coffee. It just has to be private."

This was getting more and more interesting. "Fine." She gestured toward her trusty Corolla. "How about my car? It's very private. No bugs. I mean, there might be actual bugs. But nothing that can record."

She opened the passenger door and ushered him in. He was so tall, he had to grip the metal frame and duck down to fold his body inside the car. He closed the door behind him. As she rounded to the driver's side, she realized her heart had picked up its pace and was practically pitter-patting. She spent a lot of time in her car, driving from one interview or story to another. It was almost like inviting Will into her home.

Which she would never do.

She and Will didn't get along. They never had, not since she'd first taken the job at the *Gazette* and started pestering him for information. Every time they saw each other, whether in a professional context or out and about in Jupiter Point, they got into it. They were complete opposites. He moved slowly, she practically ran everywhere she went. He was from Jupiter Point, she was a transplanted city girl. He was a law-and-order type, she made a career out of questioning authority.

Also, he was bossy and arrogant.

"I see you put my seat back," she said as she slid into the drivers' seat.

"So my legs would fit." They still didn't, exactly. His knees were spread apart so they wouldn't slam into the glove compartment.

"There's no need to get comfortable. I don't have much time."

"Yeah, I don't think 'comfortable' is on the agenda," he said dryly. He reached behind his back and dislodged a chew toy in the shape of Shrek. He looked at it quizzically. "Friend of yours?"

"Stress ball. Helps me relax."

"You? Tense? Never would have guessed it."

She sighed and drummed her fingers on the steering wheel, which had a shaggy purple cover that made her smile. "I don't have time for chitchat, Knight. Why are you here? What do you want?"

He squeezed Shrek, creating a breathy squeak. "Your, uh, speculation about the rise of opioids and the campground fires. I wanted to give you a heads up about that."

She turned toward him eagerly. "I knew it. I knew there had to be a connection. My gut never lies."

"You need to drop it," he said flatly. "It's not something you can pursue right now. If you let it go for now, I promise you'll be the department's first call once they can say something."

The hairs on the back of her neck lifted the way they always did when she was getting close to a real story. "So there is something to it, but you want me to ignore it? That's going to be hard to do. My brand-new boss will be very interested in a story like this."

"Right, I heard you got a new editor over there. What's he like?"

She grimaced, then quickly tried to pretend it was a smile. It didn't work; Will saw everything with those gray eyes of his. She'd noticed that fact before.

"He's...uh...young and very dynamic." That was code for aggressive and obnoxious. Will lifted one eyebrow, looking genuinely interested. She found herself continuing. "He says he wants more drama and conflict in our stories. He uses the word 'big' a lot." She waved her arms the way Douglas Wentworth had in the staff meeting. "'*Big* headlines. *Big* emotion. Feuds, battles, tears, fears.' That's a direct quote."

Will chuckled. "Did he get on the wrong plane? This is a small town, not Los Angeles."

"Hey, small towns have drama too. Just ask Mrs.—"

"Murphy," Will finished the sentence along with her. They both laughed at the mention of Jupiter Point's biggest rumor-monger. Merry knew for a fact that Will used Mrs. Murphy as a source just as much as she did.

Then she remembered that she and Will were adversaries, not friends, and turned her laugh into a cough. "Anyway, this story sounds important."

"Can you stall him? You'll get your big story at the right time. Just give us a little space on this one."

She eyed him, assessing how serious he was. Could she negotiate? Get more out of him in exchange for backing off this story temporarily? "I don't know, Will. Opioid addiction is a big story all over the country, you know that. Our readers are concerned. I'm not sure I can justify ignoring it completely. Do you have anything else you can give me in its place?"

She batted her eyes at him innocently. Pointless—he knew exactly what she was up to and he was no doubt immune to her wiles anyway.

"Such as?"

"You tell me. You must have something interesting going on out here."

"We like it boring. That means we're doing our jobs." He rested his big hands on his thighs. They looked so powerful, muscles bulging against the gray fabric of his uniform. She tore her eyes away.

"Well, my job is to get as many eyeballs as possible to look at the *Gazette*. I'm open to suggestions. Pin the Tail on the Deputy? Spin the Mugshot?"

He snorted as a brief smile passed across his face. Will Knight wasn't a big smiler, in her experience. He took his job seriously, though sometimes a dry sense of humor snuck out from behind his stoic manner. "Tell you what. How about a behind-the-scenes exclusive at Knight and Day Flight Tours? It's opening soon. Whole town's talking about it. You can be the only reporter to go inside. We can even take you up in a plane."

She was plenty familiar with the new flightseeing business,

which was set to open in the next few weeks. Every single woman in Jupiter Point was speculating about the two sexy Knight brothers who had recently moved back to town and bought the abandoned airstrip with its ramshackle buildings.

"You said 'we.' Are you part of the crew?"

"Investor and moral support. Two of my brothers are the main guys. But they'll do what I ask."

He spoke in such a tone of quiet authority that she had no doubt of it. "Are you the oldest?"

With a lift of one eyebrow, he nodded. A moment of awareness zinged between them. They didn't usually talk about anything personal. Best to keep that safe professional distance.

There had been one time—and *only* one—that they'd breached that distance. That was when she'd woken up on his couch a few months ago. The whole episode was blurry, thank goodness. It involved a robber, a tranq gun, and an epic hangover. They still hadn't talked about that incident. She didn't want to, because from the little bits and pieces she remembered, she might have gotten a little *too* personal that night.

She cleared her throat. "I can probably work with that. An exclusive tour, interviews with both your brothers—is it just the three of you?"

"No, we have another brother but he's in his first year of college."

"Hm." With a quick sidelong glance, she estimated his age at a bit over thirty. She looked him over again just to confirm—and to appreciate his rangy, muscled physique. She swallowed a sigh. "Your parents must have known how to keep the love alive."

His expression shut down as quickly as if he'd drawn a window shade. "So are you interested in the story? I'll set it up if you are."

She thought about it. She didn't care all that much about Knight and Day Flight Tours—it sounded like a fluff piece to her. But Jupiter Point was big on supporting local businesses, so readers would love it. And if Will Knight was going to be covering for Sheriff Perez, it would be smart to accommodate him.

"Yes, I'm interested. I'm sure our readers, especially the ladies, will want to know all about the new flightseeing service. Rumor has it your brothers are single. And I never doubt Mrs. Murphy about that sort of thing."

He opened the door of her Corolla, causing a scrunched-up bag of Doritos to tumble to the ground. He bent to pick it up. Merry had never gone for "men in uniform." She'd always preferred the nerdy type; glasses were like catnip to her. Nevertheless, she watched Will's muscles flex under his regulation tan uniform shirt with reluctant appreciation. Maybe the uniform wasn't designed to show off the officers' innate sexiness, but in his case, it sure did.

With the piece of trash in hand, he extracted himself from her car. "Are you saving this for some reason or can I toss it?"

The disapproval in his voice made her bristle. "Don't judge me. I eat on the run a lot. My car is my home away from home."

She glanced around at the interior, which was a comfortable jumble of old coffee cups, laptop bag, tubes of lip balm (some missing their caps), spare items of clothing that might come in handy, a yoga mat in case she got inspired, phone chargers, water bottles, Clif bars, protein bars, granola bars, chocolate bars, camera case, accordion file folders, extra shoes, and the cosmetics case that held everything she needed for an impromptu interview.

"If your actual home is anything like your home away from home, I ought to call the fire marshal." Will squinted at the stockpile of snack bars on the backseat. "Do you ever eat anything you can't hold in your hand while you're driving?"

She lifted her chin. "I'm a multitasker. Eating while driving saves a lot of time."

He shook his head and stuck out his other hand, the one that didn't have any trash. "Anything else you want to throw away while I'm at it?"

"Hey, Boy Scout. You don't have to take out my garbage."

That ever-so-slight smile, more of a tease than an actual smile, touched his mouth again. "Turns out I do. I won't rest easy knowing you might have trash flying around your head if you take a turn too fast."

She looked at him blankly. He spoke as if he cared. But why should he? "Why is it any of your business?"

"Public safety. Could be a road hazard."

"Excuse me?" She wagged a finger at him. "I've never even had an accident. Admit it, you're just a control freak who can't stand a little mess."

And just like that, his calm control slipped and she caught a glimpse of another Will Knight. One with a lot more passion than he usually revealed. "Good Lord, Merry. Do you have to make everything difficult? I know it's your job during a press conference, but I'm offering to *collect your trash* from your car. Why do you have a problem with that?"

The way he said her first name—it gave her chills. He usually called her "Ms. Warren," in a sort of overly formal, almost ironic tone. Calling her "Merry" had a whole different effect on her system. It sent butterflies tumbling through her belly and made her pulse ramp up.

For a surprised moment, they stared at each other. Slowly, his expression returned to what she was used to: somewhere between calm and mildly irritated.

"Fine. If it's that important to you, I'll take you up on that very civic-minded offer." She bent over and rummaged around the floorboards for the plastic grocery bag in which she'd stashing her old coffee cups. It was so full that one seam had ripped and old coffee had dripped down the outside of the bag.

Normally, she'd be embarrassed, but he'd asked for it. With a sweet smile, she handed over the dripping mess. He took it, looking like he now regretted ever bringing it up. "I'll have my brothers give you a call."

"Great. Thanks."

He closed the passenger door with his hip, since both of his hands were filled with debris from her car. With one last nod, he turned back toward the sheriff's compound. Because she couldn't help herself, she watched his truly fine ass as he cruised across the lawn with those long strides.

Will Knight was one attractive law enforcement officer. That didn't change the fact that they were total opposites, though. Now she had one more example. He was a neat freak. And she was too busy to worry about tidiness.

Although she had to admit, as she drove down the highway back toward Jupiter Point, it was easier to drive when she wasn't kicking old coffee cups away from the accelerator. Not that she'd ever tell Will that.

2

WILL DUMPED MERRY'S TRASH IN THE BIN INSIDE THE RECEPTION area. The office assistant, Cindy, gave him a curious side-eye look, but he fended off her curiosity with his famous blank stare. The one that came easily with everyone except Merry.

Then he went to the men's room to wash his hands, mentally grumbling the entire time. *Control freak, my ass.* Every time he tried to do something nice for Merry Warren, she pushed him away as if he'd threatened to off her pet gerbil or something. What was wrong with that girl?

And why did he react to her, every single time? No matter how hard he worked to hold on to his cool, one look from her sparkling brown eyes and he lost his bearings. Was there any other explanation for why he'd offered up an interview with his brothers? Or why he'd collected her damn trash?

Without even trying, she made him do things he didn't do for *anyone* else. It had to stop. It was freaking embarrassing. And it could cause all kinds of trouble if he wasn't careful.

He poked his head into his boss's office. Sheriff Perez was pretty new on the job, having been elected only a year ago. His brothers had urged him to run for the position, but he'd rather eat dirt than have to deal with networking and politicking and schmoozing.

"That went pretty well," he told the sheriff. "Merry agreed to give you a little time. But knowing her, she'll be back at it before too long. She's persistent."

Perez looked up from his computer. He was a handsome guy who wanted to run for higher office someday. He lived on coffee and wintergreen Altoids, which he claimed to be addicted to. "Hard to believe the press picked up on this. This ain't exactly *New York Times* territory out here."

Will didn't like the condescending tone in Perez's voice. Just because he wanted to move up didn't mean he should look down on Jupiter Point. "Merry Warren's sharp. Good reporter."

"Well, she'll be your problem soon. I'll be on a beach with my lady, sleeping off the champagne toasts and getting ready for round eighty-nine."

"Yes, sir." He rapped on the doorjamb and turned to go.

"How's the kid doing?" Perez asked, almost as an afterthought.

Will's heart swelled with pride, as it always did whenever he thought about Aiden. "Doing great. Loves his classes, hit it off with his roommate. Couldn't be better."

"Bueno, bueno. He needs anything, you let me know. My cousin went to Evergreen."

And that was exactly why Perez was so successful. Good memory for personal details and quick to extend a generous hand.

"Thanks, that's a nice thought."

"And how about you? The nest is empty, yeah? Time to take advantage. Spread those wings."

"Right. I'll do that." Will rapidly backed up before Perez roped him into a setup or a blind date or Lord knew what.

"My fiancée knows someone she wants you to meet. Hair stylist at her salon. Says she's a doll and perfect for you."

"Really, Sheriff, I can handle—"

"Oh, is it set-up-Will-Knight time?" Cindy appeared at his elbow. "I've been waiting for this moment. I have a long list I've been compiling. Do you know how many women come in here who ask if you're single? I kept their names for you in a file."

"That's incredibly well-organized of you, but I'm not—"

"I divided the list into witnesses, suspects, victims, and people unrelated to any criminal investigations. I thought it would be good to give you options." Cindy was twenty-two, Vietnamese, and all attitude. As efficient as she was snarky, she wore cat-eye horn-rimmed glasses with rhinestones and funky vintage dresses.

"I can handle my own personal business, thank you both very much." He fled down the hallway, pursued by Cindy's voice.

"By the way, Merry Warren is on the list too," she called after him.

He spun around. "Excuse me?"

"I put her there myself, in the category of conflict of interest. So you don't forget." She gave him a saucy finger-wag and whisked herself into Perez's office.

Will swung around the corner to the open-plan area where each deputy had a desk. He nodded to the only other deputy at his desk, Keith Jernigan. Jernigan was the main guy coordinating the opioids investigation, while Will had pulled campground arson duty. They were working the case from two opposite ends, but everyone was starting to suspect a connection.

The working theory held that fentanyl was being smuggled from China in small shipping containers, then transferred to motorhomes for distribution. In case of problems, the motorhomes were torched to destroy the evidence. It had seemed crazy at first—Jupiter Point didn't have a deep harbor and was used strictly by fishing boats and pleasure crafts. But the fentanyl was so powerful, even a small amount could generate a huge profit. A small-scale operation like this might fly under the radar.

The idea of synthetic, highly addictive drugs filtering into the Jupiter Point area made Will furious. Jupiter Point was a small town, but it had a lot of beauty and community spirit. He refused to see it destroyed by drugs.

He settled in at his desk and propped his legs on the surface. The coffee he'd poured for himself earlier was still sitting next to his computer. He stuck his finger in it, not surprised to find it ice cold. He rarely got to drink his coffee hot. Something always interrupted him.

Before he forgot his promise to Merry, he dialed Tobias's cell phone.

"Hey bro. Got a sec? I hooked you up with some free publicity," he said when Tobias answered.

"We don't need any." His brother had a voice as deep as a river running through a canyon. "We could hold a bake sale with all the stuff people keep bringing over. Is that some kind of welcome wagon thing?"

Will didn't dare tell him it was more of a matchmaking thing than a welcome wagon. "Sure. You have a problem with free pastries?"

"At this rate, I won't be able to get a plane off the ground," Tobias grumbled.

Will grinned. God, it was good to have his brothers back. Too bad Aiden was now in college, so they'd all only be together during holidays and the summer. But Will wasn't complaining. It just felt too damn good to have Tobias and Ben at the other end of his phone instead of in various hot zones around the world.

"Just take down this number and call her. It's Merry Warren, she works at the *Mercury News- Gazette* and I owe her a favor."

"Is she going to bring us cupcakes like the others?"

Will snorted at the very thought. If Merry brought cupcakes, they would probably come from Ralph's supermarket and be laced with truth-telling serum. "Don't count on that. But you can definitely expect some attitude."

"I like attitude. Is she hot?"

"She's hands off. This is a professional thing. Do I need to call this off, asshole?"

"Touchy. Jesus. Warning received. I'll give her a call. All professional-like. Maybe I'll put on a tie first. Catch you later, big brother."

Will hung up and swung around to his computer. He pulled up the list of witnesses from the campground fires. He needed to re-interview them based on the new working theory of the case. But before he did that...

After a quick glance at Jernigan to make sure he wasn't watching, Will clicked on the Flirt icon on his phone. He shouldn't do this at work. If anyone—especially Cindy—caught him, he'd never hear the end of it.

But he couldn't help it. One message from AnonyMs could make his whole day go better.

His pulse jumped at the sight of the red notification symbol. The Flirt app slogan was, "If you're looking for love, look somewhere else." The whole point was that it *wasn't* a dating site. It was designed to connect users with someone of like mind, someone to chat with, to share jokes with, someone who expected nothing emotional, physical, sexual or even social. Perfect for someone like him, who didn't want any entanglements.

He opened the message. AnonyMs had sent it this morning around six.

Crazy dream last night! It was like a disaster movie. I was running from a giant tsunami wave and people were running all around me screaming and cars were flying through the air. Then I reached up and grabbed the tire of one of the cars and it turned out YOU were driving it! I knew it was you even though I couldn't see your face, and I don't even know what your face looks like IRL. But I just knew. You shouted at me to hang on and then you drove through the air until we reached a little meadow filled with yellow wildflowers. You hovered over the meadow so I could drop down into the grass. I yelled, "Come for a hike with me!" But the car turned into a spaceship and zoomed away. Isn't that a wild dream? Interpretation, please! I have mine.

She ended with a wink emoji.

He read the message again, paying attention to every detail. AnonyMs always had vivid dreams with lots of detail. As a kid, she'd gotten into the habit of writing them down, and said someday she wanted to write a book that wove them all together. In his imagination, she was a shy, dreamy, artistic girl. The type of girl he never met in person because he mostly dealt with criminals or the victims of criminals.

He thought for a while, then typed out his answer. *Easy. Your curiosity about me is like a tidal wave.* He threw in an emoji with its tongue sticking out. *You're afraid you'll never know who I really am. Either that, or you recently watched Chitty Chitty Bang Bang. Don't know the significance of the yellow wildflowers, since your favorite color is orange. And hiking? Why? You hate to hike.*

He pressed the "send" button. Amazing that he knew those details about her, but he didn't know her name or anything else. All he knew was that she lived somewhere in central California and she was under forty.

And that he really looked forward to those messages from her.

He heard rapid footsteps behind him. Lightning fast, he closed out the app and shifted his focus to his computer screen.

Cindy appeared with the morning's mail, which she set on his desk. "I hope I didn't interrupt something. You had a funny expression on your face. A...what's that word...*doting* expression."

"Doting?" He snorted. "I wasn't doting. I was researching. Crime-solving. That's what I do. I'm a crime-solver."

"And so you are," she said in a kindergarten-teacher voice. "You're so good at it, too. Would you like a powdered donut with your coffee?"

He narrowed his eyes at her as he picked up his phone. "Why do all the women around here have so much attitude?"

She kicked up one heel and flung her arms wide—an exaggerated show-off pose. "Because you can take it, that's why."

He grunted and dialed the first number on the list. "Get out of here. I need to get some work done."

"Right. Work." She gave him a wink then turned to go. "Tell your 'work' you have real work to do." And she skipped off before he could lecture her on appropriate sheriff's department behavior.

He shook his head, feeling like a grandpa having a "get off my lawn" moment. God, he was in a rut. He was only thirty-two, and he was turning into a fossil. Duty, responsibility, work—he barely recognized himself anymore. Where was the wild and reckless Will Knight he used to be? He never let loose anymore. The most fun he had was with an anonymous woman on a goddamn app.

Correction: he had fun with Merry Warren, too. But that didn't count. She didn't like him, despite the chemistry that lit him up when he was around her. She'd been especially distant since that time he'd rescued her. It was like they'd made a pact to never mention that night. So he hadn't, even though every moment was engraved into his memory in neon.

They just didn't get along, and never would. Merry was too independent to appreciate a rescue. Especially from a Knight.

3

AMAZINGLY, MERRY'S DAY KEPT GETTING EVEN BUSIER.

She finished her article on the campground arson fires—with no mention of her suspicions. Douglas Wentworth took one look at it and proclaimed it "too boring to publish."

Thanks, Will Knight.

To avoid letting her temper get the best of her around her new boss, she hauled her laptop down to the Venus and Mars Cafe.

When she'd first arrived in Jupiter Point, the cutesy business names had seemed absurd to her. The Milky Way Ice Cream Parlor, the Goodnight Moon B & B, the Orbit Lounge and Grill... she'd rolled her eyes all the way down Constellation Way. But tourists loved it, which was the entire point. This area was known for its clear skies and outstanding stargazing. By playing up the star theme, Jupiter Point had transformed itself from a struggling fishing community to a favorite destination for honeymooners.

Merry honestly didn't care what the Venus and Mars was called, as long as it kept serving her favorite cinnamon lattes and caramel-drenched sticky buns.

After snagging a corner table, she set down her latte and drew her imaginary cone of silence around her. Big Bose headphones, check. Open laptop, check. Furious focus on the screen, check. This was her happy place—work. To her, work wasn't "work"—it was a chance to claim her place in the world. A chance to matter, a chance to shine.

She loved every part of being a reporter for the *Mercury News-Gazette*. She loved interviewing people, digging for information, exposing injustice. Of course, most of her assignments involved tedious city council meetings or budget hearings—but she did her best to make those stories interesting as well. Seeing her byline on the front page thrilled her every single time.

Face it, she was a nerd at heart.

A detail had been nagging at her. Recently she'd written a story about the challenges faced by single mothers. She'd interviewed a waitress who worked at a bar near the waterfront. The waitress had talked about sticking with a job longer than she wanted to because she needed the money. But eventually she'd quit because they offered her some kind of illegal opportunity. She wouldn't say what, but Merry got the definite sense it involved drugs.

To Merry, that amounted to a lead worth following up on.

Of course, she intended to honor her promise to Will about the opioids story. Pissing off the best sheriff's deputy in town would not be a good idea. But just because she'd committed to not publishing something didn't mean she couldn't *explore* it. That way she'd have something ready to go when he gave the all-clear.

She pulled up the notes she'd made on that interview and scanned through until she found the name of the bar. The Rootin' Rooster.

On the restaurant's website, she found more nuggets of information. Its slogan: "Where *you're* the cock of the walk." It offered "eats, drinks, and good company," along with a cartoonish busty woman winking. It also claimed to be the "home of the world famous Roosterburger."

Okay then. Not a place she would ever go voluntarily. Nevertheless, she clicked on the "employment opportunities" tab. Waitresses wanted. Minimum wage plus tips. Night hours required.

Normally, she wouldn't be caught dead in a place like that. But for a story, she'd take a chance. At the very least, she could pretend to interview for a job just to check the place out.

She was about to call the number when her phone beeped.

"Tobias Knight here," a deep voice rumbled. "Will gave me your number."

That was Will Knight for you. For all his annoying qualities, he always followed up. Solid as a mountain. "Right. Thanks for calling. He mentioned a tour, and said you guys could take me up in a plane."

"Did he? Well, whatever Will said. You tell us."

"Do you always do exactly what Will says? Is it the badge or the bossiness?" Apparently, all members of the Knight family brought out her sass.

"Huh. He mentioned something about attitude."

Her face heated. "Sorry. Will and I, we...have our issues."

"Uh-huh." Amusement deepened his voice. "Good to know. So when can you come out here?"

She set up a time to visit Knight and Day Flight Tours. From the sounds of it, Tobias was a lot like Will. Alpha man, bossy, arrogant. She had their number.

After they'd set up the appointment, she glanced at her watch and realized she had to leave for the weekly evening class she taught at the community college. She ordered a sandwich to go and ate it on the drive to the campus, smiling as she remembered Will's comment about only eating foods she could consume while driving.

Will had a good sense of humor, when he chose to. Too bad most of the time he was such a stern, impassive guy.

At the college, she raced into the classroom to find her students laughing at someone's Instagram feed. She quickly brought the class to order and tackled the week's subject—how to distinguish a legitimate source from a false one. A passionate discussion about "fake news" followed, which Merry enjoyed to the hilt.

Afterward, she poked her head into her friend Carolyn's office. Carolyn lay flat on the floor with her legs propped against the wall. She had a guest-teaching gig at another college for the semester, but she came back once a month to oversee a few ongoing thesis projects. The schedule exhausted her.

"Uh-oh, one of those days?"

Carolyn groaned. "I can't even. I just need my happy place right now. I'll call you later, okay?"

"Sure. If you need to ditch the Zen and get cocktails, let me know. My treat."

"You're a bad influence."

"I try." Merry blew a kiss at Caro, who waved backwards from her flat-on-her-back position.

"Oh wait," Caro called as Merry turned away. "Someone was looking for you."

"A student?"

"No, he said he's from New York. He seemed really anxious to meet you. He said he emailed you but you didn't answer."

And that was when Merry's day turned from busy to utter disaster.

Only one stranger from New York had emailed her lately. And she hadn't answered for a reason. "Where'd he go?"

"I wasn't sure if he was legit, so I told him to wait in the snack room." Caro drew her legs down the wall and scooted back on her butt. "He seemed harmless enough, kind of bouncy and eager. Like a golden retriever in human form. Who is he?"

Merry put a hand on her stomach, which was roiling from tension. "No one. No one important."

Caro shifted onto her knees on the yoga mat she'd spread on the floor. She brushed her ash-blond hair from her face and twisted it behind her neck. "Okay...."

"Don't tell him I was here, okay? I don't want to—"

"Merry? Merry Warren?"

The sound of a male voice behind her made her spin around. *Golden retriever in human form*...that description ran crazily through her brain because it was so perfect. Golden brown hair, eager manner, innocent eyes fixed on her as if pleading for her to toss a ball with him.

"I'm—"

"I know who you are. You shouldn't be here. You need to leave." The words came out harsher than she'd intended. A wounded expression came over his face.

"Please don't say that. We're fam—"

She interrupted with a glare. "No, we're not. Not even close. Just turn your ass around and go home."

She must have looked extra fierce, because he glanced nervously at Caro, who jumped up from her yoga mat.

"Do you want me to call security, Merry? Also, I know a few Krav Maga moves." Beneath Caro's Zen-like surface, she could be a true warrior.

Chase looked even more hurt. "Why would you do that? I'm her—"

"Don't say it!" Merry practically shouted. The drab little office felt more like a tilt-a-wheel knocking her off balance. How dare he show up here uninvited? "Just don't say anything. I have to think."

Caro put an arm around her shoulder and lowered her voice. "Merry, what is going on? He's just a kid. You deal with them all the time in class."

"He's not just a kid. He's—" She couldn't say it. From the time she'd first learned of Chase's existence, at the age of nine, she'd tried so hard not to hate him. And now he was standing right in front of her, and—

"I'm her brother," Chase said in that same eager, hopeful tone as before. "Half-brother," he added. "But that's more than nothing. I thought I didn't have *any* sisters until about a month ago. That's why I came out here. I had to meet you, Merry. I just want to get to know you, that's all."

He stepped forward, but Caro shoved out a hand to stop him. "Hang on there, buddy. She has a choice in the matter, you know."

A choice in the matter. The words resonated through Merry. She hadn't had a choice in any of it, from the moment of conception onwards. She hadn't chosen to be rejected and ignored by a father she'd never even met. She hadn't chosen for this kid to show up in Jupiter Point.

"Listen, why don't you leave your number," Caro was saying to Chase. "If Merry wants to talk to you, she'll call you."

Merry dug her fingernails into the heels of her hands. *Get a grip, girl.* She never had any trouble speaking for herself. Her mother called it "personal power"— relying on yourself, standing up for yourself, claiming your space in the world. But right now she felt her power leaking away, thanks to this confused-looking golden-haired kid.

"That's okay," she told Caro. "I got this."

With a big effort, she faced her half-brother, Chase Merriweather. She knew all about him, but seeing him in person was a shock. She studied his face for any resemblance between them. Since he was entirely Caucasian and her mother was from Brazil, their skin tone was nothing alike, nor was their hair. His was dirty blond, his eyes an eager hazel-brown. Everything about his face read 'anxious to please.' But she could see a few similarities between them, especially when he smiled. His lips curved in exactly the same off kilter way that hers did. And his ears stuck out the same as hers did.

But that was no doubt the end of the resemblance. He'd been

raised in the wealthy, sheltered cocoon of the Merriweather family and their high-end department stores, while she'd grown up in a dicey neighborhood in Brooklyn. Also, he seemed kind of ... well, clueless.

"I can't believe I have a sister," he said happily. "Like a *sistah*, sister."

"If you want anything to do with me, don't ever say that again," she told him sternly.

He shook his head quickly. "I won't. Promise. That was inappropriate. I get it."

She clenched her jaw tight. Somehow she doubted that he "got" anything about her perspective on this situation. How could he?

"Look, I know this is strange. I was so pissed at Dad when I found out that you existed and that he just sent your mother away with a check and an NDA. It's so unfair and so typical and I...I guess I want to...I don't know. I know I can't make it right. But I thought, maybe, if *someone* in our family reached out to you, maybe that would make it a little bit better."

Merry folded her arms across her chest. "If you think I've been pining away for some attention from the Merriweathers, you're completely mistaken."

He gave a frustrated groan and hunched his shoulders. "I'm screwing this up so bad. I knew I would. Okay, look, I'm staying at the Goodnight Moon bed and breakfast until I find a place, so whenever—"

"Find a *place*? What are you talking about? You're *staying* here?"

"Yeah, I'm serious about this. I want to know my only sister. It's like a quest. A personal quest. You can check out my Tumblr about it."

"A Tumblr? My name better not be in it."

"It's not. I kept you completely anonymous. I'm not here to make trouble. I swear."

When he set his jaw, she found one more striking resemblance—the "you're not the boss of me" expression she herself had perfected.

She found that particular similarity endearing, but she still wasn't ready for this.

"Look, uh, Chase. Let me think about this. I know where you're staying. You already emailed me your number. If I decide to get in touch, I will."

He nodded reluctantly, took a step back, then stopped. "You know, I read all of your newspaper articles from the *Gazette*. You're so smart, but I didn't know you were so pretty."

She lifted her eyebrows at him. "I like compliments as much as anyone, but you know what I like even better?"

He shook his head.

"Free choice. I'll call you. Or not."

"Okay." He shoved his hands in the pockets of his khaki trousers. "I understand. Hey, are you hungry? I could really use a burger—okay, I'm going now. It was nice to meet you." With that last word, he finally left.

When he was gone, Merry let out a long breath and slumped against the wall.

"Wow." Caro touched her arm. "Are you okay?"

Merry tilted her head, not sure of the answer to that question. "Probably?" She laughed. "Hey, it's not that weird to meet your half-brother after twenty-one years, right? Just another average day."

"He seems nice enough," Caro said cautiously.

"I'm sure that's what my mother thought about his father, before he got her pregnant and abandoned her."

Caro winced. "Ouch. Sorry."

"It doesn't matter," Merry said wearily. Her anger with Chase drained away. Her whole life, she'd been quick to lose her temper, then just as quick to let it go. She wondered if her half-brother had the same quality. "We were fine without him. Without any of them. Why should that change now?"

"No reason. Except that he's here and..." when Merry frowned at her, she shifted course. "What was that you were saying before, about cocktails?"

Merry laughed. "Is this a blatant attempt to get me buzzed so I tell the whole story?"

Caro squinted at her. "Would that work?"

Merry shoved herself upright and fluffed her hair, which had gotten flattened against the wall. "Probably. But I should get home. I have to make a good impression on the new boss tomorrow. How about the thumbnail version over a quick bag of chips from the vending machine?"

"You sweet-talker, you."

In the student lounge, as they shared a bag of Doritos, Merry summed up her childhood. "My mother's a singer from Brazil. She came to New York to further her opportunities, but couldn't exactly make ends meet. So she took a job cleaning house for a wealthy family, the Merriweathers. Their son took one look at her and fell hard. My mother's gorgeous, by the way."

"Not surprised," said Caro loyally.

"They got together, Mama got pregnant with me, but he couldn't take the heat from his family. They didn't want the likes of us messing with their lineage. So they gave her a big chunk of cash. She signed a non-disclosure agreement and promised to stay away. And that's about it. A couple of years later, my secret father got married to the right kind of girl and they had Chase. That's how I ended up with a white half-brother. I never met my father, and I sure never expected to meet Chase." She balled up the empty bag and checked her watch. "I need to head out."

Caro prepared to leave as well, gathering up her backpack and yoga bag. "But you know all about him. Did your mother fill you in?"

"She never said much about them. You know me, too curious

for my own good. The Merriweathers were one of my first research projects." She grinned. "I had to know about the people I got my name from."

Caro tilted her head, not getting it at first. Then— "Merry's short for Merriweather?"

"Bingo. Mama always liked that name. And the NDA didn't say a thing about what she could or couldn't name me."

"I like her style."

Merry smiled with pure affection at the thought of her mother. "She's really something. Anyway, now you know my deep dark secret life."

"I guess I do. Want me to sign an NDA?" Caro winked as she slung her yoga bag over her shoulder.

"Hey, I trust you more than ever after you threatened to call security on Chase. I bet that's the first time anyone did that."

They headed for the exit. "You're going to see him, right?" Caro said. "How can you resist, with all that curiosity you keep talking about?"

Merry groaned. "You know me too well. Okay, I admit I'm curious. But I'm pissed too. I know his kind. Just like my *non*-father, so used to getting whatever they want. If I'd wanted him to come here, I would have emailed him back. So I'm not in any hurry. I'm crazy busy with work right now, not to mention a new boss, and a big story I'm investigating. If Chase is serious about this, he can stick around and contribute to the Jupiter Point economy until I'm ready to see him."

Caro lifted her hand for a high-five. Their palms met with a satisfying smack, and Merry felt her personal power flooding back.

4

Why isn't everyone as cool as you are? SAID THE NEXT MESSAGE from AnonyMs. *What's wrong with men?*

Will frowned over the keyboard. Interesting. This was getting more personal than usual.

I don't believe in generalizations. I need specifics.

Okay then, she answered. *A specific male relative just popped into my life completely uninvited.*

Tell him to leave.

Just like that? Wow, is that how you roll with the ladies in your life?

He'd chosen the name StarLord as a joke, because he'd just seen *Guardians of the Galaxy* with Aiden and he hadn't ever intended on actually continuing this Flirt thing. But then he'd "met" AnonyMs and somehow they just kept writing. *I keep my relationships breakup-proof. Clean and simple, no drama. If a woman wants to leave, I don't argue. If I want out, I just go.*

That's cold.

That's real. I've had a kid to raise for the past eleven years. He didn't need a fake mother-figure around. So I kept my sex life separate.

Mentioning "sex" was another first. But she'd brought up the topic of relationships. That opened up a big old can of worms.

Only a man could think that makes any kind of sense, she sent back. *But I like it. I keep my sex life separate too—separate from other people*. Big smiley face. *I can satisfy my own self without all the drama, know what I mean?*

Oooh, now this was getting good.

Will rubbed his hands together and glanced around the living room. His computer was set up in the corner. Right now, the room was empty, but either one of his brothers could walk in at any moment. They were both staying with him until they found their own places, and neither seemed in any hurry to do so.

Not that he wanted them to. It was great to have more Knight brothers in the house.

After he was granted guardianship of Aiden, he'd sold the old property and bought a big rundown farmhouse closer to Jupiter Point. Neither of them wanted to live in the house where the murder had happened. Will thought fixing up the farmhouse would be a good hands-on project they could both focus on. The work wasn't even close to being done, but he and Aiden had learned a shit-ton about construction.

He stretched out his legs under the vintage writing desk that had come with the house. He'd just gotten back from a night run and still wore his workout clothes. He really ought to jump in the shower, but this convo with AnonyMs was too juicy to cut short.

I'm not sure I understand, he typed with a smirk. *Maybe you can go into more detail.*

Can't you use your imagination? the reply pinged a second later.

All too well. It's a good thing you can't see into my head right now.

Are you sure I can't? What's that I spy in there...looks like naked people! Then again, that could be the inside of any man's head.

He laughed out loud just as Ben walked into the room. He typed a quick "x"—the symbol they'd agreed on as meaning someone in real life was interrupting them. Then he closed out the app and rose to his feet.

Ben had a free weight in each hand. He was alternating arms, working his biceps as he strolled around the house. Shirtless.

"What the fuck? You're going to drip sweat everywhere," Will grumbled.

"Okay, Grandpa." Ben grinned at him. After spending five years as an Air Force pilot, he was used to teasing. "Who were you chatting with?"

"No one."

Chatting, to him, didn't quite describe it. That sounded like "chitchat," like boring conversation that didn't mean anything. His communications with AnonyMs were so much more than that.

Ben shrugged and dropped his weights onto the couch.

"Do you mind? We have a whole gym for that. It's outside. In the barn."

"It was lonely out there. I need someone to talk to while I work out. Want to come throw some iron around?"

"I was just headed for the shower."

Ben threaded a hand through his sweat-stiffened hair. It was finally growing out after years of the typical precision brush-cut. Of all the brothers, he looked the most like their mother. Sometimes the sight of his honey-blond hair and deep gray eyes made Will's heart hurt. Mom was out there somewhere. Grieving, running, hiding, who knew what. Occasionally Cassie sent a postcard letting him know she and Mom were both okay. He'd always sent copies to his brothers when they were overseas.

It wasn't enough, and yet it had to be.

"Better hurry, Grandpa." Ben teased. "You're getting sweat everywhere."

"Yeah, yeah." Will shut down the computer and slid his chair back. "How did the interviews go?"

"Pain in the ass. Why do people apply for a job they have no qualifications for? One of the applicants barely just got her pilot's license. I had to break it to her that she needed at least two years' flying experience." He cracked a grin. "I did offer her some copilot action. We're having dinner next week."

"Copilot action? Is that what they call it these days?"

"Hey, don't knock it. You could use some yourself. You act like an old man, Will. I've been keeping an eye on you and I'm not liking what I see. I'm worried. So is Tobias."

Will grabbed a gym towel from the back of his chair and wiped his face. "The hell you are. I'm fine. Jesus. Having the time of my life."

"That's the thing. You should be, but you're not. How about a beer? Barstow's, what do you say?"

Normally he'd jump at the chance to hang out with his brothers at everyone's favorite brew pub. But he'd much rather get Ben out of his hair so he could quiz AnonyMs some more. Her last provocative comment had all kinds of images flying around in his brain.

"Another time. I have to work tomorrow. Big investigation going on. Big by Jupiter Point standards, anyway." He brushed past his brother, but Ben jumped up and followed him toward the stairs that led to the bathroom, pumping his free weights as they went.

"You know, this strong and silent act only goes so far. I went away and worked out my emotions defending our country. You had to stay here and be Mr. Mom. Ever think you might have a few problems built up? Some shit you stuffed down and never thought about?"

Will wheeled around to face his brother. "I think about everything. Often. I haven't forgotten and I never will. But we don't have to dwell on it either."

Ben backed away, raising his hands—which were still full of iron—in a defensive position. "Okay, okay. It was just a thought. Jesus."

The front door swung open and Tobias walked through. Even

though he had the most intimidating appearance of the three of them, he was perceptive as hell. He stopped in the hallway and glared at them. "What happened?"

"I told Will he needed a woman and he ripped my face off." Ben worked his jaw back and forth. "Surprised I still have feeling in my jaw after that right jab he gave me."

Will rolled his eyes. "You're an idiot. What happened is that Ben doesn't know when to quit. And I *have* a woman. Roxy. She's a peach."

Both of his brothers gave him the "cut the crap" look.

Roxy was their former neighbor, and she and Will had been sleeping together off and on since high school. It was the ultimate relationship of convenience, and neither one had ever pretended otherwise.

Tobias turned to Ben. "Don't worry about the woman situation. It's covered. And I don't mean Roxy."

Will frowned at him. "What are you talking about?"

"Our free publicity."

Ben did a few more biceps crunches, looking thoughtful. "I'm intrigued. What's her name?"

"Merry Warren. She's coming out to the airstrip next week to interview us."

"Interview *you*," said Will. "I'm a silent partner, remember."

"Nope. We all have to be there. That means you too, Will. The Knight brothers, united."

"Can't do it. I have a job. Solving crimes, protecting and serving. Why do you want me there?"

"Just a little something I picked up on when I was talking to Merry. She sounds hot, by the way."

Ben was grinning like a madman. "This ought to be good. Tell you what, Will. You be there for the interview, and I'll stop hassling you."

Will gave in—mostly so he could get to his shower faster. "Fine. Text me the time and I'll work it out."

He loped up the worn stairs toward the second-floor bathroom. If Tobias thought there was anything between him and Merry, he was dreaming. Merry had made her feelings perfectly clear. She didn't like him.

AnonyMs, on the other hand...

He smiled as he stepped into the shower. AnonyMs was everything he wanted in a woman. Funny, real, honest, smart. And now they were starting to talk about sex. The next step seemed logical to him.

What if he could talk AnonyMs into becoming a little less...anonymous?

THE ROOTIN' Rooster was located in an old warehouse in the industrial stretch of the waterfront. If Merry had to choose one word to describe the place, it would be "disgusting." She couldn't even find a spot on the bar the application didn't stick to. She figured no one would care enough to check her references, so she made up a few food service jobs for the past work history section.

Of course, she left out the fact that she was currently employed by the *Mercury News-Gazette*.

When she finished filling it out, the bartender gestured toward the back office. "Go on in there. Pete's the one who does the hiring."

Pete turned out to be a black man in his thirties wearing a satin gym jacket. He looked her up and down. "You're looking pretty uptown for someone going for a waitress job."

Crap. She'd overdressed. It probably didn't matter, since she didn't actually want the job. She just wanted to see the interior of the place and talk to the management. Her goal was to see if anything set off her reporter's Spidey sense. "Is that a problem, dressing nice for a job interview?"

He bared his teeth in a smile. "Feisty, now. Okay then. Tell me why you want this job."

"I need the money. I heard the tips are pretty good here."

"They are, if you work for them."

Merry hid a shiver of repulsion. She could just imagine what kind of "work" he meant. Not anything she wanted to do, that was for sure.

"Well, you're a looker, you got that light-skinned exotic thing happening, a little sass, a little ass, I think we can find a few shifts for you. You work nights?"

"Sure. Nights are better for me."

"You got a man? A kid?"

"Do I have to answer that?" She didn't want this scumbag knowing anything about her. "Whatever shifts you give me, I'll be there. I'll figure it out."

He looked down at her application. She used the opportunity to quickly scan the office. A filing cabinet in the corner, piles of file folders. Some balled-up bartender aprons. Everything sloppy and uncared for. If something criminal was going on here, they'd keep much better order. They wouldn't take a chance on leaving files out like this.

She relaxed. No way was this the headquarters of some kind of drug-smuggling enterprise. It was exactly what it looked like, a sleazy club for losers.

Just then the phone on the desk flashed a red button. Pete stiffened, a subtle reaction that she wouldn't have noticed if she hadn't been paying such close attention. "Gotta take this call," he said, forcibly relaxing his shoulders. Body language. It told the tale.

She lingered, curious to know who was calling and why Pete had suddenly gotten so tense. "It's okay, I don't mind."

The phone kept flashing. With a muttered curse, Pete pressed the button and answered with a low, "Yo."

He listened, then said, "I'll be there. Yeah. Got a waitress in here interviewing. Yes, sir. Thanks." He hung up and pinned her with a glare. "What are you waiting for? A raise?"

"So I'm hired?" Everything about his manner set off alarm bells. Her reporter's Spidey sense was definitely going crazy.

He snorted. "You ain't too bright, are you?"

She put on her best dim bulb look and planted a hand on her hip. "I'm plenty bright to wait tables. So am I hired or what?"

"Yeah, yeah, you're hired. This a good number for you?" He checked the application. "I'll call you with your shifts."

"Thank you, you won't regret it."

She backed out of the office.

As she hurried out of the bar, she looked with disgust at the clientele, who mostly seemed to be down and out members of the fishing industry, and the waitresses, who wore ridiculous costumes with tail feathers, like the rooster version of Playboy bunnies.

Was she seriously going to do this? Wear a *rooster* costume? For a story?

She knew firsthand how addiction could ruin lives. To keep her away from the menace in their own neighborhood, her mother had used all the Merriweather money to send her to private school in Manhattan. Ironically, three of her wealthy classmates had OD'd senior year. She knew perfectly well that no community was immune.

Before Merry had gotten the job offer from the *Gazette*, she'd never even heard of Jupiter Point. But now she loved the charming, quirky little town. If she could do anything to stop drugs from taking hold here, she would. This story could help Jupiter Point, and it could help her career. To quote her new boss, it was *big*. If she had to wear rooster tails to get the scoop, she'd damn well cockadoodle-do-it.

5

A FEW DAYS LATER, MERRY, RUNNING LATE, DASHED INTO THE *Mercury News-Gazette* on her way to Knight and Day Flight Tours. The *Gazette* occupied one of the original Jupiter Point buildings from the early 1900s. Over the years, the sun had faded its red bricks to a deep rose color. The gilt paint on the art deco sign was chipping and the gables provided shelter for squirrels' nests. But Merry loved the old-school feel of the place.

Still juggling her cinnamon latte, she made a quick stop in her office to grab her favorite jacket. Call it childish, but she wanted to look her best for this step into Will Knight's domain. She found her jacket draped over the back of her chair and tugged it on over her brown camisole. A Dolce & Gabbana knock-off, the sharply cut cream-colored blazer was the most expensive thing she owned. It gave her skin a deep bronze glow. She was busy adjusting the cuffs when two men stepped into her office.

One was Douglas Wentworth, wearing a pink button-down shirt, horn-rimmed glasses and a soul patch on his chin. The other, she saw with a shock, was Chase. Her half-brother whom she still hadn't called.

"Merry, I'd like you to meet our new intern. This is Chase

Merriweather. He just graduated from the University of Virginia and he's a whiz at social media. I'm hoping he can juice up our online presence. Get us up on Instagram, that sort of thing. He can start with the Knight and Day story, it's nice and visual."

She plastered a smile on her face and shook Chase's hand. Since she was already on thin ice with Wentworth, she couldn't object without a good reason. The fact that he was her secret half-brother didn't seem to qualify and definitely wasn't something she wanted to spread around. "Welcome aboard."

He shook her hand, looking hopeful and apologetic at the same time. She dropped the smile as soon as she politely could. "Are you ready? I'm running a little late."

"Sure."

"Make it big," Douglas reminded them.

She hurried out of the building, with Chase on her heels. As soon as she hit the sidewalk, she turned on him. "Seriously?"

"I'm sorry. Are you really mad? I promise I won't get in your way. It just kind of happened. I hadn't heard from you, so I came to see you at the newspaper, but you were out on a story. Then I saw the ad for an intern and it felt like it was meant to be."

"I asked you to wait until I was ready."

"I know. You can still ignore me until then. But maybe it'll be easier to get to know each other if we're working together."

He fixed pleading puppy dog eyes on her. For such a preppy-looking kid, he got points for persistence.

"I'll quit if you really want," he added meekly.

She folded her arms across her chest and surveyed him. He was clueless but harmless, she supposed. She could deal better with an intern than an overeager half-brother.

"It's okay," she finally said. "You don't have to quit. Come on, my car's that way." She gestured down the street at her Corolla.

He grinned, but pointed to a brand new, shiny black BMW right behind her car. "That's me. I can drive if you want."

She clenched her teeth so hard her jaw spasmed. Of course

he would have a fancy sports car. And of course he would assume his ride was better than hers. Well, it might be more expensive, but it wasn't *better.* She had all her stuff in her car and it was her home away from home and he could just go fly a kite.

"Good idea." She unclenched her jaw to smile at him. "You can follow me there. Just stay close so you don't get lost."

She walked away before he could protest. Okay, so maybe she still had some anger toward the Merriweather family. Not that any of it was Chase's fault. Logically, she knew that. Even so, she couldn't seem to speak normally to him.

She headed for her Corolla, passing the Sky View Gallery on the way. Evie McGraw Marcus was sweeping the sidewalk outside her little shop. Evie waved at her with a big smile that included Chase, who was trailing just inches behind Merry. Normally she would have stopped and introduced them, but she wasn't ready to explain why she suddenly had a very white half-brother.

So she cruised past with nothing more than a "call me" gesture.

"Margaritas tonight!" Evie called after her. "Suzanne has a babysitter, so get ready for some fun!"

"I'll be there!" She'd probably need an entire pitcher of margaritas by tonight.

When she reached her car, she turned to Chase. "I'm heading that way down Constellation. Better keep up."

"I'll be right behind you."

The road to Knight and Day wound through the foothills clustered around Jupiter Point. This time of year, September, the hills glowed umber brown and the valley held deep purple shadows. As she drove, Merry thought about the earthquake currently shaking up her life.

A difficult new boss, a confusing new half-brother.

Ugh. *Men.* If only all men were more like StarLord. Thoughtful, soulful, funny, smart.

Speaking of StarLord, he'd sent her a message this morning

but she hadn't had a chance to read it. As she rounded the last curve toward the ocean, she opened the app.

Reading while driving...very bad idea. She could just imagine how Will Knight would lecture her about that.

Smiling, she read the message in quick glances.

It was a poem. She loved it when StarLord wrote poems, even silly ones. It confirmed her sense that he was exactly the sort of sensitive man she wanted to find.

If you were a star, I'd be a telescope. If you were an island, I'd be a breeze. If you were a clock, I'd be high noon. If you're just a dream, can I keep hitting snooze? (P.s. I know "breeze" and "snooze" don't rhyme.)

She laughed, then swerved to avoid a creature scampering across the road. Behind her, Chase honked his horn.

She swung the steering wheel to get her car back in the right lane, barely seeing the road in front of her. Chills chased through her, filling her up like bubbly at a wedding.

She had to meet his guy, this StarLord. He was totally different from the men she knew. Even if he turned out to be hideous, she wouldn't care. She knew who he was on the inside. That was all that mattered.

She crested the last hill before the airstrip. From here, meadows filled with wildflowers stretched toward the Pacific Ocean, which slumbered under the hot September sky.

Even if she never met StarLord, knowing that someone like him existed made it easier to deal with the other men in the world.

Deputy Will Knight, for instance.

If Will pulled his bossy, arrogant moves, all she had to do was think of StarLord and his tender, funny messages.

WILL HAD to hand it to Merry. When she turned on the charm, no one could resist her.

As soon as she stepped onto the freshly resurfaced pavement next to the newly painted reception building, Tobias and Ben fell all over her like moths to a flame.

He didn't, of course. He knew all about Merry and her reporter wiles. She had a way of asking questions that kept you talking and before you knew it, you were sharing details meant to be kept quiet. He'd been burned early on with her and had never made that mistake again.

Instead, he hung back and watched her flash that smile, tilt her head, fix her sparkling eyes on his brothers, and turn them into pigeons eating out of her hand. While they took her into the hangar to show off their Cessna 206, the Piper Matrix, and the Robinson R44 II Raven helicopter, he stayed on the tarmac with the intern, Chase, who explained that he was taking pictures for Instagram.

"If you're on Insta, I can tag you," he said.

"You'll have to ask my brothers about that. I'm just a bystander."

For some reason, the kid seemed fascinated by the fact that they were all brothers. "All of you work together? Do you play sports together? Football? Tennis?"

Will lifted an eyebrow at him. "We're more of a basketball family."

"That's cool, that's cool. So you do all live together? Is that fun, kind of like a sitcom?"

Jesus. What was with this kid?

"Will!" Tobias called to him from the area of the hangar. He and Ben were rolling the Cessna 206 six-seater onto the tarmac. The propellers quivered in the constant breeze that came off the ocean. "Come on over for the family interview."

At the edge of the tarmac, Merry was watching the rollout of the Cessna with her head cocked, her eyes sparkling with curiosity. He allowed himself a moment to stare at her, since she wasn't looking his direction. She was so beautiful, with her pretty amber skin and unruly fluff of hair. How soft and springy would it be to the touch? His fingers itched to feel for himself.

But knowing Merry, she might turn on him like a spitting cat. She'd probably be shocked at how attracted he was to her. He barely admitted it himself. Around her he turned into a strait-laced stiff who barely cracked a smile. And he knew exactly why —because he was afraid of giving himself away. Letting on how incredibly appealing he found Merry Warren.

He left Chase, who was busy composing a tweet, and ambled toward his brothers. As he reached them, Merry was asking Tobias about the bidding war for the property. "I understand several real estate developers were interested. People were talking about vacation homes, condos, that sort of thing."

"That was thanks to Sean Marcus," answered Tobias. "He felt the community would be better served by bringing back a flight-seeing service like the one his parents had."

"Also, he's been wanting some more air support for the Jupiter Point Hotshots," Ben added. "We agreed to offer resources for search and rescue, firefighting, whatever Jupiter Point might need."

Merry scribbled notes in her reporter's notebook. It looked a lot like the notebook Will used during interviews, which amused him for a second. He and Merry had nothing in common—except those things they had in common.

"So the two of you are both trained pilots with military experience. And you, Deputy Knight?"

Will started. He'd been watching her smooth brown hand manipulating that pen. The sight was oddly sexy. "Nope. They're the flyboys. I keep my feet on the ground."

Ben slung his arm over Will's shoulders. "This guy right here is the roots. We're the leaves. Because we left, get it? He stayed in Jupiter Point and held down the fort."

Will gave him a narrow-eyed look. He didn't want Merry knowing about their family.

"Where's your sense of humor, bro?" Ben turned back to Merry with a shrug of apology. "Don't mind Grandpa here."

Merry gave him a somewhat sympathetic look. "So is it just you three running the family business?"

"We have a younger brother who just started college," Tobias said. "He's got a summer job here if he wants it, but school comes first."

"All boys. Wow. And your parents?"

Awkward silence descended, so fast and complete that the distant sound of waves on the gravel shoreline could be heard. A soft whir came from the gentle circling of the propellers. The scribbling of Merry's pen paused as she looked up.

Tobias cleared his throat. "Ah, we have a sister too. Our parents aren't part of this. They're—not around."

Will's stomach felt tied in a hundred knots. Merry glanced at him again, but he kept his face completely impassive. If she wanted to know more, she'd have to figure it out herself. She was a reporter, it shouldn't be too hard.

Luckily, she changed the subject. "Have you guys been in touch with Suzanne Finnegan at Stars in Your Eyes? She plans tour packages for honeymooners, and I bet she'd love to work with you once you're up and running."

Will relaxed, as did his brothers. None of them liked talking about their parents.

"Suzanne's coming out here tomorrow to meet with us," Ben answered. "We'll be catering to the tourist crowd, of course, but we also plan to offer a special rate to locals. We live in such a beautiful spot, especially when you see it from up there. It ought to be easier for people who live here to take advantage of that. Speaking of which, are you ready to get airborne?"

Merry stopped taking notes. "Um." She folded her lips, her confident manner disappearing completely. That one small moment made all of Will's stiffness melt away.

"First time in a small plane?" he asked her gently.

"Well, I'm not in it yet." She darted a nervous glance at the Cessna. At that moment, Chase jogged over to them. "Maybe Chase should go instead. He can take pictures for Instagram and all that."

"Sure!" the kid said eagerly. "I can get some great shots for you, Merry."

Will eyed him, amused by his eager-beaver manner.

"We can take you both," said Tobias. He buckled up his flight jacket. "There's plenty of room. Will, you come too."

Will was about to decline—he was due back at the station—when he caught another glance from Merry. A pleading one. How the hell could he resist that? Merry Warren, queen of attitude, was nervous about strapping herself into a Knight and Day Cessna 206?

He nodded, then added a teasing, one-sided smile. "Sure thing. Just don't hold my hand too hard, Merry."

She made a face at him. Good. He was used to sass from Merry. It was a lot easier to handle than panic.

IF SOMEONE HAD TOLD Merry that by the end of the week, she'd be holding Will Knight's hand, she would have laughed in their face. But there she was, ten thousand feet in the air, squeezing his big hand for dear life. She was probably crushing his bones, but she couldn't seem to loosen her grip.

The land was so far away, and as for this little tin can they were packed into...whose genius idea was this? Was this legal? Would someone really pay to do this?

Cotton tufts of clouds floated around them. She had the wild impulse to reach out and snag one, catch a ride with something that belonged up here. She'd ridden in airplanes before, of course. But on a commercial flight it was easier to pretend you weren't rattling through the air in something that belonged in a pantry. The outside air was *right there. Inches away.* And damn, was that a bird?

Will pried his hand out of hers and moved it to the base of her neck. Warm. Solid. Calming. Even through her ear protection, the drone of the engine drowned out other sounds. The plane hit an air pocket—or maybe it was a mountain, what did she know?—and dropped. She shrieked and clamped her hand onto his thigh. It felt like warm steel under her hand—another anchor in this crazy, free-floating cork bouncing on an air current.

His hand, still on the back of her neck, tightened. One thumb traced circles along her skin. Slow, calm movements. He gave her a reassuring smile and mouthed something, but she couldn't make it out over the engine noise and the hammering of the blood in her ears. But the motion of his thumb spoke its own language. *Everything is fine,* it said. *If this was a crisis, I wouldn't have time for such a thorough, slow-moving, sense-drugging caress, now would I?*

Slowly, surely, she relaxed. Her chest eased enough for her to take in a shaky breath. Will's thumb pressed harder, and her body automatically translated his meaning. *Take another breath. Deeper. That's it. Everything is fine. Close your eyes if you want. I'm here. I'm solid as a rock. And I'm not leaving.*

She clung to that reassurance as she forced her eyes back open. In the front seat next to Ben, Chase was snapping photos of the ocean below. He didn't seem bothered by the turbulence. Maybe he'd spent plenty of time in little private planes. LearJets, yachts, BMW's. The world was his oyster. She'd be more envious if she weren't so terrified.

Finally, the Cessna stabilized and the bouncing up and down changed to a smooth chug-a-chug.

And then, thanks to that soothing hand on her neck, she relaxed enough to appreciate the beauty of it. The vast sparkling sea. The hazy offshore islands, the puffy clouds, the endless horizon.

Chase turned around and flashed a delighted grin at her. For one moment she forgot her annoyance and smiled back.

The breathtaking vista out the plane's window drew her attention again. They were passing near an island, a wooded peak with creamy lines of foam lapping at the shoreline. Out of nowhere, a line of poetry came to her. One of the lines in Star-Lord's poem. *If you were an island, I'd be a breeze.*

She whispered the words under her breath because they fit the spellbinding beauty around her so perfectly.

Will looked at her sharply. "What did you say?"

Had he heard her random line reading? Unlikely, with all the engine noise. "I said, I can practically feel the breeze!"

She smiled at him, so giddy with relief she could practically kiss him. Those gray eyes would close in, those firm lips cover hers, that stubble brush against her cheek—

Kiss *Will*? What was she *thinking*? And oh my God, she still had her hand on his thigh.

She snatched her hand away.

Deputy Will Knight better not ever mention this moment. It was going in the vault, right along with that other incident-that-shall-not-be-named.

6

"OKAY, I GOT MY PITCHER. WHERE'S Y'ALLS?" MERRY WRAPPED HER arms around the plastic pitcher of neon-green liquid the waiter set on the table. Safely in her favorite booth at the Orbit Lounge and Grill, with her friends Evie, Suzanne, and Brianna around her, life finally felt normal again.

Brianna Gallagher flung up her hands. "Hey, if you need it that bad, it's all yours. I'm driving you home, though."

"Hell no. I'm driving myself from now on. I figured something out today." Merry filled the stack of plastic glasses that the waiter had provided along with the pitcher, and handed them out. "I am not a good passenger. Especially if the vehicle is basically the size of an airsickness bag"

Across the table, Evie's lovely face brightened. Merry privately considered her to be one of the most beautiful women she'd ever seen, with her silvery eyes and peaceful manner. She was married to Sean Marcus, who had sold the airstrip to the Knight brothers.

"The flight tour!" she said. "Did you take a ride in one of those little planes?"

"Yes, I did. And I kissed the ground that used to belong to Sean when we landed."

Brianna laughed. "I'm with you. Ground is good. The sky provides rain and sun and stars and looks pretty, and that's more than enough. I don't need a close-up view."

Since Brianna was a gardener who spent most of her time with her hands in the soil, this didn't surprise Merry. She lifted her glass to click it against Bri's.

"All of this is beside the point," Suzanne declared. With her long blonde hair and carefree attitude, one would never guess she was a new mom, except for the spot of spit-up on the shoulder of her blouse. "What we really want to know is what the hot cop's brothers are like now."

"I thought we agreed not to call him that?" Merry grumbled into her margarita.

"Did we?" Suzanne blinked innocently. "Pregnancy brain."

"You're not pregnant anymore," Brianna pointed out. "Unless...oh my God. You haven't touched that margarita. Oh my God! Suzanne, are you?"

"God no." She picked up her drink and drained it. "It's more of an all-purpose excuse," she gasped as she lowered the plastic glass. "I'm planning to use it as long as Josh lets me get away with it."

The others all laughed. Merry gazed at her friends with affection. Evie and Suzanne were cousins, and Evie and Brianna were childhood best friends. They'd all known each other forever, but they'd accepted her into their little group without hesitation. She loved that about Jupiter Point. New arrivals got the benefit of the doubt. As a city girl, she'd always imagined small towns to be close-minded and intolerant. She couldn't speak for other small towns, but Jupiter Point had accepted her easily.

"Back to our main topic of conversation here," said Suzanne. "The famous Knight brothers. They've been gone so long, I'm not sure I'd recognize them."

Merry waved her hands in the air. "Hold up, hold up, hold up. You know the family?"

They all stared at her in surprise. "Of course," Evie said. "From afar. They lived outside of town, so they didn't go to our high school. But everyone knew about them anyway. Four wild brothers and one spoiled sister. People told crazy stories about them. They were hell-raisers, every one of them."

"Excuse me, are we talking about the same Will Knight? The one who singlehandedly upholds the rule of law with that stick up his ass?"

Brianna laughed at that description. "He wasn't always like that. He changed after—" She broke off, then lowered her voice. "Well, after the murder."

"The *what*?" Merry waved her hands about again. Maybe that margarita had been stronger than usual, because she sure hadn't seen *that* coming. "What are you talking about? No one gets murdered around here. This is honeymoon-stargazing territory. Murder's bad for tourism."

"Well, strictly speaking, it didn't happen in Jupiter Point," said Brianna. "They lived outside city limits."

"I feel bad even talking about this," said Evie softly. "It's been so long, and it really tore their family apart. I've never heard Will mention it. And the other brothers joined the military right afterward. I think they just wanted some space from all the talk."

Merry sloshed the last of her margarita around. "Can someone please give me the details here because I'm really not used to being the last to know something."

The other women exchanged glances. Merry jiggled her foot impatiently. She could always look it up in the archives, but she burned with curiosity and wanted the details now.

Suzanne finally stepped into the silence. "It was their father. He was found murdered at their house. Stabbed, I think. No one ever found out who did it. Some people said it was a random stranger, other people suspected Mrs. Knight. I guess they had a lot of problems in their marriage. After she was cleared, she had a meltdown and left town with Cassie, the only daughter. I think she was maybe sixteen then. Will was twenty-two and he took charge of the family. He was in law school then, but he dropped out and came back home to deal with everything."

Brianna was shaking her head at the memory, her ginger-cinnamon hair gleaming in the overhead light. "It was so awful. Poor Will. The whole family was a mess. The youngest brother, Aiden, was like, eight. His father had been murdered and his mother abandoned him. Poor kid. But he's doing well now, or so I've heard."

Merry realized her mouth had dropped open. All this time, no inkling of this story had reached her ears. In three years, no one had thought to mention an unsolved murder involving someone she worked with on a regular basis.

And then she remembered that moment when she'd asked the brothers about their parents and they all froze. She'd even made a note of it. "Parents?" she'd written. The shock of that plane flight had chased the memory right out of her head.

"No one talks about it," she marveled. "I haven't heard anything until this very moment."

Evie nodded thoughtfully, her sleek dark hair spilling over her shoulder. "It's out of respect for Will, I think. Everyone around here loves him. He could have run for sheriff and won in a landslide. He probably didn't want to stir up any talk about the murder. It has to be tough, the fact that it was never solved. The family never got any justice."

Stunned, Merry thought about the three brothers she'd spent time with today. Suddenly she saw Will, Tobias and Ben in a fascinating new light.

Especially Will, to be honest. She'd always known he was smart, but law school? That part was news to her. The fact that he'd left school to take care of his family gave her a new level of respect for him. Actually, it explained a lot. His sense of responsibility, his sternness, even his slow-mo-ness. He wasn't just a thorough deputy, he was a de facto parent.

"I wonder why no one at the paper ever mentioned any of this?"

"Because it's in the past," said Evie firmly. "The Knight brothers are back home, and everyone's happy to have them. It's great for the community. Not to mention all the single girls around. No one wants to stir up something that's going to hurt them. What's the point?"

"It's an unsolved murder right here in Jupiter Point" Merry pointed out. "That sounds pretty interesting to me."

Suzanne used her napkin to dab a drop of margarita from her upper lip. "Merry Warren, don't even think about digging up that story. You know how you're always complaining about Will, saying how slow he is and how he never gets back to you in time. You call him Deputy Slow-mo."

"Yes, so?" Merry shifted uncomfortably in the booth. She liked to vent her frustrations in the safe space of the Orbit, but Will had a lot of good qualities as well. When it came to his police work, he was the best—thorough, fair, highly respected. He was one of the good guys, and she knew how important that was. Also, he'd rescued her from that idiot who had shot her with a tranquilizer dart at Finn's place. And that wasn't even including his rock-hard thighs and a warm hand that felt perfect against the back of her neck.

"He won't talk to you at all, ever, if you mess around with that," Suzanne finished. "It's like the third rail of the Knight family. They don't talk about it."

"And neither does anyone else. They dealt with the trauma in their own way, and they deserve the space to do that," Evie said softly.

Merry sucked on her straw to avoid commenting. Silence might work for the rest of Jupiter Point. But she was a reporter.

Curiosity was her superpower. Ignoring this story might be beyond her abilities.

"So back to our original question, how'd those boys turn out?" Brianna asked.

"If you like 'em big and good-looking, not too bad." Merry smiled at the others. "As it happens, that's not my jam. I'm more into the cerebral type."

"Cerebral?" Lisa Peretti slid into the booth next to Merry and they shared a quick hug. They'd become good friends earlier in the year, when Lisa had been hiding out in Jupiter Point to escape a criminal who was after her. They'd proclaimed themselves Team Cynic, until Lisa had fallen in love with Finn, another firefighter. "Are you talking about your online mystery man?"

"Ohh!" Suzanne clapped her hands with excitement. "No wonder you're immune to the Knight brothers. You have a mystery man? Do you know anything about him?"

Merry sighed. Maybe she shouldn't have mentioned her adventures on Flirt to anyone.

"I have no idea who he is, but I think he's from somewhere near here. And he's amazing. He writes me poems. He's soulful, sensitive, and nothing like the men I usually meet."

"To be fair, the men you usually meet are often under investigation," Brianna pointed out. "Or the ones doing the investigating."

"Exactly, that's why I want someone completely different. You girls can keep your macho firemen with their washboard abs and so forth. I'll go for the sweet poet who makes me smile every time I open one of his messages."

The other four women exchanged amused looks. "It's not the abs we love, Merry," said Evie. "It's what's underneath all those muscles. The heart and soul."

"A man who stands by you," agreed Suzanne, her aquamarine eyes misty.

"Who always has your back," said Lisa. "Even when you think you don't need it."

"Who will *literally* save your life," threw in Brianna.

Merry had heard enough. This sentimental shit was *so* not her scene. She dug through her laptop bag for her wallet. "I don't need a man to save my life or take care of me or any of that. I take care of my *own* self. Nothing against men, but you can't rely on them. Men are good for two things—sex and a good laugh. And half the time, I'm laughing *at* them." She found her wallet and fished out a twenty.

Lisa stopped her before she could put the bill on the table. "Put your money away. This round's on me. I just got a job at the Urgent Care and I'm celebrating."

"Girl, congratulations!" Merry gave her a little side hug. "I feel safer already. See? Who needs a man? We ladies got this. We got the power. Just like my mama always said. We're strong, we're smart, we can handle our own business." She stashed the wallet back in her bag. "Me and my mystery poet, we're the perfect match. With a little vibrator action on the side."

She winked as everyone burst out laughing.

"Whatever works for you, Merry." Lisa squeezed her hand with a smile. "We just want you to be happy. So when are you going to meet this man?"

"Meet him!" Merry pulled a comical face. "That might ruin the whole thing."

"Oh come on, you must be curious. Are you telling me that Merry Warren, superstar reporter, doesn't have the teensiest, tiniest desire to meet him in person?"

Of course she did. Hadn't she just been thinking the same thing while driving to Knight and Day?

"I'm a little curious," she admitted. "Actually, I've been putting together the clues he's dropped."

Brianna bounced on the vinyl seat. "This is fun, like playing detective. What have you figured out?"

"I think he's a professor." Merry ticked off qualities on her fingers. "I think he's a single dad, I'm guessing a widower. He teaches something like law, or criminal justice, something like that. He writes poetry on the side, just for his own pleasure. He doesn't have much time to date because he's raising a child alone. And his secretary is named Cindy."

"That's impressive detective work," said Lisa. "How do you know about his secretary?"

"Once he sent a message to me that was meant for her. I think it was a cut and paste error." Merry grinned at her friends, who all looked appropriately impressed. "Have y'all forgotten I'm a reporter? This is what I do. I figure things out."

"Yeah, but you won't know if you're right until you actually meet him," Suzanne said. "And *when* you do, I'll take care of everything through Stars in Your Eyes. I'll create the best blind date you could ever imagine. It will be destiny in action. Ooh, this is going to be amazing!"

"*If* we meet," Merry reminded her. "*Big* if."

None of her friends looked convinced by that "if." Honestly, neither was Merry.

"Oh," said Evie suddenly. "I forgot to ask you about the new guy you were with this morning. Mrs. Murphy made me promise to ask, or she'd ban me from the bookstore. It doesn't mean you have to answer," she added quickly.

"He's, well...he's the new intern. And—" She broke off. It hadn't been *terrible* hanging out with Chase today. But she still wasn't ready to claim him as her brother. "He's new," she added weakly.

Evie took a sip of her drink, eyeing her with amusement. "A new intern who's new. My work for Mrs. Murphy is done."

7

I've been putting things together and I think I've figured out who you are. Will flexed his fingers in preparation for dropping his truth-bomb on AnonyMs. He only had a couple minutes before he had to leave for a re-interview of an arson witness. He aimed to wrap up all the interviews before Perez left for his honeymoon.

But he always had time for AnonyMs.

You're a novelist who writes mysteries. Someone like Sue Grafton. You're either divorced or you've never been married. You're cynical when it comes to the opposite sex so you've probably had some bad experiences. He flexed his hands again, debating his next statement. Once he broached the idea of meeting, it would be hard to back off. *You live within driving distance of Jupiter Point. One more thing. You've been thinking about whether we should meet in person, but you're not sure if it's a good idea.*

He checked the time on the computer. He needed to hit the road.

I'm not sure either, but here's the thing. What doesn't move forward dies before it has a chance to live. I don't want this to wither away from lack of oxygen. If we don't meet, that's what might happen. I'm willing to take the risk. Are you?

He hovered his index finger over the "send" button. This was it. Once he let this message out into the ether, there would be no going back.

"Will, help us out here." Tobias's voice came from right behind his back.

Quickly he clicked on the other tab he had open—the front page of the *Mercury News-Gazette*. Merry's article had just come out. Its headline read, "Knight Flight to the Rescue," along with a shot of Tobias and Ben in their leather flight jackets, arms crossed over their chests, posing in front of the Cessna.

"Oh good, you already have it up. Did you read the article? She did a good job."

"Yeah, I read it. She made you guys sound like fucking heroes."

His favorite line read, "Both Tobias and Ben Knight have distinguished records of military service, but they each echoed the same sentiment. It was time to come home and serve the community in the best way they could."

"She mentioned you, too."

"Yes, I noticed that part. I quote: 'They join their oldest brother, well known to Jupiter Point as Deputy Will Knight, who says he's a silent partner in the new enterprise. In a perhaps unrelated side note, Knight and Day Flight Tours is promising a hundred percent on-time policy."

Tobias's laugh rumbled like a front-loader pouring gravel. He leaned his hip on the edge of Will's desk. He was such a huge dude, Will worried he might tip it over. "Nice dig. I like that girl."

"Yeah? Well, good luck with that."

He winced at how harsh that sounded. Merry could be aggravating, but he respected her. He admired her work ethic and her bright mind. And he was trying like hell to pretend he wasn't wildly attracted to her. That was another reason to meet AnonyMs as soon as possible. He needed a distraction.

"We want to send her something as a thank you for the article," Tobias said. "Maybe flowers. Any idea what kind she likes?"

"Tiger lilies," he said promptly.

Tobias lifted one black eyebrow. "You send her flowers a lot?"

With a start, Will realized he was thinking of AnonyMs. He had no idea what kind of flowers Merry liked. "Nah, that was just a bullshit answer off the top of my head. For Merry, I don't know. Something with thorns? Something that makes you break out in a rash?"

Tobias snorted. "Get your head out of your ass, bro. I like her. If I thought there was a chance she'd say yes, I'd ask her out."

The idea got under Will's skin in a major way. Tobias and Merry—nah, he couldn't see that working out at all. Tobias liked biker chicks and tattoo models and strippers. And Merry liked... anyone but Will, probably.

"I wouldn't bother," he said, trying not to let his discomfort show. "Merry keeps her personal life very private. I've never heard of her going out with anyone. She's very focused on her career."

Tobias's dark eyes, a blue so deep it looked black, scanned him closely. "Any reason I shouldn't try?" He tucked his thumbs in his pockets with the swagger of a man who never left a bar without someone's phone number.

Will gritted his teeth. He didn't have a legitimate reason to tell Tobias to stay away from Merry. But he couldn't keep his mouth shut either. "This is a small town, dude. People respect Merry. She has a lot of friends here. A lot of them are married or engaged to firefighters. In other words, watch yourself."

"You know, all you have to say is that you want her for yourself. You don't have to make up a bunch of reasons."

"Excuse me?"

"Like I'm afraid of some firefighters. Come on." Tobias

smirked at him. *I've kicked ass on five continents*, said that cocky grin. "Man up. Admit you're interested."

"You have her number. Go ahead, call her. Just don't blame me if she laughs in your face. Now get out of here. I have to finish up some work."

God, would he ever leave? Will burned with impatience to get back to his unfinished message to AnonyMs. Tobias pushed himself away from the desk.

"We'll go with the tiger lilies," he said over his shoulder as he left.

Will barely heard him. As soon as Tobias was out of the room, he clicked over to the Flirt tab and reread his message. Oh man. He was really putting it out there.

If she said no, things would be different. If she said yes, things would be different.

Fuck it. He hit the red "send" icon and watched his message evaporate from the screen.

WILL STRUCK gold with the re-interview. One of the witnesses was a teenager who'd been camping with his family. During the first interview, he hadn't said much. But this time, Will interviewed him where he worked, at one of the loading docks on the waterfront. Away from his family, the kid talked much more. He remembered jogging past a man wearing a t-shirt from a private local gym called Heavenly Hardbodies. Finally, a break.

Afterwards, driving through the waterfront, Will spotted the borderline offensive sign for the Rootin' Rooster. The one time he'd come out here to investigate a drunk and disorderly call, he'd noticed that the burgers didn't look half bad. And he was hungry.

It was a forty-five-minute drive back home—might as well get some food in his stomach first. He swung into the gravel lot, which was filled with pickup trucks, Harleys and an RV. Good thing he wasn't wearing his uniform. Maybe no one here would recognize him or give him any trouble. He fished a cowboy hat from his backseat. Maybe it would disguise him enough to avoid any recognition from anyone he might have arrested at some point.

Inside the Rootin' Rooster, Toby Keith was blasting so loudly you would almost think the bar was a happening place—until you noticed the half-dead demeanor of the clientele. Mostly men slouched at the tables, fondling their shot glasses and eyeing the waitresses.

The last time Will had been here, he hadn't paid attention to the waitstaff. He definitely hadn't noticed their uniforms. Every server—they were all attractive women—wore a strange kind of outfit with feathers sprouting from the back of their waistband.

Good Lord. The burgers better be good. He felt dirty just walking into the place.

He grabbed a chair at an empty table and sank into it. He rested his arm on the table, wincing at the sensation of old beer sticking to the fabric of his shirt. Screw this—what were the chances the hamburgers were any good when they couldn't even clean off the tables? It offended his love of cleanliness and order.

He was trying to peel his sleeve off the table so he could leave when someone stuck a menu in front of him.

"That's okay, I changed my mind," he muttered as he finally freed his shirt.

"Really? Is something in here not as advertised?"

That voice sounded familiar. He finally pried his shirt away from the sticky mess on the table and looked up at the waitress.

Sparkling, mocking brown eyes, smooth amber skin, full lips curved into a merry smile, full *breasts* cupped in the ridiculous chicken costume all the waitresses wore.

Holy rootin' rooster. "*Merry?*"

OH, for God's sake. Will Knight? *Seriously?* The only non-heinous man to walk into this place in the last two hours, the man hiding underneath a cowboy hat, rocking an ass-hugging pair of jeans and a damn fine leather jacket, that man had to be *Will Knight*?

"Of all the sleazy bars in all of Jupiter Point, you had to walk into mine," Merry said dryly. "But it looks like you're walking right out again, so don't let me stop you."

"I changed my mind. I'll have a Roosterburger and fries."

She scrunched up her face. "Try again."

He picked up the menu and squinted at it. He'd taken off the cowboy hat but stashed it on his lap. He probably didn't want it touching the disgusting table. She'd tried to wipe it off but really, the job required some degreaser and a chisel. "Roosterburger and coleslaw?"

"Better. The oil in the fryolator hasn't been changed in a decade, apparently. There's always a chance of *e coli* from the salad though. Consider yourself warned." She started to leave but he snagged her wrist.

"Hang on a rootin'-tootin' second. What are you doing here?"

"Oh, that's funny. Rootin'-tootin'. Very quick with the mockery there, aren't you? I'm working and I just took an order. Wouldn't want to keep our high-class customers waiting." She made a face at him and tried to leave, but still he kept ahold of her wrist.

"You have a job. A pretty demanding one, last I checked. Seriously, what are you doing here?"

"Is there some kind of legal problem with me working two jobs? Because otherwise, I'm really not seeing how this is any of your business."

He was watching her closely, those deep gray eyes penetrating right to her soul. Something fluttered in her lower belly, the kind of sensation that always meant trouble. Sexual excitement. Lust. AKA catastrophe.

"This isn't the kind of place I'd ever picture you working. For sure, I never thought I'd see you wearing something like *that*." His gaze skimmed briefly across her rooster uniform. All of a sudden, she was much more aware of the way the rooster bustier left the upper curves of her breasts bare. "If you need extra money, we can always use part-time help at the department. I could put a good word in for you."

Pride stiffened her spine. "I don't need your charity," she snapped. "I love this job. The tips are fantastic and I get to meet so many fascinating people. I'd work here for free, just for kicks."

His eyes narrowed, making the gray of his irises stand out in the low illumination. "I don't believe a single word you're saying. I know you, Merry. You're the last person who wants to prance around in a corset and tail feathers. This is for a story, isn't it?"

She quickly reviewed her options. Should she tell Will that she was chasing a story here? She still had one training shift to go before she was off probation. If the manager—or the big boss—knew she was chatting up a cop, she'd be out on her ass. Her best chance to follow up on this lead would evaporate.

If she told Will her reason for being there, would he leave quietly and let her do her thing? Or would he make a fuss and drag her out of the place? Knowing the bossy, control-freak, straitlaced Will the way she did, she figured on an eighty percent chance of the latter.

She couldn't take that risk.

Lifting her chin, she cocked her hip and planted a hand on her red-satin-covered hipbone. "That just shows you don't know me as well as you think. I *love* to prance. *Especially* in tail feathers." She spun on her heel and hip-swayed her way across the floor as if it were a catwalk. Every eyeball in the place followed her. She knew it, she felt it, and she didn't care. The only thing she wanted to do was wipe that look off Will's judgmental face.

~

WILL WANTED to tear his gaze away from Merry's perky rear, but that would have required a complete brain transplant. God, was any woman ever more infuriating? She seemed to go out of her way to irritate him and get under his skin. He was trying to look out for her, for Chrissake.

No matter what she said, he'd bet his truck that she was here on a story. But what kind of story could the Rootin' Rooster possibly have to offer?

The place was a haven for lowlifes. They drank, they brawled, they left big tips, and sometimes they crossed the line. Assault and battery cases weren't uncommon. The owner was a complete sleazeball; some said he was mobbed up but no one had ever proved it. Will often heard rumors of drug deals taking place here...

And then it clicked. *Goddamn it.* Merry was here following up on the story she'd promised to put on pause. The link between the campfire arson and the flow of opioids into the area. She must think the Rootin' Rooster had something to do with it.

Nothing else made sense. If she wanted to do a story on the life of a cocktail waitress, she could find a place closer to home. To take a temporary job in the worst part of town, the story had to be worth her while. Only something big would fit that bill.

Stewing, he watched as she darted around the room, taking orders and delivering drinks. In typical Merry fashion, she moved fast and smart, so efficient, so on point. She had a good manner with the customers, too. Just friendly enough to earn her tips, but not so much as to encourage conversation.

Who was Merry Warren, anyway? He knew so little about her, he realized. All he knew was the outer layer—the quick-witted reporter who always had a comeback and who wrote clean, precise articles that actually got the facts right. The woman who never dated, as far as he knew, but had tons of friends. The woman who, after she'd woken up on his couch, had ghosted before they could discuss what had happened.

What else? Merry had no patience for bullshit. He'd seen her roll her eyes during press conferences when someone made a statement that didn't add up. Her car was a godawful mess. She liked to laugh. She worked hard. And damn, she really knew how to move in tights, a bustier and tail feathers.

Everyone else was noticing exactly the same thing. Goddamn, it wasn't safe for her here. What was she going to do, work past midnight, then drive back to town in her crappy, messy Corolla? What about all the drunken deadbeats who might follow her to her car?

He dug the heel of his hand into his forehead. A headache was developing, he was exhausted from traveling, and all he wanted to do was get home. But no way was he going to leave Merry here on her own. He'd have to stick around until closing.

When she sashayed over to deliver his Roosterburger, he told her as much. As predicted, she didn't take it well.

"You're insane. Do you know how many cocktail waitresses work here? Are you going to babysit every one of them?"

"Only if they have a knack for getting into trouble." Serenely, he ignored her protests and poured ketchup on his burger.

"I'm just doing my job."

He glanced up at her. She held the tray under her arm, the opposite hand planted on her hip. Her golden-brown eyes snapped with outrage.

"That's just it. Which job are you *really* doing?"

The flash of self-consciousness told him he'd hit the bull's-eye. She skimmed a glance across the nearby tables, probably making sure no one could hear them.

She lowered her voice. "Again, it's really none of your business. Isn't there some kind of rule about interfering in an investigation? You're always accusing me of that."

He burst out laughing. "Dream on, Lois Lane. There's no law against me interfering in your investigation, especially since you promised you'd let it rest."

"I said I wouldn't *print* anything. That doesn't mean I can't do my research."

"So you *are* researching. Damn it, Merry. That's a bad idea." He leaned closer and gripped a hand around her forearm. "Drug dealers are dangerous. You aren't trained to handle this kind of situation. Why don't you let the police take over?"

"I'm not getting in anyone's way." She jerked her arm away. "I'm just waiting tables. Jesus. Now eat your burger and go along home. We don't like customers hogging the tables."

"I already told you. I'm not leaving. If you make a fuss, I'll let the manager know he hired himself a fake waitress."

Her face tightened with anger. "You wouldn't."

"Try me. Face it, Merry, you're a magnet for trouble. You nearly got kidnapped off a hiking trail. Then you got shot with a tranquilizer dart. Now you're wearing that," he waved a hand at her outfit, "around fifty men who are quickly losing all their inhibitions. I'm not leaving here without you."

She stared at him for a long moment, then shook her head as if resigning herself to putting up with a watchdog. "Fine. If you're going to be so stubborn, the least I could do is bring you some sustenance. You like fries?"

"Very funny."

She screwed up her face at him. "Should have figured you wouldn't forget that comment. Let me ask you something, Deputy Annoying. Are you single?"

He stabbed a fork into his coleslaw. "Why do you ask that? I'm not trying to hit on you. I'm trying to keep you safe."

"The reason I ask is because you really ought to think about lightening up. I'm a grown woman. Did you ever think maybe you're scaring away all the good ones with your bossy attitude?"

"Is that an honest question?" He laid his fork down and held her gaze. She nodded, though his sudden intensity made her draw back a bit. "Honest answer, then. No, I've never considered the possibility that my bossiness scares women away. For most it's a turn-on, as a matter of fact. I've never heard a complaint from anyone except you, out of all the women in Jupiter Point. So I guess that means we won't be going to bed anytime soon."

Her pupils widened and he caught the subtle sound of her breath quickening.

Jesus. It was a damn good thing he was off duty. He'd never talk to her like this if he was on the job. He usually kept himself under better control.

"Some men are sensitive to a woman's feelings," Merry was saying. "They *ask*, instead of issuing orders. Maybe you should consider giving it a try sometime."

He snorted. "Let me guess, you have some fantasy about a New Age guy who plays the flute and rubs your feet and listens to all your problems."

She gaped at him.

Ha. He'd hit the nail on the head. "Maybe that's why *you're* still single. Those guys only exist in, I don't know, ads for a juice cleanse or something."

Her nostrils flared. She looked like she was about to bonk him on the head with her tray. Maybe he'd gone too far.

He softened his tone. "I'm just trying to keep you from getting hurt. It's part of the whole 'protect and serve' mentality. Are we on the same page here?"

"Put it this way," she said in a voice that shook ever so slightly. "I accept the fact that I'm not getting rid of you tonight. Likewise, I accept the fact that you are the last man in Jupiter Point that I will *ever* go to bed with. So I guess we *are* on the same page."

"Good." Emphatically, he lifted his burger and ripped a hunk of meat off it. Cold. Damn it.

As he savagely chewed his burger, he knew one thing for sure. If Merry had disliked him before, multiply that by a thousand now. Maybe a lawman and a reporter were doomed to be at odds forever.

Thank God for AnonyMs. At least with her, he could have a

civil, adult conversation. Something that was clearly impossible with Merry Warren.

8

THE FACT THAT WILL DIDN'T TRUST HER ENOUGH TO LET HER DO her job in peace made Merry furious. Out of the four cocktail waitresses at the Rootin' Rooster, she was the only one with her own tagalong rent-a-cop. He didn't watch her *every* move, but it felt like it. Sometimes she glanced over and saw him talking on his phone, or jotting down notes on a notepad.

Maybe he was actually picking up some clues while he was hanging around. Which would be helpful, since she hadn't gleaned anything since she'd started working here.

Not that he would share any clues with her. Of course not. He didn't respect her or what she did.

One bright side was that the other customers took note of his presence and left her alone more than usual. Since he'd taken his seat, all long-legged and quiet and forceful, not a single drunkard had put a hand on her ass.

As the night wore on, her anger drained away. She'd always been quick to react, but her temper usually cooled just as quickly.

Really, sticking around to protect her was a thoughtful gesture. Obviously Will was tired. The dark circles under his eyes made them a smokier color than usual. Grooves bracketed his mouth. His firm lips cut like stone into the dark grain of his scruff. He didn't have his usual stoic patience with an undercurrent of irritation. Tonight, that irritation came right out into the open. He seemed edgier, rougher, and face it—hotter.

She'd always considered him an attractive man, though she'd fought against it. But out of his uniform, in an open-necked shirt and worn jeans...Jesus take the wheel. He was really something.

And he was dedicating his night to watching over her. Solid, trustworthy, *good* Will Knight. Fighter of evil, defender of Jupiter Point.

Honestly, it was difficult to be too upset with him. Besides, she'd just have to nose around on her next shift. He couldn't stalk her every night.

At the end of her shift, she changed into her regular clothes in the staff bathroom. She carefully slipped her tail feather costume into a garment bag and hung it in the closet set aside for the waitstaff's uniforms. She stuffed her tips into her purse then slung it across her chest, messenger-bag style.

The other waitresses were hanging out at the bar for one last nightcap. Ordinarily, Merry would join them in case anyone dropped a tidbit she could follow up on. But not tonight. Not with Will waiting. Besides, she wanted her bed and her own apartment. It felt like weeks since she'd been there.

And because of that decision, she got the first break in her "investigation." As she was slipping out the side door, which was reserved for employees, she spotted a large, beefy man whose mass was large enough to seem gravitational. His manner, his posture, all reeked of "lord of all he surveys" arrogance. He was in the midst of approaching a dark sedan with tinted windows—a hired Town Car, she guessed. A driver waited inside, the engine idling. Another man stepped out as he approached and opened the back door for him.

He inserted his huge body inside and gave a signal to drive away.

A chill rippled through her. She had no doubt that man had something to do with whatever criminal activity was taking place at the Rootin' Rooster. Even though she hadn't seen much of him, she fixed the details of his appearance in her mind. Weight, close to three hundred pounds. Height, six feet. Coloring—who knew?

If only she'd left just a little bit earlier and had been sitting in her car. She would have had a crystal-clear view of him...

She glanced across the parking lot and caught sight of Will's Tacoma right next to her car.

In perfect position to see that man.

She waited until the sedan had completely disappeared from the lot, then dashed across to the Tacoma. Will rolled down the window as she approached.

"Did you see that man?" she asked him.

He maintained that implacable calm that always irritated her. "What man?"

"The one who just got into that sedan. I'll bet you anything he's involved in this thing. If you were paying any attention at all, you would have noticed him."

"Hm." He shrugged his broad shoulders. Her glance dropped to the seat next to him. His hand was tented over an object that looked suspiciously like a smartphone.

"Oh my God. You got a shot of him, didn't you?"

He lifted one eyebrow at her but refused to answer her question. "You're probably ready to get home. You must be tired. I'll wait until you drive away. I want to make sure you leave safely."

Merry felt as if the top of her head might blow off from sheer frustrated rage. "Are you seriously telling me that after my long night of slinging flat beer and poison fries, *you* got the best lead, and you aren't even going to share it with me?"

"I told you what I think. Investigators investigate. Reporters report. Now are you going home or do I have to get out and physically put you into your car so I can get some sleep?"

The nerve. The colossal, unmitigated, inexcusable *nerve* of the man. She hauled off and kicked his front tire. She was wearing her favorite half-boots, suede with a zipper up the side, so she didn't kick too hard. The gesture hurt her toe more than the tire, for sure.

Even so, it wiped that smirk off his face. "Seriously? You're going to assault a law enforcement officer?"

"No. Just his vehicle." She kicked again, the sharp toe of her boot slamming into the rubber of his tire with a satisfying *thunk*. "And you'd better keep a close watch on that phone too, because I'll snag it the first chance I get."

"You're going to *rob* an officer? You're really asking for trouble, aren't you?" Amusement threaded his voice.

"Don't laugh at me. I'm really mad at you."

"Yeah, I got that. My truck got that. My tire got that. I'm sorry you're mad that I can't just share police evidence with you until I know what it means."

"It's a *photo*. If you're so worried about my safety, you should show it to me so I can avoid that man. How am I supposed to recognize him if I never see his face?"

If that argument moved him, he didn't show it. "You should get home."

She threw up a hand. "We're done. Don't follow me. Don't talk to me." She took a few steps away from him, then whirled around again. "Did you ever wonder how I got to the age of twenty-six with no major injuries, a master's in journalism, and a portfolio full of award-winning press clippings? Did you ever think, 'Hm, maybe she's smart and knows what she's doing and doesn't take stupid chances? Maybe I should offer her a little respect instead of shutting her down? Hm, maybe that Merry Warren cares just as much about the well-being of Jupiter Point as I do?'" She shook her head, the frustration cracking around her like static. "*This* is why you can't trust a man. This is why us women are better off standing up for ourselves."

At least she got the last word. Will said nothing else as she stormed away from his truck. She marched to her car, which she'd parked under the brightest light in the lot. Despite what Will seemed to think, she knew how to keep herself safe. She had the power. She worked out, she'd taken self-defense training, she didn't put herself into dangerous situations. If she found herself in a sketchy spot, she knew how to de-escalate and squirm her way out of it.

Failing that, she knew how to dial nine-one-one. And ask for anyone *except* Deputy Will Knight.

Still fuming, she drove out of the lot, thoroughly aware of Will's close attention to her exit.

Back home, she was still so worked up that she changed into Tommy Hilfiger boxers and a ribbed T and danced around to her "power" playlist, which was a weird mixture of old school hip-hop and Brazilian afro-pop that her mother sent her. Her mom showed up in the mix too, though her songs were mostly jazz ballads.

Still vibrating with adrenaline, she sorted through her mail, then drank a tall glass of lemonade. She watered her plants, which she kept in her kitchen sink because the leaky faucet was their only source of water if she was on a deadline. She took a stab at cleaning up her living room. Mostly that meant carting piles of books and papers from one place to another. She thought of her apartment as a nest, which meant everything was soft and cushiony. She'd chosen plush chocolate carpet, the most comfortable couch ever designed, and a color scheme of bronze and green that she found very easy on the eyes.

When she'd finally worked off all that energy, she pulled out her laptop. She could really use a sweet message from her favorite online mystery man. The best way to counteract an obnoxious man would be a chat with someone completely different. Honestly, sometimes she found it amazing that two members of the same gender could be so opposite.

In her email inbox, she found a message from Chase. *Great*

article!! You killed it. Did you like my photos?

She answered with, *Yes. Nice job.* She had the sense she was patting a friendly dog on the head. He was so eager to please, and if he maintained respect for her boundaries, maybe they could start talking in a more genuine way.

She switched to the Flirt app and saw that a message had been waiting there since Friday. She'd been so busy with her weekend Rootin' Rooster shifts that she hadn't checked. She scanned through it quickly, her heart rate amping up all over again.

I don't want this thing between us to wither away from lack of oxygen. If we don't meet, that's what might happen. I'm willing to take the risk. Are you?

Oh my God. This was it. Decision time.

StarLord was right. If they never met in person, they'd eventually lose steam. On the other hand, if they *did* meet in person, who knew what would happen?

She thought about Will Knight and his infuriating behavior. Damn it, she wanted to meet StarLord just to spite Will. To prove that men could be sensitive and sweet.

Stalling for time, she clicked over to her email. A new message had come in about ten minutes ago, probably while she'd been dancing around in her underwear. It was from Will Knight's personal email account, which she'd never actually seen before.

The subject line read, "Friend of yours?"

The body of the email was nothing but an attachment. A photo of the man at the Rootin' Rooster. The photo had been snapped at the moment when he was getting into the sedan, so the interior dome light illuminated his features. She didn't recognize him, but he sure looked like a hard man.

She downloaded the photo onto her laptop, then tapped out a reply. "I appreciate this. Your next Roosterburger is on me. How's your tire?"

A few seconds later, he replied to her email. "I'd rather eat my tire than another one of those burgers. But thanks."

She smiled and jiggled back and forth in her chair. When Will relaxed, he was kind of cute. He was attractive no matter what, of course. But when he let his sense of humor come out, he was positively endearing. And she really couldn't believe she was saying that—even silently, to herself, in the privacy of her own apartment. She sent off one more email. "Since sharing is caring, I'll remember this. Good night."

Once again, it took mere seconds for him to respond. Will was a lot quicker with the comebacks than she'd realized. "Saving this email for posterity. Good night."

She smiled again, all of her previous anger with him dissipating in a flood of warmth. He was a good guy. Better not to be at odds with him. Much better to have Will as a friend than an enemy.

As for something beyond friends...

Well, she had StarLord for that.

She went back to the app and tapped out her acceptance before she could think better of it. She added, *One catch: I get to make the arrangements. I'll message you tomorrow with the details.*

Amazingly enough, StarLord also answered right away. Jeez, was everyone online late on a Sunday night?

I leave it completely in your hands. Standing by for instructions.

See? That was the kind of respectful approach every man ought to have. If only she could show Will. He could learn a thing or two from StarLord. Although—he was probably too stubborn to change. Once a cop, always a cop.

Before she went to bed, she fired off a quick text to Suzanne. *Mystery man meeting is on. You're in charge! Just make sure it's a public place in case my instincts are way the hell off. Xoxoxo.*

She logged off her computer and, finally exhausted, flopped into bed.

9

THE NEXT MORNING, SHE GOT A MINOR SHOCK AT THE *MERCURY News-Gazette*. A bouquet of tiger lilies sat on her desk in a curved glass vase. Tiger lilies! Who could possibly know that she liked tiger lilies? Unless Chase had somehow figured it out and was trying to work his way ...

She grabbed the vase and marched down the hallway toward the break room, where the interns and copy assistants hung out. Chase was there alone, feet propped on a metal folding chair, elbow resting on the table as he scanned his phone.

She placed the vase of flowers on the table next to him, jarring his elbow from its position. "I reject your flowers," she told him. "That sort of thing is not going to work on me, and how did you know about tiger lilies anyway?"

He straightened up and pulled his feet off the chair with a metallic clatter. "What are you talking about? Those aren't from me."

"They aren't?" She frowned at them, completely confused now. StarLord knew she liked tiger lilies, but he didn't know where she worked or even who she was...*did he*?

"How would I know what kind of flowers you like?" Chase was

saying in a wry tone. " I know hardly anything about you. So far, all I know is that you work a lot."

"That's right. I'm a workaholic and proud of it. Some people have to work for a living, though that might come as a shock to you."

He snorted. "Dad works all the time. Maybe that's where you got it from."

She flinched backwards. She'd never considered that her work dedication might come from her non-father. "I doubt that," she said stiffly. But oddly, she felt an unexpected urge to know more about Gordon Merriweather. She knew the publicly available facts about her missing parent, but nothing else. Nothing intimate. "Does he, uh, like his work?"

"I don't know. I guess. He likes making money and he kind of has to keep the family business going. Hey, look." He poked his finger between the stalks of the lilies. "There's a tag."

She snatched it from him and scanned it quickly. "Thank you for the very well-written story. You're welcome back anytime. (If you dare!) Tobias and Ben Knight, Knight and Day Flight Tours."

Huh. She stared at the tag, completely puzzled. How on earth would either Tobias or Ben have any clue that she loved tiger lilies? Maybe she'd mentioned something during the tour? Possibly when she'd been on the edge of vomiting in the plane? Maybe she'd blacked out and babbled something about tiger lilies. Maybe one of them had psychic powers. Maybe they also liked tiger lilies and bought them as a matter of routine.

Or maybe it was just a strange coincidence.

That explanation seemed as good as any.

"Thanks," she told Chase, still mulling over the mystery.

"Don't you mean, 'thanks, little brother?'" He gave her an impish grin.

"Don't push it."

She caught sight of the photos on his phone. "Are those from Knight and Day?"

"Yeah. I heard this crazy rumor about a stash of money hidden somewhere on that airstrip. Kind of like a treasure hunt." His face lit up with enthusiasm. "I'm great at finding things. Every time Mom loses her glasses or her wedding ring or—" He broke off at the look on Merry's face. "Sorry. All I mean is, it's a skill. Look how I found you."

She ignored that remark. "It's just a crazy rumor. Nothing's ever been found. And it's none of your business."

"I know, but wouldn't it be cool to be the one who finds it?"

"Please just...don't get into trouble, please? This is my town, I'm still not sure about you being here, but I definitely don't want you poking around someone's property."

He gave her a sunny smile. "Sure thing, sis. Hey, do you want to have lunch?"

"I'll think about it. Maybe sometime this week."

"Sometime this week is great! Anytime!"

Sighing, she tucked the vase back under her arm and headed out of the break room. For sure, she couldn't keep saying 'no' to Chase. He was too likable, and she had too many questions.

In the hallway, she collided with Douglas, spilling some of the water from the vase onto his shirt.

"Merry, I'm glad I ran into you." He didn't look glad as he dabbed at his shirt. "We need something for the new Sunday edition, something big."

Of course. "Big." She wished she could ban the word from his vocabulary.

"The metro desk says you've been working on a story about opioids."

Crap. You couldn't hide anything from the damn metro desk. Will still hadn't given her the go-ahead on the story, so she deflected. "That story's not ready. It's complicated, and I want to get it right. Maybe I'll have it for you soon. I'm working as hard as I can."

He narrowed his eyes at her. Today he wore a plaid bow-tie

and a vest—as if he went out of the way to look like a jerk. "You know, I'd heard you were a real go-getter. Future star and so forth. I have to say, so far I'm not seeing it, Merry."

Her stomach dropped in a sickening plunge. Ice swept through her veins. Never in her life had she disappointed a boss, or even a teacher. They always loved her because she worked so hard for them. But Douglas had never once seemed impressed with her.

"I'll just...you'll see. It'll be a good story. I promise."

"Not good. *Big*."

"Right. Big." She hurried away from him and shut herself in her office.

Maybe she should call Will and get the go-ahead on the opioids story. He'd sent her that photo last night, after all. It was worth a shot.

And honestly, secretly, she kind of wanted to talk to him.

She dialed his number, feeling her pulse pick up as she did so. "It's Merry Warren from the *Mercury News-Gazette*."

"I know who you are, Merry," came his dry response. "I'm an officer of the law. Can't get much past me."

She smiled. For some reason, hearing his voice chased away the anxiety from her conversation with Douglas. "You know, there's something wrong when you have to reinforce the fact that you're an officer every few minutes. Are you starting to doubt it? Because if you are, just call me up and I'll confirm it. Like, three days later, in my own sweet time."

"Was there a reason you were calling, or is this just your regularly scheduled 'give Will a ration of shit' call?"

She laughed. Okay, so he won that exchange. "I need a story. My boss is on my ass and I know you still want to hold back on the opioids ... right?"

"Right," he said firmly. "But I can probably throw you a bone."

"That's all I want. A bone." As soon as she said that, her face flamed. "That didn't sound right."

"Sounded just fine to me," he said innocently.

She bit her lip. These conversations with Will Knight were getting much too flirtatious. "So can we meet? What do you have for me?"

"Today's pretty booked, and I have a thing tonight. Can it wait until tomorrow?"

"Sure, that's great." She had a "thing" tonight too. A StarLord thing. Every time she thought about their date, she shivered with anticipation. "Let me know when you have time tomorrow."

"Will do."

"Ha ha, that's funny."

"Excuse me?"

"You said 'Will do.' You're Will. And then there's 'do.'" She cringed, realizing just how ridiculous that sounded. A long pause followed her embarrassing non-joke. He probably thought she was the biggest dork in the world. Lately she kept making a fool of herself with Will. Grabbing his thigh during that plane flight. Kicking his tire. Wearing tail feathers in front of him. What was going on?

Let this be a lesson. She had to keep that professional distance. No more slipping into "he's not so bad," or "he's so hot," or "I can trust him." Reporters and deputies should stay in their corners, on opposite sides of the ring.

"Are you making merry at my expense?" he finally said. "Making merry. Get it? You're Merry."

She laughed. "You know something, Will? Sometimes you really surprise me. Maybe you aren't the big stick-up-your-ass I thought you were."

"And maybe someday you'll surprise me and manage to carry on an entire conversation without insulting me."

"Dream big, Deputy. Dream big."

~

WILL HAD a hard time focusing on his work, knowing that tonight he'd finally be meeting AnonyMs. She'd sent the plan halfway through the day. He was supposed to meet her at the Jupiter Point Observatory at sunset. He was supposed to bring a bottle of champagne—that would be the tell that she'd recognize him by.

So he was right. She did live near Jupiter Point.

It occurred to him that maybe he'd met her before but hadn't realized it. Maybe she worked at one of the businesses in town. Maybe they'd both been drinking at Barstow's at the same time. Maybe they'd reached for the same peach at the supermarket or passed each other jogging on Stargazer Beach.

Or what if he knew her even better? What if she worked at the hardware store or did his taxes or cut his hair?

Whoever AnonyMs was, she knew a lot about him. She knew him on an intimate level that he didn't share with many people. If anyone. In fact, she might know him better than anyone else did, other than his brothers. Possibly including his brothers.

After all, his brothers had no idea that he liked to fool around with poetry. No one in the world knew that, except for AnonyMs.

At the end of the day, he drove home and changed into his nicest jeans and a sweater. It was always colder at the observatory and there was often a wind blowing. He happened to have some champagne in the cupboard, ready for the grand opening party of Knight and Day, whenever that eventually happened.

He'd almost made it out of the house when his brothers drove up in Tobias's Land Rover. Ben gave a whistle as he hopped out, swinging from the roll bar.

"We're going to Barstow's, but it looks like you're way ahead of us. Hot date?"

Will kept walking toward his truck. "Business meeting."

Tobias slammed the door of the Land Rover and tucked his thumbs in his pockets. "What kind of sheriff's deputy business meeting calls for champagne?"

"A 'none of your business' meeting."

"Nice!" Tobias reached out a hand for a high five. "I like it." He turned to Ben. "Translation: a date so hot he can't even talk about it."

"Right?" Ben looked Will up and down and shook his head, looking very unimpressed. "Dude, if you're going on hot dates, you might want to level up your wardrobe. What's on your feet?"

"Boots. Steel-toed."

"Translation: the better to kick your ass with," Tobias told Ben. "Leave Will alone. He deserves some fun. And if Grandpa's found a girl in this town who wants to put up with him, I like her already."

"Fine." Ben made way for Will. He opened the door of his truck and slid inside. "What's her name? Maybe I've met her. It's a small town, and I've met a lot of single girls over the past two months."

"Eaten a lot of casseroles, too," said Tobias.

Will's grin broadened. "I might have spread the word about the two lonely bachelors needing some attention."

"Son of a bitch," said Tobias good-naturedly. Then he reflected on it for a minute. "Good thinking."

Ben rapped on the hood of the truck as Will shifted into reverse. "Good luck, man. Hope it works out. It's past time for one of the Knight brothers to settle down, and I nominate you."

"I second that motion," said Tobias.

Will flipped them both the bird and pressed his foot to the accelerator to zoom down the driveway. He could have had a nice, peaceful post-child-raising life right now. But no, he'd had to invite his two wild brothers to live with him.

He drove the long series of switchbacks that took him up the hill—almost a mountain—where the observatory was located. The Jupiter Point Observatory had a medium-sized infrared telescope and a small staff of astrophysicists. They offered tours and rented the spectacular grounds for parties and other occasions. The closer he got, the more his stomach tightened and a sense of nausea wanted to take over. This was essentially a blind date. Who the hell subjected themselves to a blind date anymore? Everyone knew they were doomed to failure.

This one in particular had a lot riding on it. He and AnonyMs had gotten so close since they'd been writing. The chance of failure, of shattered expectations...fuck, it was huge.

10

HE PARKED IN THE BIG VISITOR LOT AND HEADED FOR THE GAZEBO. Fancy fundraisers and weddings and other events were held at the gazebo because the view from the terraced grounds was so spectacular. Right now, at sunset, the ocean looked like liquid gold shimmering at the feet of the mighty sun god.

Smiling at that whimsical image, his vision still blown out by gazing into the setting sun, he bumped into someone hurrying across the grass. With his free hand, he reached out to steady his victim.

"Sorry about that," he murmured. "Wasn't watching where I was going."

"Will?"

He blinked down at Merry Warren's still-blurry face. "Merry, hey."

Oh, for Chrissake, couldn't he catch a break? Of all the people he didn't want busting him at a moment like this, Merry would be at the top of the list. She would mock him, she'd dig all the embarrassing details out of him, she'd manage to squeeze it into a story. He could imagine the exact wording she'd use. *Deputy Will*

Knight, last seen showing up for a blind date in steel-toed boots and his best jeans, declined to comment.

"Hi. Sorry, the sun was in my eyes," she said, looking nearly as embarrassed as he felt. "I didn't mean to crash into you like that."

"Don't worry about it. It's a beautiful sunset. Worth getting gut-checked over."

She smiled, but without her usual sass. He detected hesitation, maybe even nerves.

They both stood there for a moment, as if waiting for the other to make their move. Finally, he went for it. "Well, nice running into you." He took a step toward the gazebo.

So did she.

He stopped. With a strange look on her face, she glanced at the brown bag tucked in the crook of his elbow.

"What's in the bag?" she asked slowly, as if she didn't really want to hear the answer.

He stared at her. He looked ahead at the gazebo. The pretty Japanese-style structure was empty. No one else was anywhere nearby.

Holy hell.

Slowly, one inch at a time, he drew the bottle of champagne from the brown paper bag, revealing the gold crinkled wrapper at the top.

"*What?* No. *You're* StarLord?" Merry covered her face with her hands, so only her appalled eyes peeked over her fingers at him. "No. No no no!"

He cringed, wishing the entire terrace hillside of the observatory would just crumble away, taking him with it. "AnonyMs?"

He was half-hoping she wouldn't recognize the name, proving this was all a mistake. But that didn't happen.

"Oh God. Oh God! This is a disaster." Merry turned away, then did a complete rotation, ending up facing him again. "No. You *can't* be StarLord!"

He felt as if he'd taken a step into the twilight zone. "I can't?"

"You're nothing like StarLord! StarLord is sensitive, he's soulful, he writes beautiful poetry. And you're...you're a *cop*!"

She said the word as if it were an insult. He bristled in response. "And you're nothing like AnonyMs. You're impossible to get along with and I can actually converse with AnonyMs without being called Deputy Slow-mo. Or worse."

She covered her face again. "You're supposed to be a professor! A single-father professor!"

"You're supposed to be a shy novelist." All the intimate things they'd talked about raced through his mind. Poems. Dreams. Sex. "Oh shit. This is bad."

"Why are *you* so worried? I told you about my *vibrator*!"

He stared at her, then gave a snort of laughter.

So did she, even though her face was still crimson under her hands. And suddenly they were both laughing so hard they could barely stand. He bent over, resting his hands on his knees, the champagne bottle slipping to the ground. She dropped into the grass, tears rolling down her cheeks.

"Oh my God. I never, ever, *ever* would have imagined this," she gasped. "I'm a *reporter*. How could I not figure it out?"

"Hell, I'm the cop. If anyone should have put it together, it's me. Nope. Not a clue."

She just laughed all the harder, and so did he. They laughed for a while, until they were both sitting on the lawn, completely breathless and wiping tears off their faces.

"So now what?" she finally asked.

He clawed a hand through his hair. "We can pretend none of this ever happened. Rewind to before I suggested that we meet. Rewind to before that first message."

"Maybe rewind to before the birth of the Internet. I'm going to need a good amount of distance." She hugged her arms around herself. She wore a nubby sweater in a deep nightshade purple, along with tight black pants and a pair of half-boots whose heels sank into the grass. One thing about Merry, she always looked good.

Would it kill them to at least spend some time talking? Right now, he had a million unanswered questions. She probably did too, considering Merry *always* had questions.

He pulled the bottle of champagne out of the bag. "You know what might help this moment? Alcohol."

"Amen to that." She hesitated, glancing toward the gazebo. "So...this is going to sound silly now, but Suzanne put together a whole package for us. One of her Stars In Your Eyes experiences. I suppose we could...nah. Never mind."

He looked at the gazebo, which had room for several long picnic tables under the lovely carved roof. One of the tables was set with a blue-and-white checkered tablecloth and two wine glasses, as well as hurricane lamps and plastic-wrapped trays of food. "A picnic?"

"Yes, nothing elaborate. Not romantic at all. Really." Her smooth brown face looked rosier than usual.

Her embarrassment brought out all his protective instincts. "Look, I know this isn't what either of us expected. But we're the only ones who know, right? So we're in this together. As long as neither of us caves under questioning, our secret is safe."

He stood and extended a hand to her. One corner of her mouth twitched upwards. She took his hand and pulled herself back to standing. "You know, the girls are going to practically waterboard me to find out who you are."

"I've never heard of waterboarding with margaritas," he said dryly.

"How do you know about the margaritas?" By mutual unspoken agreement, they drifted toward the gazebo.

"I've seen you girls at the Orbit." He remembered the occasion perfectly. He'd been working on the armed-assault case on the Breton trail, the one in which Merry had nearly been kidnapped. He'd been pissed as hell that she'd been in danger. "Now that I'm looking back, I can't believe I didn't figure out that you're AnonyMs. I was close, you know. I guessed mystery novelist, remember?"

Reaching the gazebo, he placed his hand on her lower back to guide her up the steps. The slope between her rib cage and hip bone settled perfectly under his palm. He felt the micro movements of her muscles as she climbed the first step. The sensation electrified him.

Jesus. This was really happening. Merry was AnonyMs. AnonyMs was his perfect woman. Therefore... He shied away from completing that math.

"I was close too. I guessed criminal law professor single dad." She laughed over her shoulder at him. The setting sun turned her skin to dark gold and her eyes to sparkling stars.

His throat tightened. He'd worked so hard to focus on her professional side instead of the fact that she was a beautiful woman. But now? Impossible.

He drank in the sight of her as she stepped toward the bench on the far side of the picnic table. He touched her elbow before she got too far. "You can take this side. You'll get a better view of the sunset."

"Now that's exactly what my sweet, sensitive StarLord would say."

He twisted his face and groaned. "You're going to torture me with this forever, aren't you? Can't a guy just be thoughtful?"

"Yes. A guy *can* be, in an ad for a juice cleanse or something."

He laughed. She reached out and took his hand.

"And now I know the tough and mighty Deputy Will Knight can be thoughtful too. How about we both sit on this side and watch the sunset?"

"Sounds disturbingly romantic."

She grinned. "Not at all. We're just two people who know each other on a professional basis, who communicate secretly on the

Internet, and who are about to get drunk so we can deal with the situation. Not romantic at all."

"Right. When you put it that way..." He peeled off the gold wrapper on the champagne bottle and worked the cork free. The trapped air released with a hiss. He filled two glasses with the foaming bubbly, and lifted one of them high. "Cheers."

11

THIS HAD TO BE SOME KIND OF COSMIC JOKE, MERRY KEPT thinking. Of all the people in Jupiter Point, Will Knight would probably be the *last* man she *ever* would have connected to Star-Lord. She would have thought it was some kind of hallucination except for the sharp fizz of champagne on her tongue. That was real. So was the scent of Will's aftershave, something light and spicy, like cedar shavings. His strong, lean body stretched next to hers on the picnic bench.

The more buzzed she got, the more ridiculous the situation seemed. She kept remembering new details and bursting into giggles.

"The tiger lilies! Did you tell Tobias and Ben I like them? But how did you—"

"They asked me, but I was thinking of the other you. I had no idea you liked them too." He shook his head, confusion clouding his gray eyes. "That didn't make sense, did it?"

"None of this makes sense."

"Man, did I have this all wrong. I told my brothers you probably preferred flowers with thorns."

She had to laugh at that. "Touché. I like people to be a little bit afraid of me, if you know what I mean."

"I do. I'm the same way. Makes enforcing the law a hell of a lot easier."

She angled her body toward him. The revelation of this other, softer side of Will Knight was really blowing her mind. "So it's all a front? The big tough lawman act is just for your job?"

"I can't tell you that. You might use it against me." He shot her a sidelong glance filled with amusement. A flutter sparked to life inside her. Attraction, curiosity, interest, desire...a heady mix, on top of the champagne.

"I thought we agreed that we're bound to secrecy."

He laughed and reached for the tray of appetizers Suzanne had left for them. He unpeeled the plastic and offered first choice to her. She smiled to herself. He really was that sweet, thoughtful guy she'd imagined StarLord to be.

"It's not all an act. I am a cop, after all. Also, I was a wild twenty-two-year-old kid in charge of a grieving eight-year-old. He acted out a lot. Sometimes I handled it well, sometimes I had to lay down the law."

"You couldn't just write him a poem?" She winked and selected a cherry tomato and tore the stem off with her teeth. His gaze followed the action.

Okay then. Attraction: mutual.

He cleared his throat. "About that...any chance you can—"

"Nope." She didn't even let him finish. "I love your poems. I think you should publish them."

"Hell no." He filled one of his palms with salted almonds from the tray. "I'm a cop. Do you know how much shit I would get? Suspects would be laughing their asses off."

"You could read them their rights *and* recite them a poem. It would be glorious."

He glowered at her. "Not happening. I don't write them for anyone to see. It's more like...doodling. Images come to mind, different thoughts, and I work them out on paper. It's private. Not even my brothers have read any of them." He popped an almond into his mouth, as if that was the end of the topic.

She cocked her head at him. Now that his stern-faced facade had cracked, she was fascinated to see what else lived behind it. "You don't like people seeing anything personal, do you?"

He tossed another few almonds in with the first one. Stonewalling by almonds. Then finally, he spoke again. "It's not exactly... I've been in the spotlight. And under a microscope. My whole family went through it. Made me protective."

A chill shivered over her as she realized what he was referring to. "Your father?" she asked delicately.

He shot her a sharp, resigned look. "I guess it's no surprise you've heard about that."

"I'm just surprised it took so long. You have a lot of fans in Jupiter Point."

"But you've never been one of them."

She brushed a crumb off her sweater. "I admit, Deputy Slow-Mo, that we've had our run-ins. We're natural enemies, after all. An officer and a reporter, that's kind of like oil and water. We're adversaries. Just look at the way you keep stepping in the way of me doing my job."

"Hmm." He nodded thoughtfully. "I do see what you mean. Like how I sent you that photo. Police evidence, sent directly to your inbox. Are you sure I'm the enemy?"

She nudged his side with her elbow. "It's true, every once in a while, you do something that makes me think you've turned over a new leaf and crossed over to our side."

He snorted. "That will never happen. I'm about solving crimes and protecting the populace. It's who I am and who I always will be."

"And I can see why." Now that she was putting all the pieces together, it made sense. Often a tragedy changed the trajectory of a person's life. She'd seen it over and over when interviewing crime victims. She squinted at him thoughtfully, imagining a young Will vowing to catch his father's killer.

He waved a hand in front of her face, interrupting her fantasy. "I can see the gears turning, but you're wrong. That's not why I work in law enforcement. I was headed there all along. I just ended up in the first half of *Law and Order* instead of the second."

With a sigh, she drew up one knee and rested her chin on it. "I love that show."

"So do I."

"Well, I guess maybe we're not complete opposites."

"No comment," he answered dryly.

She burst out laughing. Another thing they had in common—sense of humor. When Will relaxed, like now, with the last sunlight reflecting in his gray eyes, he was pretty irresistible.

"I can think of a few things we have in common," he added. "We both work hard. My brothers say I work too much. They worry about me."

She tipped champagne to her mouth. "Oh, I'm a hopeless workaholic. I don't even use my vacation time unless it's for a story. I've been that way since junior high."

"What got you into journalism?"

She gave him a searching look, but detected nothing beyond sincere curiosity in the question. "Well, I got hooked early on. I always had a foot in two worlds. I lived in a low-ish income neighborhood in New York with my mother, but we had money from my father that went toward my education. I took a subway every day to a private school uptown. I knew how to blend, no matter where I was. Anyway..."

Jeez, she was getting off track. Will's attentive manner made her want to tell him all sorts of personal stuff.

"When I was fourteen, a reporter came to our neighborhood investigating a story about landlord abuses. But no one wanted to talk to him because they were afraid they'd get evicted. They didn't trust him to protect their names. So I helped him out. I interviewed people, I took photos for him, I got him copies of the illegal notices people were getting. The story was published in the *New York Times* and it was the most incredible feeling. And it worked—repairs started happening that never did before. And it was all because someone came and shined a light on a problem. After that, I knew I had to be a reporter."

She paused to take a breath.

"Don't stop. Tell me more. What's your mother like?"

"She's a singer. She's fierce. She never babied me. I had to stand on my own two feet, which is how I liked it anyway."

"She sounds impressive."

Any compliment about her mother always made her glow. "She is. We're still close, but she's on tour right now in Japan, along with my stepfather. He's her manager, we both took his name when they got married, that's where my last name 'Warren' comes from. You know, she could have used that money from my bio-father for herself, but she kept it for my education instead. That's one reason I work so hard. She sacrificed for me and I don't want to let her down."

"Jupiter Point's best reporter? Not likely."

She smiled, then shifted the tone of the conversation to something lighter. "You know what I want to do? I want to go back through all the StarLord messages and reinterpret them based on what I know now."

"Yup, a few little tidbits are coming back to me."

The evil gleam in his eye told her exactly what he was referring to. She changed position so she sat on her knees and heels and swatted him on the arm. "How much will it take for you to delete some of my messages and forget you ever saw them?"

He laughed, fending her off easily. "Bribing an officer of the law?"

"Totally justifiable."

"What's the problem?" he teased. "There's nothing wrong with being an independent woman in charge of her own sexuality."

The word "sexuality" shifted the atmosphere between them. Her throat tightened and her lower belly clenched with excitement.

"Yes, but I told that to StarLord, not Deputy Will Knight."

"You know me. I don't tell secrets. I'm the king of 'no comment.' It's one of the things you don't like about me."

The secrets part was true. As for the rest of it... "I never said 'don't like.' That's not an accurate quote."

They smiled at each other. The last light from the sinking sun kissed their faces. The moment seemed to last forever, the two of them wrapped up in the spell of the whispering ocean breeze, the deepening dark. She had the sense of being perched on top of the world here in this mountaintop gazebo with a man who kept revealing new layers.

She wrenched her gaze away before things got too intense. "Sunset," she reminded him.

They both watched the sun's last glimmer of goodbye. A star winked into visibility, like Tinkerbell coming out to play. Merry was acutely aware of Will next to her, as if her body was communicating with him on a level her mind didn't quite grasp. Her heart kept skipping to a different rhythm, the little hairs on her arm prickled. Her mouth went dry, her throat tight.

Looking out at that far horizon, where the last streaks of persimmon and violet shimmered, time shifted. The world suddenly felt both bigger and more expansive than she'd ever imagined, and at the same time, cozier. More intimate. As if she was perfectly safe right now, and forever. As long as Will sat by her side.

She shook off the impossible thought. Their weird relationship hadn't gotten any less strange because they now knew they'd been communicating intimately for months. In fact, it was stranger.

"We should probably talk about what happened before," she said reluctantly. "At your place. After the tranquilizer gun."

12

Will drew in a deep breath at the forbidden topic. He still remembered the panic of spotting Merry unconscious outside of Finn's guesthouse. The dynamic, ball-of-energy girl he knew wasn't supposed to be splayed out like a rag doll in the flower bed. He'd charged across the lawn, and when he'd found her still breathing, he'd actually uttered a prayer to God—not something he often did.

He had enough EMT training to confirm that her heart was beating normally, her pulse strong. She'd been rendered unconscious, but nothing was fundamentally wrong with her. So instead of taking her to Urgent Care, he took her home and settled her onto his couch. He'd called into the office to file a report, and stayed home the rest of the afternoon as she slept it off.

Thinking she might end up spending the night, he brought her a fleece blanket. He was kneeling next to the couch and tucking it around her when she suddenly sat bolt upright and grabbed him. "Where am I? What happened?"

"Whoa whoa whoa." He put his hands on her shoulders, hoping to calm her. "It's okay. You were attacked at Finn and Lisa's guesthouse. Nothing serious, you just got knocked out. I brought you here to sleep it off."

Her pulse was jumping in her throat. He smoothed his thumb over her collarbone in slow, gentle circles. Her eyelids drooped and her head sagged to the side. He realized the drug wasn't out of her system yet.

"Come on, why don't you lie down. I promise you're safe here. I think you have some more sleeping to do." He eased her back , but when he tried to pull his hands away from her, she resisted. She took one of his hands and tucked it under her cheek like a pillow.

"Feels good," she murmured, sounding half drunk. "I like your hands. They're very sexy. Do you know hands are the first thing I look at in a man? If a guy has big hands, that's a good sign, that's all I'm saying."

He froze. He clamped down on the laughter trying to fight its way out of his mouth. Poor Merry didn't know *what* she was saying. If she did, she definitely wouldn't be using words like "sexy." Hands weren't sexy, or at least his weren't. They were big and calloused and sported a few scars here and there.

She snuggled her cheek against his palm. He was still reeling with the shock of that move when she did something even more provocative. She licked the heel of his hand like a cat. The surprise of her wet tongue on his skin sent shockwaves all the way up his arm.

"Bet you didn't know I think you're hot. I think you're a little hottie two-shoes," she murmured. "A hotsa-matzoh. A hot-ten-tot. A hot cross buns, a hottie van winkle, a—"

"Okay, settle down." He shushed her, mostly because he was afraid he might laugh if she kept going. So Merry Warren thought he was hot, did she? Or at least she did when she was stoned out of her mind on some kind of tranquilizer. "Just go back to sleep now." He did what he'd always wanted to do—tucked a bit of her springy halo of hair behind her ears. It felt soft and alive under his fingers.

"Don't you think I'm p-pretty?" Merry, stammering? He'd never heard that before. Usually she spoke at a rapid clip with barely an *um* or an *er*.

"You're very pretty," he told her. Because it was true. "You're beautiful."

"You're just saying that." She stuck out her lower lip, so plump and delicious he wanted to lick it.

"I'm not much of a sweet-talker. If I say it, I mean it. But you should sleep now, you'll feel better after a nice rest..."

"Even my big butt? I got that from my mama."

"Yup, yup. That part's good too. It's all good, from what I've seen." As soon as those words left his mouth, he wished he could take them back. They were much too flirtatious for this moment, with Merry impaired by a tranquilizer.

She immediately struggled to sit up.

"Merry, lie back. You need to sleep."

"You need to see *all* of me," she insisted drunkenly. "So you can know for sure."

"That's a bad idea. Jesus, Merry." She was trying to pull her arm through her sleeve, but her bent elbow got everything mucked up. Still, he saw enough creamy brown skin to make him want to cry. "Please leave your clothes on. I beg you."

"See? I knew it!" She jabbed an index finger at his chest. "You don't like me. You don't want me naked."

"I do, I swear I do. But you're under the influence and, my God, Merry, please stop this, I'm only a man, I have only so much willpower—"

"Will! Power!" She burst into giggles. "You *are* Will. And you have all the power you want. You got the power, you got the power..." Now she was waving her arms over her head, couch-dancing. Jesus, this was a nightmare. Maybe he should just get the hell away from her before they did something they really regretted.

He was easing away from her, sitting back on his haunches, when she swung toward him and flung her arms around him. She yanked him toward her and planted a kiss right on his mouth.

The shock of her soft lips against his reverberated through his system. With all the fast-talking, quipping and interrogating Merry did, he'd never imagined her lips would be like *this*. Like caressing velvet, or drinking perfectly aged Scotch. Rich like a vein of gold, deep like an underground lake. Despite his better judgement, he responded, using his lips and tongue to savor the sleek texture of her mouth. Her flavor made his head swim.

He took hold of her shoulders, her soft flesh giving way under his hands. Everything about her was so much more tender and feminine than he would have expected. Merry wasn't just a wise-cracking, pain-in-the-ass reporter. She was a warm, passionate, lusty woman.

And she was *all shot up with tranquilizers*.

With both hands on her shoulders, he thrust her away from him. This time he laid her down on the couch and wrapped the blanket around her entire body, arms and all, like a mummy. "Go to sleep," he told her sternly, as if he were talking to Aiden. "I mean it, Merry. Sleep. Now."

She blinked at him, her eyelids already starting to drift shut. Maybe his kiss had put her to sleep. Or maybe she'd used up the adrenaline that had jolted her awake. She snuggled into the covers and within a few minutes was drooling into his grand-mother's throw pillow.

The next morning when he came stumbling out of his bedroom looking for Merry, she was gone. She'd left a note. "Called a taxi. Thanks for the rescue. Now we're even. (Remember last month's puff piece about the sheriff's budget request? You're welcome.) P.S. I don't remember a thing."

Okay then. He'd crumpled up the note and tossed it in the trash. And worked damn hard to erase the whole thing from his memory.

NOW MERRY WAS BRINGING it up of her own accord. She held a long match and was in the midst of lighting the hurricane lamps set out on the picnic table. As she lit each lantern, a flame flared within its glass globe, then subsided to a firefly flicker.

"I thought you didn't remember that night."

"It's foggy, and I'm not sure I remember it all. But I think I got the basics down. I told you what a hottie you were and tried to kiss you. You were embarrassingly patient and made me go back to sleep."

He frowned at her. "That's not exactly how I remember it."

"Oh no? What am I leaving out? Did I try to take all my clothes off?"

He lifted an eyebrow at her. "Just your top. Don't worry, you were too woozy to get it all the way off."

She shook the match until the flame was out, then tossed it aside. "Oh goodie. That's a relief. Okay then, what am I remembering wrong? If it's too excruciatingly mortifying, you can give me the CliffsNotes."

"It's not mortifying. You can stop beating yourself up. You were hit with a freaking tranq gun. Nothing you said or did meant anything. I put it all out of my mind as soon as I saw your note."

"Yeah, but now it's different. Now we're here, on this...well, I supposed you would call it a date. And that night happened, so we might as well get it all out in the open. What am I leaving out?" She settled back down on the bench next to him. The flames glowed steadily in their glass bubbles.

"You didn't leave anything out. You said you tried to kiss me."

Her expression brightened. "So I didn't try to kiss you?"

"You succeeded. You *did* kiss me."

Looking aghast, she turned to him. "I kissed you?"

"You don't remember? Great. Talk about a blow to the old self-esteem."

She put a hand on his arm, laughing with dismay. "You said yourself I was impaired. I just remember bits and pieces. I remember how sexy your mouth looked and how I *wanted* to kiss you. The next thing I remember after that was snuggling into the pillow while you wrapped me up like a burrito."

Maybe it was ridiculous, but his pride objected to that whole scenario. How could she forget that kiss? "I was holding back," he pointed out. "You weren't yourself. I didn't want to take advantage."

"Come on now, you don't have to make excuses." She patted his shoulder in mock sympathy. "It's nothing against you. Not all kisses are everything they're cracked up to be."

He glared at her. "Mine. Are."

"Whatever you say, Deputy. I really think you're overreacting." The demure glance she gave him from under her eyelashes made him growl. "How about we just agree that the kiss was amazing and unforgettable and move on to some other topic. There's something I've been meaning to talk to you about, as a matter of fact. It's not a case, really, just something I want to give you a heads up about."

Her voice receded into a distant buzzing. She kept talking, but all he could think about was the movements of her mouth, the way her full lips wrapped themselves around her words, the upward tilt of the left corner of her mouth, a quirk that made it look as if she was always on the verge of laughter. Her skin glowed like burnished bronze in the light of the lanterns. She was so beautiful and brilliant, she took his breath away.

Forget his kiss? Hell. No.

He cupped his hand around her chin, stopping her in mid-sentence. Her eyes went wide, the pupils dilating. "I'm correcting the record right now."

"You are?"

"I'm going to kiss you and you're not going to forget about it." He paused for just enough time to give her a chance to pull back if she wanted.

She didn't. In fact, her lips parted and a curious spark lit up her eyes.

That was his Merry. She could never turn down a chance to learn something new. Or something she'd forgotten, in this case.

He tilted her face up and softly skimmed his lips against hers, just the merest brush. "One thing to remember," he murmured in low tones against her lips, "is that you initiated the last kiss. I'm sure it wasn't your best either, since you were zonked out. So it didn't begin the way I would have preferred."

She shivered, goose bumps lifting on her skin. Already he was liking this kiss even more than the first one.

"Normally I like to take my time. You know me. Deputy Slow-mo." He demonstrated by slowly sliding his tongue just under the curve of her upper lip. Her lips were ever so slightly chapped, the rough bits tickling his tongue. "When you do something slowly, you have time to make sure it's right. You can be thorough. That's how I like to kiss. Thoroughly. Completely. I don't leave anything on the field when it comes to kissing." As he talked, he explored the full swell of her mouth with his teeth, his tongue, pulling out just enough to form words.

Her breath came faster, her pulse jumping a mile a minute in her throat. "Do you," she cleared her throat, "do you always talk this much when you kiss?"

"Nope. This is for you, my favorite wordsmith. I figure the way to your heart is through words along with kisses. Am I wrong?" He tugged at her lower lip, using his teeth to add a little edge to the move.

"You're not wrong." Her voice was getting shaky. Triumph

filled him. She was not going to forget this kiss. He was going to kiss the living daylights out of her if it was the last thing he did.

So he plunged his hands into that soft profusion of hair, tilted her head back, and kissed her so deep and long and wild that he lost track of time. His entire focus, one hundred percent, was devoted to her. He forgot they were alone in a gazebo lit by hurricane lamps, that not far above them, an infrared telescope was aimed at the stars, that an ocean stretched all the way to Japan from the cliffs below. He forgot the day, the time, his name, everything that wasn't Merry and the taste of her lips and the warmth of her mouth and the soft sounds she was making and the feel of her hands gripping his back, the magic springing to life between the two of them and wrapping them up in a shower of sparks under the stars.

She broke off the kiss with a ragged gasp. "Will. My God."

Instantly he released her. Had he gotten too carried away? His head was swimming from the intoxication of her kiss, the candlelight, the night breeze. "Sorry." God, his voice sounded like a rusted-out hinge.

"No, no. I don't mean it that way. I just mean, Jesus. That was some kiss." She touched her tongue to her lips. Her eyes gleamed with liquid light.

Satisfaction spread through him like his favorite smoked ale. At least she wasn't so dismissive of *that* kiss. And he could do even better. If he could just get her alone and naked somewhere, get past those thorny defenses, get her relaxed and loose and deadline-free...

"Okay, we need to set down some boundaries," Merry declared, fluffing her hair where his hands had disturbed it.

His little fantasy shattered, just like that. "What do you mean?"

"No more kissing. And definitely not like that."

He drew back and scowled at her. "What are you talking about? You liked that kiss."

"You put your finger on the problem."

"Problem?" Now his head was swimming even more. Confusion gave way to irritation. Merry really knew how to keep him off-balance. "You wanted me to kiss you."

"I did. I know." She scooted away from him, putting a couple inches between them. "And it was...great. You're right. You really know how to kiss. I must have been out of my mind on tranquilizers to forget the first one."

Hurt pride officially soothed. "So what's wrong?"

"Think about it, Will. We work together all the time. And now it turns out there's this other connection. I'm still getting used to the idea that you're StarLord. I feel like on a virtual level, on Flirt, we're really great friends. And then on a professional level, there's another whole dynamic. I pester you with questions, you stonewall me. It's a truly magical relationship."

Her dry tone made him laugh. "I don't stonewall. I'm deliberate. I only share what I feel needs to be shared."

"Okay, well, leaving that aside. I respect you as a deputy, despite my complaints. And I hope that's a mutual thing."

"Yes. You do good work. I've always respected you, that's why I'm extra careful around you."

She shot him a surprised look. "I'm going to take that as a huge compliment."

"Sure. But I'm still stuck on the part where you don't want to kiss me anymore."

She held up a finger to correct him. "Where I don't think we *should* kiss anymore. It's not about wanting to or not wanting to. If we had no other connection outside of Flirt, that would be a different story. I just think we should step carefully."

He rested his elbows on his knees and looked at the planked floor of the gazebo. Maybe Merry had a point. He was used to low-maintenance, easygoing women like Roxy who offered a good time *in* bed but didn't want much of a relationship *outside* of bed. That wasn't Merry at all. Merry was the kind of woman who would consume his time and attention because she fascinated him. It would be all in, no holds barred, lose your heart or go home.

"I hear you," he finally told her.

Was that a flash of disappointment in her eyes? Too bad. He might be a bossy deputy, but he never pushed a woman where she didn't want to go. If Merry wanted to put the brakes on, he'd go along with it.

For now.

Until she saw the benefits of more kissing. And more than kissing.

"So what now? What about StarLord and AnonyMs?"

She twisted her mouth in thought. "It seems kind of silly to use code names now. It's just so strange, like annoying Deputy Knight is gone and soulful StarLord is gone, and instead there's this new person. You. And you're some kind of combination of the two."

"So you're saying I'm kind of a stranger."

"I guess so."

"Maybe that means we should start over from the beginning."

"What do you mean?"

He didn't know exactly what he meant. But he did know that he wasn't letting this go. Not yet. He was too damn attracted to her. He knew AnonyMs so well, knew how her mind worked, and despite Merry's take on it, to him, they were the same person. He planned to use all his knowledge to lure her where he wanted her —into his bed.

But he kept that intention to himself.

"Jupiter Point is a small town. We have friends in common. We'll probably run into each other. We can just see how it goes." He spoke as casually as he could, but inside he didn't feel casual at all. Determined would be a better word.

She nodded thoughtfully and stuck out her hand. "Friends, then?"

He reached his right hand across his body to shake hers. "Close enough."

As their palms met, he gritted his teeth to keep from pulling her into another kiss, another embrace. The pull between them was so strong, it felt tangible.

She felt it too, he would swear it on his life. Their eyes met and magic pulsed between them.

Far too soon, she pulled her hand away. "We need to pack this stuff up. Suzanne left a garbage bag here somewhere."

Fighting disappointment, he helped her clean up the remains of the picnic. They blew out the lanterns and left them in a crate under the table. He claimed the garbage bag—"that's my job, remember?"

That made her giggle, but as they walked across the lawn toward the parking area, she sobered.

"If we're really going to be friends, there's something else I should tell you."

"Shoot." A warning bell clanged in his brain. What could be more of a shocker than finding out that AnonyMs was Merry Warren?

"You know that intern, Chase, who came out to the airstrip with me?"

"The one who took all those pictures?"

"Yup. He's—" she hesitated, and he wondered for a stark moment if she was going to say that she was dating him. "He's my half-brother."

13

Poor Will. Honestly, there wasn't enough champagne in the world for all the bombshells Merry kept dropping on him.

He blinked at her. "Your what?"

"We have the same father. I'd never met him before, but recently he showed up out of the blue. He got the internship at the paper and he's been hanging around ever since. He says he wants to get to know me."

He nodded a few times. "And how's that going?" he asked dryly.

"Not well. He seems nice enough, harmless. But maybe I'm just naturally suspicious. Why did he all of a sudden want to track me down? And why stick around even though I'm not really into it?"

He laughed. "If you ever want to go into law enforcement, you're off to a great start."

"Do I sound paranoid?" She scuffed the toe of her boot against the pavement as they reached the parking lot. "I saw him looking through pictures from Knight and Day Flight Tours. He mentioned those rumors about the missing money."

"If he wants a life of crime, he'd better learn not to blurt things out."

"Okay, I get it. I'm paranoid. But I don't trust that entire family, not after how they treated my mother." At his questioning glance, she explained. "They gave her money to go away." She bit her lip, the old hurt sneaking in the way it did sometimes. "Anyway, I just wanted to warn you."

When she looked up at him, she caught an odd expression on his face. As if he was—touched. "You don't have to worry," he said almost tenderly. "But it's kind of cute that you did."

"Cute?"

He turned her with one strong arm so she faced him. "Yeah, cute. I appreciate the thought. But the Knight brothers can take care of ourselves. I'm more worried about you and this half-brother of yours. He seemed like a dopey kid to me, but I can check into him if you want."

"No, that would feel really strange, checking out my own brother."

"You wouldn't be, I would. And he's not my brother. As far as I'm concerned, he's a stranger in town, and we don't cotton to strangers around here." He shifted into a backwoods accent.

She giggled. "You're pretty cute, aren't you?"

"I prefer 'devastatingly handsome,' if you don't mind."

She laughed again, flashing on that kiss. It still reverberated through her like the sound of a bell. Or maybe like a wake-up bell. *Rise and shine*, it called to her. *Something big is happening, something beyond exciting, something you've never felt before.*

Honestly, it scared her, which was why she'd instantly decided they shouldn't try that again. Messing around with Will would be like playing with dynamite. With his strength and authority, he made her previous boyfriends look like little boys. That kiss... there was so much behind it. So much intensity and emotion and depth.

They'd reached his Tacoma. She paused but he nudged her past it. "You don't have to walk me to my car," she protested.

He gave her a look that said "no arguments." God, he really was in rock-wall mode now. Of course he had to walk her to her car. Protectiveness was woven into the fabric of his being.

Which was another reason not to go to bed with Will. She didn't need a full-time guardian, or even a part-time one.

When they reached her car, she leaned her rear against the driver's side door. He stayed back a step, which she found oddly disappointing. One little kiss goodbye wouldn't hurt, would it?

But his mind wasn't on kissing. It was still on Chase. "Do me a favor, would you? If anything happens with Chase, if anything bugs you, or he says something that sets off any alarm bells, please call me. Anytime, day or night."

"Or Knight and Day," she quipped.

"Or Knight and Day." Finally, he smiled again. "That might be our new slogan. Anytime, Knight or Day."

"I sense a poem coming on."

He gave her a wry look, but didn't respond. He kept his steady gaze on her, giving nothing away. She'd love to know what he was thinking about right now. The kiss? Her half-brother? Their online relationship? Their non-online relationship? Something that had nothing to do with her, like what numbers he was going to play in the lottery or what he was going to have for breakfast?

She lingered one more moment, just in case he tried to kiss her again, or make any move at all. But he didn't. So she got into her car, gave him one last wave, and pulled out of the parking lot.

As soon as she got home, she logged onto her computer and fired off one last message to StarLord. "I don't regret a thing."

For the next few days, Merry obsessed over the incredible revelation that StarLord was Will Knight. The worst part was that she couldn't tell her friends, not even Suzanne, who had provided that wonderful picnic.

"We had fun," was all she said. For a writer, it was pretty much torture that she couldn't say more.

"The least you could do is share a couple of details," Suzanne grumbled. Using her stroller to box Merry in, she'd cornered her on Constellation Way outside of Mrs. Murphy's bookstore, Fifth Book from the Sun.

"Just for the record, that's no way to use your child," Merry said virtuously. "You're setting a bad example."

"Ha. I set up a romantic interlude for you and all I get is, 'we had fun'? Even my baby is disappointed in you."

"Okay, it was a lot more than fun. It was kind of mind-blowing. But I really can't say any more than that. Especially here." She cast a significant look toward Mrs. Murphy, who was dodging a line of customers to peer out the window at them.

She'd be all over this little morsel. My God.

"Somewhere else, then. We can go anywhere. Have stroller, will travel." Suzanne adjusted the visor keeping the sun off Faith's little face.

"I really can't, Suzanne."

"Because it's someone you know. Someone I know. Someone we *all* know."

Merry schooled her expression to reveal nothing. Damn, that expressionless act Will pulled off was a lot harder than it looked.

Suzanne caught on right away. "Right on all counts!" she said triumphantly.

"I have to go."

"Margaritas tonight? A little rum might make you talk."

Yeah, it probably would. No margaritas for a while, Merry decided. "Sorry, I have to work."

"Since when do you work nights?"

"I work all the time, didn't you know?"

Lisa called her later that day to offer moral support. "I just want you to know, I would never try to pry a secret out of you."

"Did Suzanne corner you, too?" Merry balanced her phone on

her shoulder as she breezed through an article on a proposal to install roundabouts in key intersections.

"Pretty much. Faith got a bee sting. She called my emergency number, then once the baby was okay, the gloves came off. But I told her your business is your business, and I refuse to pressure you."

"Thank you." Since Lisa had come to Jupiter Point with a secret of her own, Merry wasn't surprised by that statement.

"However, if you feel the need to talk, if you *want* to let someone in on the identity of your mystery man, you *know* I'm a great keeper of secrets. Just pointing that out."

"Lisa..." she warned.

"No pressure."

"*Lisa...*"

"Okay, gotta go, a patient just walked in." She hung up in a hurry. Merry had to laugh. In just a few months, Lisa had gone from jaded big-city cynic to one of the crowd. It was kind of cute, actually.

Thank goodness for Carolyn, who didn't pester her at all. Most likely, that was because she was simply too busy now that she was flying back and forth between two jobs. She didn't have time for trivial things like Merry's suddenly surreal love life.

Maybe "love life" wasn't the right term. It was more like—hot pursuit.

All of a sudden, she kept running into Will everywhere. Jogging at the beach, eating a giant stack of pancakes at the Milky Way with his brothers, breaking up a fight at Barstow's, helping the hotshots and the local fire department with fire mitigation. In public, they both acted as if nothing had changed, as if they were still prickly adversaries.

But every time she saw him, her heart did this funny thing in her chest, a kind of expansion, like a tiger lily unfurling from a bud.

And another thing...he kept doing very sweet, completely

anonymous things for her. For instance, on the morning after their date, when she stopped at the Venus and Mars for her morning cinnamon latte the barista refused to accept payment. "It's already taken care of," he told her. "Secret admirer, I guess."

The next morning, same thing. After three mornings, she pinned him down. "How long am I drinking lattes for free?"

"He left a hundred dollars and a number for us to call when the funds run out. I'd say you're drinking for free as long as you want."

Huh.

That same day, Mrs. Murphy called to notify her that her book had arrived. Mystified, since she didn't remember ordering any books, she swung by the Fifth Book from the Sun. The book was a new collection of stories by Toni Morrison, her favorite author in the world. Hardcover, signed by the author, and much pricier than anything she would have bought for herself.

Mrs. Murphy claimed to have no idea who had ordered the book. Will had actually managed to keep a secret from the biggest rumor-monger in town, which made him some kind of Superman.

"But if you want me to find out," Mrs. Murphy added in a whisper, "I have a few tricks up my sleeve. Not strictly legal or ethical, but I could bend some rules for you."

"Please, don't even consider that. You wouldn't want Jupiter Point's finest coming after you."

But Merry didn't mind a certain member of Jupiter Point's finest coming after *her*. She'd never been wooed like this before. Being pursued by Will Knight—yeah, she kind of loved that.

And it kept going. Brianna knocked on her apartment door one morning with a gorgeous terra-cotta pot filled with dirt. "Special delivery from an anonymous benefactor," she said, her vivid face alive with curiosity.

Merry peered at it suspiciously. "Dirt?"

"Uh, no. I mean, yes, that's *soil.* Potting soil. Covering up a rare variety of Lilium lancifolium from China." When Merry stared at her blankly, she continued impatiently, "Tiger lily. There are three bulbs in this pot. They'll grow inside if you give them enough moisture, but you can also plant them outside. Did you know that you can eat every part of a tiger lily plant? It's medicinal too. You can make a tincture from the flowers that helps with nausea during pregnancy."

"There will be no need for that tincture, thank you very much." Merry took the terra-cotta pot, which was heavier than it looked. She always forgot how strong Brianna was from all her garden work.

"Are you sure? If a man gave me three Lilium lancifolium bulbs, my ovaries might spontaneously go into overdrive."

Merry laughed. "You'd better tell Rollo that all it takes is a big old pot of dirt and you'll start popping out babies."

Brianna flushed self-consciously.

"Wait...are you...?"

"No, no, not yet. But we've been kicking around the idea. Suzanne's baby has no one to play with. And I always wanted someone to make fairy houses for. I was shocked when I reached high school and no one was interested in fairy houses anymore."

"Girl, you kill me. I swear, when you look up adorable in the dictionary, there ought to be a picture of little gingeroo Brianna making fairy houses in the forest. Thanks for the delivery." When Brianna planted her feet and refused to budge, she added, "And no, I'm not saying who sent this."

"But do you *know*?"

"Goodbye, Bri."

Then came the final straw. At work one day, she got a call from the front desk. The local car detailing service had arrived to pick up her car.

Very sweetly, she asked them to give her a minute.

Then she dialed Will's number. "What the hell do you think you're doing? My car is fine as it is!"

"When's the last time you had your oil changed? And your brakes checked?"

"There's a schedule somewhere." She couldn't remember exactly where she kept that information, but who really paid attention to that stuff anyway?

Deputy Will Knight, of course.

"Can you just do me a favor and let them check out your car? I'd sleep a lot easier."

"But they're going to clean it too, aren't they? I can't have that. My car is kind of like a filing cabinet on wheels."

"Fine, tell them to skip the interior. That's up to you." He coughed, burying the word "stubborn" in the sound.

"I heard that. And I can't accept your intrusive bossiness disguised as an offer of help."

He growled a little bit. "You're a helluva lot of trouble, you know that?"

"I've been told, yes. Now back to the main point. What are you up to with all these little gifts and so forth? I thought we agreed we're going to keep things on a friendly level."

"Which is why I didn't send you the moon-and-star condoms I thought you'd appreciate."

She laugh-snorted. "The what?"

"They glow in the dark."

She laughed so hard that Chase, who happened to step into her office at that moment, stopped in his tracks.

"You're laughing." He sounded confused by that fact. "And you sound like you're having fun."

She covered the receiver. "This is a private conversation. Do you mind?"

"With who? Is it a guy? Do I know him?"

"*Private*," she repeated. She really didn't want Chase to know anything about Will. Even though he'd been perfectly respectful lately, she wasn't ready to get too personal with him. Just because they shared a father didn't mean they had anything else to talk about.

When Chase's face fell, she relented. "How about lunch next week?"

He grinned, his blond hair flopping around his ears. "Seriously?"

"We'll see. But I think so."

When he finally moved past her doorway, she lowered her voice. "Seriously, Will, I can handle my own business. I don't like taking things from a man, even a friend. I'm all about standing on my own two feet."

"How's a guy supposed to sweep you *off* your feet, then?"

Her mouth quivered into a smile and that warm feeling spread through her again. Was that what Will was trying to do? Sweep her off her feet? The fact that he wanted to made her glow inside. "That's not on the agenda, remember?"

"Agenda's change."

Just then, she heard a click as someone else jumped on the line. "Hey there, mystery woman. Whoever you are, if you don't jump Will's bones, you're making a mistake. He's one of the all-time great guys. Legends will be told about him someday. Books will be written, songs will be sung."

"*Cindy!*" Will's furious voice interrupted her.

"Gotta go," Cindy said hurriedly. "But you should know I have a curated list of prospects for Will and I'm not afraid to use it." And she hung up.

Will said goodbye at that point, in such a mortified tone that she didn't dare laugh.

So he wasn't the only one feeling the heat about their off-the-radar "thing," whatever it was. Small town life...she might never get used to it.

14

DESPITE MERRY'S STUBBORN ATTITUDE, WILL KNEW HIS STRATEGY was working. Someone like Merry, with her curious mind, needed to be kept off guard. He couldn't do the normal, predictable thing and expect to make an impression. He had to reach outside the box. And all his anonymous gifts were accomplishing exactly what he wanted. If he kept the surprises coming, eventually she'd see the light.

At that point, he'd have her right where he wanted her.

Tiger lilies and books were one thing, but he knew Merry well enough to know exactly what she *really* wanted. Some women liked jewelry or chocolate. The quickest way to Merry's heart would be a hot tip on the story she was working on.

The opioids investigation, for instance.

The DEA had identified the man at the Rootin' Rooster as "Buckaroo Brown," an ex-con and drug dealer who had apparently made some new connections while in state prison. He lived just over the border in Tijuana, only coming to California every few months.

Will debated long and hard whether or not to share that information. His main concern was that it might put her in danger. According to the DEA, Buckaroo was safely in Mexico and wasn't expected back for the rest of the year. Maybe Merry would drop her gig at the Rooster once she had the scoop about Buckaroo, which would make her safer. No matter what, Will would be watching like a hawk.

Besides, he'd spotted Buckaroo thanks to her. She deserved to know who he was. And he knew how much she'd love getting an anonymous tip like this.

So, feeling slightly ridiculous, he called Merry from a phone booth and spoke in a whisper. "Are you the one working on the drug story? I got a name for you. Buckaroo Brown. Check it out."

Soon after he made that anonymous call, she shot him an email.

"Got a tip on the fentanyl story. I'm sharing it with you in good faith. It's a name: Buckaroo Brown. I'm researching him now. Pretty unsavory character. Please be careful. And please remember I shared this with you."

He emailed back right away. "Your cooperation with the sheriff's department is noted. We'll follow up on this right away. If this lead checks out, you no longer have any reason to moonlight at the Rooster, is that right?"

After a short interval, she pinged him back. "You're forgetting about the tips. Reporters don't get paid much. Can you believe I make more as a cocktail waitress in a rooster outfit?"

Damn it.

"Watch your back," he emailed back. "I've heard of Buckaroo and he's not someone you want to mess around with."

For a few days after that, he didn't hear from her. He kept tabs on Buckaroo, just to make sure he didn't make any surprise visits to Jupiter Point. He also followed up on the lead he'd gotten about Heavenly Hardbodies. He was able to match the teenager's description of the suspect with three sweaty bodybuilders.

Before he brought them in for questioning, he took a break to help his brothers at the airstrip. Forecasters were warning of a big

Pacific storm coming, and the place still need buttoning up. They worked furiously, talking little. He was grateful for that, because if they got a hint of anything going on with him and Merry, they'd give him shit the entire time.

The rain arrived with a light pitter-patter just as they were closing the last high window that let air into the hangar. They stood for a moment, listening to the rattle of raindrops on the roof and looking for signs of moisture making its way inside. When they saw nothing, they all high-fived each other.

"Knight brothers rule. No one gets wet unless we make it so," Ben joked.

"You had to make it dirty, didn't you?" Tobias pulled his jacket over his head in preparation for the dash to his car.

"No, you made it dirty. I was talking about the roof."

The rain picked up in intensity until it sounded like an entire symphony of drums on the metal roof.

As they squabbled, Will's phone rang. Merry's number flashed, along with the thumbnail he used for her—a picture of a tiger lily. He walked away from his brothers to take the call.

Her voice came fast and breathless. "Will, I'm sorry, I didn't know who else to call. I tried Triple A but they're backed up because of the storm." In the background, he heard the sound of wind gusting and howling.

"Where are you? What's wrong?"

"I'm down past the waterfront. I was at the Rooster, then I decided to follow up on something I found out about Buckaroo. When he comes to California, he stays at a lodge not far from here. And before you yell at me, he's out of the country right now so there's no risk of running into him."

"I'm not yelling. Just tell me where you are."

True, he wasn't yelling, but he was furious with himself. If he hadn't shared Buckaroo's identity, she wouldn't be stranded in a storm right now.

"I'm on Route 68, that little road that goes into the mountains after you pass the airport. I thought I'd have time to just swing by here and check it out before the storm hit. But all of a sudden it started raining like crazy and then my car stalled, sometimes it does that when it gets wet. I tried my usual trick to get it going again, but there's just so much rain. It's crazy—" The wind snatched her voice away, so he couldn't make out her last words. He was already loping out of the hangar toward his truck.

"Are you inside your car right now?"

"No, I couldn't get reception inside the car. I only have one bar now."

"Get inside your car and sit tight. I'll be there as soon as I can. I'm all the way out at the airstrip so it'll probably take me an hour. If anyone stops to help you, tell them someone's on their way. And keep your phone on. Put your hazards on."

"They're ... already... Jesus, Will." Now she sounded irritated. "I'm not ... idiot."

He grunted. What exactly would you call someone who set off to investigate a drug lord *with a storm coming*?

You'd call the person a pain in the ass.

And if that person was Merry Warren, you'd race to your truck without a second thought.

"Oh hey, I do have reception in here." Her voice sounded clearer now; obviously, she'd gotten into the car. "Listen, Will, I didn't mean for you to chase after me. I thought you might know a good tow truck service or something."

"I'm coming. Just sit tight." Rain slashed against his face. He fought gusts of spitting wind all the way to his Tacoma. Damn, this storm was a lot worse than any of the forecasters had predicted. Weather off the Pacific in this area could be unpredictable. That was one reason Knight and Day Flight Tours had invested in a high-tech weather detection system, which unfortunately wasn't hooked up yet. In the meantime, they were at the mercy of the Weather Channel.

He yelled to his brothers that he was going to meet someone

and dove into his truck. Rain beat against the window as if it was knocking to get in. As he did a reverse turn to head out of the lot, his rear tires fishtailed a little. So much water all at once meant a high risk of hydroplaning.

As he headed out of town, he called dispatch to let them know where he would be. This kind of intense storm would cause problems across the county. Even though he was off for the weekend, it might be an all-hands-on-deck situation.

He called Merry again to let her know he was moving slowly, but he'd be there as quickly as he could.

"Don't worry about me," she told him. "Be safe, take your time. I'm getting some work done while I sit here. The rain's kind of soothing if I don't think about how the water level's rising in that ditch next to me."

"Call me if it gets worse and I can radio to see if someone's nearby. But the department's going to have its hands full with this weather, so I'd rather not."

"Oh my God, Will, no, forget about me. You should be out there helping. I'm fine."

"I may have to if they call me in, but first I'm getting you out of there. No arguments." And he hung up before she could argue about the "no arguments" ban.

On the way, he helped two stranded motorists, gave a hitch-hiker a lift to a very crowded gas station, and nearly hit a panicked deer crossing the road. The rain was relentless. It came in waves, sheets of water sweeping across the road, turning visibility to crap. He kept the windshield wipers at full blast the entire time, and still squinted through a distorted layer of water to see where he was going.

By the time he reached the turnoff to Route 68, evening was closing in, adding to the darkness of the cloud cover. This road was narrower, and as Merry had mentioned, the drainage ditches were overwhelmed by the sheer volume of water. From what he could see, they were filling up fast and close to overflowing.

Finally, with his shoulders aching from their hunched position over the wheel, he spotted blinking red hazard lights ahead. As he closed in, he recognized Merry's Corolla and saw the dim outline of a figure inside. Relief sent his heart soaring. He pulled up in front of her car. The door opened and she ran out, holding a red rain jacket over her head.

"Perfect timing," she yelled over the din of the rain still coming down. "My battery's dying."

"Hazards going out?"

"No, my laptop battery. The car's fine." She laughed, then ran around the hood of his truck to reach the passenger side. The door opened in a splatter of rain drops and there she was, her damp face glowing with exhilaration. Along with the red slicker, she wore a pair of velour sweatpants and running shoes. Her sudden presence, all light and life, snatched his breath away. "I know this sounds wrong, when people are probably getting stuck in the mud and I might never drive my car out of here, but I love storms."

Her breathless excitement made him smile. "I always look at them as public emergencies, but I guess I can see your point."

She laughed. "I like chaos, I think. That's when things get interesting. As long as no one gets hurt."

"Since I haven't been called in yet, the damage must not be too bad." He looked at the rain still cascading down outside. "I can't do anything for your car right now. We can wait here until the rain lets up, or we can find a place nearby to hunker down."

"I vote for door number two. I'm starving. If we keep going down this road, we should get to that lodge where Buckaroo stays."

He glanced at her sharply. She blinked at him innocently. "Are you still trying to investigate this story?"

"I'm just trying to stay out of the rain." With a beguiling smile, she added, "They probably have a bar. I'll buy you a hot toddy."

"I'm not buying your innocent act. You came all the way out here and you want to see what you can learn."

She gave up with a shrug. "I wouldn't mind. But it's the closest shelter I know of, and I'm chilled and wet and if they have any rooms available, I'd love a hot shower. And I'm serious about that drink, or whatever else you'd like. But it's cool if you don't want to. I get it."

"Get what?" Scowling, he turned his key in the ignition.

"You don't want me to figure out that *you* sent me that tip about Buckaroo."

He threw his head back and let out a long laugh. "When did you know?"

"Are you kidding? Right away. But it's the sweetest thing anyone's ever done for me." As they pulled back onto the road, she scooted closer to him and rubbed her arm against his. "Even sweeter than tiger lilies and lattes."

"Yeah, well, I didn't expect you to go dig up some middle-of-nowhere lodge and drive out there in a storm," he grumbled. "Fine way to repay my generosity."

"It's a lodge. How dangerous could that be?"

15

BUT WHEN THEY PULLED INTO THE PARKING LOT OF SWEET Mountain Lodge, her words seemed almost prescient. A river of water cascaded down the hillside behind the stately building. It poured into the creek that ran behind the lodge, its banks overflowing. At a guess, the creek was at least five feet deep. And on the other side, a boy hopped from foot to foot.

A group of people had gathered on the lodge side of the creek. They were waving and shouting at the boy, who was crying hard. Will guessed he was probably around nine years old.

"Shit. Do you see that kid?" He checked his phone; no service. "Do you have a signal?"

Merry checked her phone too. "No. Totally dead. What should we do?"

"I'm going to go get him." He steered the truck toward the group standing on the bank of the creek and parked as close as he could. "You can stay inside if you want."

"I want to help. What can I do?"

He glanced at her. By the determined set of her chin, he wouldn't have much luck talking her out of helping, and he could use a level-headed person around. "Can you drive a stick shift?"

"Of course."

"Then I want you to take the wheel after I get the truck into position. I need to attach a safety line to the hitch. I may need you to pull forward or back. Can you do that?"

"Absolutely."

He turned the truck and backed it up as close to the overflowing creek bed as he dared. Merry slid over to sit behind the wheel. He showed her the signals for forward and backward, then pulled up his hood and launched himself into the storm. He approached the group of onlookers. A quick glance told him which were the family members of the stranded boy and which were looky-loos throwing out bad suggestions.

"Deputy Knight from the Jupiter Point Sheriff's Department," he called. "Whose child is that?"

A young woman ran toward him. "He's ours," the woman sobbed. She gestured toward a man by the shore who refused to leave his spot. He was completely soaked down to the skin. "My husband tried to cross but the current is too fast and he slipped and nearly drowned. Can you help him?"

"Yes ma'am, I'm going to do my best. I'm going to fasten a safety line to my truck and go across."

He assessed the water still pouring in from the hills. "The quicker the better. The level's still rising and it's getting dark. Has anyone called for help?"

"Yes, but they said it's going to be at least half an hour before they can get anyone out here. He was playing in those woods, he said he fell asleep." The young woman's face was white with fear. "I think he's getting cold too. I saw him shaking."

"We'll get him back, don't you worry. Go tell him who I am and that I'm coming across to get him. What's his name?"

"Nick."

The woman ran back to her husband and they both waved and called across the water to Nick. Will opened the crew cab door of his truck and fished out the cable he kept back there.

Merry twisted around to watch him. "Are those the boy's parents?"

"Yup." He did little more than grunt as he planned out exactly how to accomplish the rescue. Merry seemed to understand and didn't say anything more until he had what he needed.

"Stay safe, Will," she said softly.

"Just keep a close watch, okay?"

"I will."

For two pretty verbal people, they both seemed at a loss for words. He caught her gaze for a moment and let their unspoken communication take over. *I care about you. Don't get hurt. Not when we're just getting started...*

Then he slammed the door shut and half-jogged, half-slid to the back of his truck. He anchored one end of the cable to the trailer hitch, then clipped the other end to his belt. He didn't have a rescue harness with him, so this would have to do. In a rushing river, he wouldn't risk it. But a rising creek with a panicked boy—worth the discomfort.

With the line well-secured on both ends, he trudged through the mud to the edge. He waved at the boy, who had climbed onto the tallest rock he could find. The kid was shivering in his thin Incredible Hulk T-shirt. He was probably wishing he was the Hulk right about now.

With one last nod at the parents—Nick's father had his arms wrapped tightly around his wife for comfort and warmth—he waded into the chilly water. The current tugged at his legs as if it was trying to push him over. The muddy bottom sucked at his boots. Each step had him sinking deeper into the muck. He would make better progress if he swam, but the flow was strong enough that he might get carried too far down and have a hard time fighting his way back.

So he took it step by step, grateful for the cable tethering him to his truck. To Merry. He felt her gaze on him, felt her support urging him onwards. Of all the ways they'd communicated, this one was new. But it was real. Without doubt, he knew she was right there in the water with him, in spirit.

At the midpoint of the stream, the water came to his armpits. Each step became more of a challenge as his body took precious energy to maintain his core temperature. Nick came closer to the edge, then jumped back as a wave splashed him.

"Nick, can you hear me? Stay right where you are," Will called to him. "I'm coming to help you, but I need you to stay put." If he slipped on the rocks, all bets were off.

"I can't really swim," the boy told him in a high, anxious voice. "I been taking lessons but that water's too fast."

"It's okay. You won't have to swim. My feet are on the bottom right now. All you'll have to do is hang on to me. Got it?"

He nodded, then folded his arms across his chest, shivering. "How cold is it?"

"Damn cold," Will muttered as he pushed his chest through the rushing water. He felt like the prow of a ship cutting through the waves. When he was about two feet from the other side, the cable reached its end. He felt it tug against his belt. Should he ask Merry to back the truck closer to the water? No, too much risk of it getting stuck in the mud. Besides, he could feel the water still rising. It was lapping against his chest, and for sure he didn't want to be neck-deep in this torrent.

"Okay, dude," he said to Nick. "This is as far as I can come. But it's plenty close enough. Just jump toward me and I'll grab you. Just try not to land on my head, would you? I know it makes an easy target."

Nick hesitated, judging the short distance between the rock he stood on and Will's open arms. "Just jump?" he asked, screwing up his face.

"Just jump." Will braced his legs in the muddy bottom. His body was really feeling the strain of fighting the nonstop current, and he needed all his energy for getting back. "Any time now. It ain't exactly warm in here."

He gave the boy an encouraging smile, but still he didn't move.

"Your mom is really worried," he said softly. "She can't wait to get her arms around you. Your father too."

Nick chewed on his lip and stared down at the water. Will cast around for something else to inspire him to jump.

"Know what else? There's a reporter in that truck. She's going to want to interview you, I can guarantee it. Would you like to be in the newspaper? I bet she'll take your picture too."

Finally, he brightened. "Can I be on TV?"

"Maybe. I can't say for sure. But she's waiting back there and I know she'll write you a great story. But we have to do our part, right? Okay now, don't think, just *jump*!"

He put all his authority into that last word. Since he'd been speaking evenly up until then, it shocked Nick enough so he launched himself into the air. He landed with a big splash right on top of Will, nearly knocking him over.

Will wrapped his arms around the kid and staggered backwards. He managed to regain his footing before the current grabbed him, but the slip scared the hell out of him. He was tiring, his arms sore, his thighs on fire. "You're going to ride piggy back. Wrap your arms around my shoulders, not my neck. Got it?"

Nick was holding on to him like a monkey and seemed unable to follow any commands, so Will turned and began the trek back, his arms filled with shivering child. One mucky, watery step, then another.

On the shore, Nick's family was jumping up and down, shouting and clapping. This time when he reached the halfway mark, the water came all the way to Will's shoulders. Nick clambered farther up his body, grabbing onto his head.

For a micro-second, Will couldn't see a thing because Nick's arm blocked his vision. It wasn't long, but enough to make him lose his footing again. He lost his balance completely and toppled into the churning water.

Nick shrieked and clutched him even more tightly. Water closed over Will's head, frigid and fast, so fast. He fought to find the bottom, fought to hold on to Nick, fought to breathe. He dug his steel-toed boots into the muddy bottom. Between the drag of his boots and the cable around his waist, he was able to fight the force of the creek somewhat. But not quite enough. He kept stumbling and going under, then surfacing for just enough time to haul in a breath of air before the water pushed him over again.

And then—a miracle. Something was helping him. Pulling him toward the shore where the water was less deep.

Not a miracle. *Merry.*

He lurched through the tumbling water, drawn by the cable as if it were an umbilical cord attached to his middle.

Nice and slow, Merry, he thought, just in case their silent communication was still working. Maybe it was, or maybe she was just a smart girl, but she kept the pace of the truck's forward motion exactly the way he needed it. Slow, with the occasional pause for him to catch up.

As he got closer to the shoreline, Nick's father plunged into the water, holding on to the cable to keep from getting swept away.

When he was close enough, Nick squirmed out of Will's grasp.

"Hang on, kid," Will gasped. "Let's get a little closer to him. We're almost there."

But he was too excited to listen, and the next thing Will knew, Nick wriggled into the water and splashed toward his father.

"Daddy, daddy!" His father swept him up into a tight embrace, then waded back to shore.

"Be right back," he called to Will.

Will didn't have the energy to tell him not to bother. He kept his entire focus on moving toward the shore, toward Merry. He could see her now, looking over her shoulder as she inched the truck up the incline toward the lodge. His feet were solidly under him now, the water only reaching his knees. He gave her a weary signal to stop the truck. She did so immediately. The cable slackened as he trudged the last few feet to the bank of the creek.

As soon as he took the last exhausted step onto solid ground, he fell to his knees. He sat on his heels, drawing in air in huge gulps.

The door of the truck swung open and Merry ran down the embankment toward him. She dropped onto her knees next to him. "Are you okay?"

He lowered his head to her shoulder, too exhausted even to keep his head up any longer. She wrapped her arms around him and rubbed her hands up and down his back.

"Oh my God, you're freezing. Can you make it to the truck? We have to get you out of these clothes. You're shaking."

"Fine," he said in a gasp. "Just give me...minute. Take the cable." He gestured to the carabiner on his belt. She reached toward his waist to unhook the cable, just as a dark-haired woman came jogging over to them.

"Hi there," she said. "I'm the manager here. I saw what you did and wanted to offer you a room for the night, gratis. You're a hero. That poor kid, plus the bad publicity if anything had happened to him, and I don't even want to *think* about the liability. But mostly, we're just so glad he's okay."

Will blinked at her, then at Merry. His lips were too cold to form words and his mind wasn't quite back up to speed yet.

Merry stepped in. "You're saying he can stay the night here?"

"You both can. Hot bath, room service, the works. Courtesy of Sweet Mountain Lodge. Just a small gesture of our appreciation."

"Wow, that's really generous." Merry glanced his way, but he was too exhausted to have an opinion. She turned back to the manager. "We accept. I just have to get him to the door, that's all."

"I can send some of our kitchen crew down..." she began dubiously.

Finally, Will found his voice. "I'll be fine," he said through chattering teeth. "But thanks."

The manager presented them both with a practiced smile. "Again, our deepest thanks. Just tell the front desk that Holly comped you a suite for one night, along with anything you need from the restaurant." Tucking her hands in the pockets of her raincoat, she hurried back to the lodge.

"Wow, I wonder if she knows I'm a reporter," said Merry wryly. "I usually get booted, not comped."

He chuckled, though it sounded more like a watery gurgle. "You're with me now. And you did great. That was good thinking, to start the truck up. Gave me that little boost I needed at the end."

"You scared the living crap out of me, Will." She placed her hands on his wet, numb cheeks. Even though he couldn't feel much, it felt good. Which made no sense, just like everything else related to Merry.

"I nearly dove in after you, but I came to my senses in time," she said. "And really, all I did was drive about two feet. You risked your life for that kid. My heart was in my mouth the entire time. I was so scared."

"I told Nick you'd put him in the newspaper. That's how I got him to jump."

"Of course I will. Maybe I can get an exclusive with the hero who rescued him too." The warmth of her hands was finally penetrating through the chill. It gave him a sense of comfort, of coming home. "You really need to get inside. Do you think you can walk yet?"

"Worth a shot."

16

THAT SHORT REST ON THE MUD BANKS DID WONDERS FOR HIM. HE felt better as soon as he was standing. Since he was still wobbly, Merry slung an arm around his back and supported him all the way to the truck. He definitely didn't object to that. He'd dive into a dozen icy creeks to get Merry's arms around him.

He eased into the passenger seat and let her drive to the front door. She went inside to check in and left the heat blasting in the cab. He almost dozed off while she was gone.

"Adrenaline," he explained sleepily when she hopped back into the truck. "After it wears off you feel like a truck hit you."

"Well, a truck didn't hit you, it saved you." She gave him a teasing smile. "And now it's giving you door-to-door service. They gave us a ground-floor suite so you don't have to climb any stairs. Oh, and it has a hot tub. Fancy, huh?"

He groaned in anticipation. Immersing himself into warm water sounded like the best idea in the entire world. Maybe Merry would immerse herself along with him. A guy could dream...

She insisted that he stay in the truck while she found the room, parked as close as possible, then ferried their few things inside. Her laptop, his emergency duffel, her purse, and that was about it. By then he'd regained enough energy to leave the truck under his own power. His clothes and boots were so saturated that he squished like the Swamp Thing on his way into the room. When he saw that the room was carpeted, he stopped at the doorway and bent down to take off his boots.

Except that his fingers were still too numb to manage the laces, so Merry knelt next to him to help.

"Don't get used to this 'waiting on you hand and foot' thing," she joked. "I only do this for genuine kid-rescuing heroes."

He straightened up and held onto the doorjamb while her nimble fingers undid his laces. He tried, oh so hard, not to imagine her fingers doing other things to him, but it was impossible. He didn't have the energy to deny his attraction to her, or to hide it. He couldn't act casual either. All he could do was stare at her as if she were an angel come to take care of him.

When she eased his boots off, muddy water dripped onto the carpet. She put them in the hallway, then had him lift his feet one by one so she could remove his socks. His toes were red, the rest of his feet white and clammy.

"Well, Deputy Knight, I wouldn't have chosen this body part to be the first that I got to see naked, but I guess that's how it worked out." She smiled up at him while his still-numb brain tried to process her words.

First? Naked? First of how many? Which body part would she have chosen?

He was still pondering her words when she rose to her feet and bundled him toward the bathroom. "I already got the water going in the bath. Take your time. I'll order us some food in the meantime. Any requests?"

"You in the tub with me?"

She grinned at him in delight. "I can see that your brain function is returning. Or at least one of your functions."

"One of the best ones," he pointed out. His tongue still felt a little clumsy. If he kissed her now, it would probably feel like a block of ice to her. Even so, he desperately wanted to. "Thank you, Merry. I really appreciate this. You. I appreciate *you*."

She gave a low laugh. "No, Will. You're the one who's appreciated. You came to my rescue and ended up saving a little boy. You're amazing." They stepped into the bathroom, which held a spacious Jacuzzi-size tub mostly filled with steaming water. "Can you get your clothes off by yourself or do you need a hand?"

By now, Will was done feeling like an invalid. He spoke slowly and carefully, making his clumsy tongue enunciate. "When I take my clothes off with you, it's not going to be for a bath." He lifted one frozen eyebrow.

Her eyes widened. "Um..."

Good. He'd surprised her.

She cleared her throat. "I'll be right out here, so if you need anything *G-rated*, let me know."

He held her gaze, pouring heat and promise and so much more into that one look. He shrugged off his jacket, which fell to the floor with a sodden thud. She didn't budge; instead she seemed riveted to his movements. So he put his hand to the bottom of his thermal shirt and tugged it over his head.

With his head still swaddled in fabric, he heard her quick intake of breath. But when he pulled the shirt off his head, she was gone and he had the bathroom to himself.

HOLY WOODWARD AND BERNSTEIN, she was *not* expecting that. Merry shut the bathroom door and leaned against it. She shut her eyes and shook her head, knees weak from the image of Will's smooth muscles flexing in his spectacular torso.

That just wasn't fair. First he saved a kid, then he took off his shirt right in front of her. How was she supposed to maintain that professional distance when he did stuff like that?

She crossed to the desk that held the room service menu and opened it. The words might have been Pig Latin for all the sense they made. She stared at it blindly, seeing Will instead of the dinner listings. Will struggling through that gray water. Will holding a squirming kid against his chest. Will nearly disappearing in the churning floodwaters.

He was never in any danger, she told herself. That's why he'd had the cable. He was tethered to the truck the entire time.

But he could have drowned. Or at least it had looked that way from the shore. His head kept going under, then bobbing up, then going under.

She buried her face in her hands, tears leaking through her fingers. The emotions that had powered through her in those desperate moments still had her heart pumping. If she lost Will... no, she couldn't lose Will.

Will was the one she'd turned to in a crisis. Will was the one she could count on. The one who looked out for her. The one who made her heart glow and her blood sing. The one she told secrets to. The one who kept surprising her, over and over.

She wanted him. Her body vibrated with the knowledge. She wanted him with a power that knocked her off her feet. Just like that flooding creek out there.

She picked up the phone and ordered a selection of food she thought he'd like. The moment called for comfort food—meatloaf and mashed potatoes—but knowing him, he probably liked the spicy stuff too. He had all sorts of little surprises like that hidden away in his personality. So she ordered some potstickers and spicy chili as well. Then threw in two big slices of apple pie and whipped cream, along with some coffee. The macaroni and cheese was for her, because nothing said "everything's going to be okay" more than mac and cheese. Unless it was SpaghettiOs, which weren't on the menu. In her opinion, more restaurants ought to serve SpaghettiOs.

After she'd hung up, she called again and added an extra

order of bread and butter. After a near-death experience, a guy should eat whatever he wanted. And the girl who'd nearly watched him die shouldn't worry about calories.

She heard splashing in the bathroom and smiled to herself. Will was fine. He was a tough guy. She'd never seen him in a situation like this before, but she shouldn't be surprised. Once, she'd seen him arrest someone, and the speed and force with which he'd moved had taken her breath away. He'd be fine, and they were here in this amazing hotel suite for the night, with a truckload of food coming and a bed the size of Arizona...

Sure, she'd told him they should keep things strictly friend-level. But a girl could change her mind, right? It was worth considering, wasn't it? A handsome hunk of a hero was on the other side of that bathroom door and it was getting harder to remember *why* they shouldn't tumble into that bed.

After the food arrived, she left it all set up in its covered dishes and tiptoed to the bathroom door. The splashing had stopped. Maybe he was clean by now. Clean and getting dressed. Disappointment made her sag against the door. The moment had passed.

Then she remembered that he didn't have any clean clothes with him.

She tapped on the door. "Will, how's it going in there? Everything all right? Do you need some clothes?"

No answer. Had he survived a raging flood only to drown in a bathtub? She'd better make sure.

She pushed open the door and found him sound asleep, his head resting on a folded towel on the edge of the tub. His long, muscled body was stretched out, one knee bent up, bits of him visible under the floating islands of soapsuds.

She quietly pulled the door closed, her mind filled with images of those hard muscles and long limbs. Naked Will Knight was just as magnificent as she'd always imagined. And yes, she had spent some time imagining it. She could admit it now.

"Hey Merry." Low and amused, his voice traveled through the door. "Was that you?"

"I was just making sure you hadn't drowned in there."

"Nope. Still breathing. But you're right, I could use some clothes."

Clothes? Who needs 'em! She pressed her lips together to keep those words from escaping. "I'll get your bag. Hang on."

She found his emergency gear back in the bedroom and brought it to the bathroom door. "I'm just going to set this right inside—"

The door swung open and there he was. Tall and wide-shouldered, with a towel wrapped around his hips, riding tantalizingly low. He'd dried himself off, but moisture still studded his skin and his hair curled damply around his ears. It was an endearing look on him, she had to say. Instead of his usual impassive manner, he looked relaxed and loose and mouthwatering. His gray eyes shone like beacons through the steam of the bathroom.

Wordlessly, she held out his bag. He took it and pulled out a pair of sweatpants. "Thanks. That was great. I feel a thousand percent better now."

She nodded, but couldn't seem to make herself move. Behind him, the water was draining out of the bathtub. The steamy warmth of the little room was so relaxing, so seductive.

"It's your turn now," he told her. "Shower or bath?"

She shook herself to attention. "A long hot shower sounds good to me." It would sound even better if he got in with her. She wanted to suggest it, all sassy, but if he came into the shower with her they would have sex for sure, and if that happened...well, she wanted that...let's be honest...but there'd be no going back and—

Will interrupted her confused thought process. He curled one warm, damp hand around the back of her neck and hovered his face over hers. "You're thinking too much," he murmured. "Take your shower. Then we'll go from there."

Swallowing hard, she nodded like a marionette. *Go from there.*

Go where? Right now, she'd go anywhere with him, and that was a dangerous thought. He eased past her, a knowing smile curving his firm lips. The chemistry between them felt like a tractor beam pulling her toward him. She watched him walk toward the bedroom, his rear flexing under the towel, his loose strides those of a man thoroughly confident in his power to please a woman.

Gah! *Get a grip.* They had an entire night ahead of them, a king-size bed, and a planet-size mutual attraction.

Maybe she should make that shower a cold one.

17

"So," he said after she'd showered. "I'm digging the new look."

With hair like hers, she didn't dare use any of the hotel's shampoo—it would strip the oils right out. So she'd pinned it up out of the way during her shower. Now she had it in two fluffy puffballs, probably looking a lot like Minnie Mouse. Since she didn't have spare clothes, he'd lent her one of his clean t-shirts. It was huge on her, hanging to mid-thigh, and proclaimed her to be a member of the "University of Arizona Athletic Department." Luckily, her underwear hadn't gotten too wet from the storm.

While she was showering, he'd uncovered all the room service dishes and set everything on the desk. They were both so hungry, they'd barely said a word until they'd consumed most of the chili and mac and cheese.

"Thanks." She grinned at him. "I like to mix it up. Rooster feathers by day, extra-large boy T-shirts by night."

"Call me crazy, but I'll go for the T-shirt." His scorching glance told her he'd also go for removing the t-shirt. She shivered with anticipation.

"How did you know I love chili, by the way?"

She tapped the side of her forehead. "I'm a journalist, and I have amazing powers of deductive reasoning."

He lifted an eyebrow. "Deductive reasoning?'

"Sure. Want to hear my thinking?" He twisted his face into a wary expression, but she continued anyway. "You're kind of a homebody. You like order and stability, traditional stuff. Maybe because you were the oldest and you had to keep things together after your parents were gone. Or maybe that's your natural personality. But you also have an adventurous streak. That's why you went onto Flirt. And that's why, even when you found out who I am, that I'm this hot mess who never cleans her car, you still want to hang out with me."

"Huh. And all that says chili to you?"

"It does. I bet you can't argue with that logic." She gave him a sassy smile over a big forkful of mac and cheese.

"Right, because that's not logic. But if we're analyzing food choices, let's talk about that macaroni and cheese you're shoveling into your mouth."

She swallowed her current mouthful and daintily patted her lips with a linen napkin. "A lady doesn't shovel. A lady nibbles. That was a nibble. An overenthusiastic nibble."

"Okay, wordsmith. You can describe it however you want. But you can't deny what it says about you."

"Oh, this ought to be good. What does it say about me?"

"That you can't wait until we're naked in this big bed together."

"*Excuse me?*" She nearly choked mid-swallow. She wasn't sure if she was more shocked by that statement—which was totally true—or by the fact that he was turning the "food choice" tables on her. "You're going to have to walk me through that one."

"It's obvious. Macaroni and cheese is pretty much the whitest food you can eat. White flour, cheese made from milk, which is white. In case you hadn't noticed, I'm a white guy. Also, it has two ingredients, macaroni and cheese. There are two of us." He waved his fork between the two of them. "Put it all together, it's clear that you want me."

She snorted as she dug into her food again. "I see what you're doing there. You're making fun of my chili statement."

"Why would I make fun of that?" he asked mildly. "Just because you're pigeonholing me?"

"Touché. But you have to admit you ate up that chili pretty fast. And you didn't deny my analysis."

"Actually, I *do* deny it. I mean, I like chili, don't get me wrong. But me wanting you has nothing to do with some 'adventurous streak.' And you're not a hot mess. You're just busy. And hot. I'll accept the hot part."

She let those words settle over her. He'd said he wanted her. He said she was hot. And he got that she didn't prioritize cleaning her car because other things were more important. "What does it have to do with?" she finally asked. "If it's not your adventurous streak."

Even though their tone up to now had been light, he put down his fork and settled his penetrating gaze on her. That was the thing about Will—he always took her seriously. He never brushed her off. He might refuse to comment if he didn't think he should, but he didn't dismiss her.

"What *doesn't* it have to do with? You're smart. You're gorgeous. You're passionate. You're funny. You're sexy as hell. You're thoughtful. You're dedicated. You're impressive in every way, Merry. Maybe a little too single-minded sometimes, a little too reckless when you're on a story. But that's just my opinion. You put a hundred percent of yourself into what you do, and I can't really criticize that. I'd be a hypocrite if I did."

The room seemed to shift around her, the ground dropping away beneath her feet. She'd been longing her entire life to hear words like that. Under everything Will said ran a current of *respect*. And that was all she'd ever really wanted.

Maybe it was due to being the disposable cast-off child of the Merriweathers. Maybe it was being her mother's daughter, driven to excel. Maybe it was growing up mixed in a black and white world. Whatever the reason, all her life she'd craved respect. She wanted to be *seen and heard*.

And here was Will Knight, a deputy sheriff, law and order personified, handing that to her like a fact of life. Something without question.

Except that he wasn't "law and order personified." She had to stop thinking that way. She always hated the idea that she had to represent women of color, or biracial people, or anyone except her own self. He was Will Knight, an individual. A big brother, caring friend, respected member of the community, secret poet, and all-around beautiful man.

One who wanted her. And whom she wanted.

She put down her fork and shoved aside her plate. "Will..."

He looked at her alertly. "Merry..."

"I'm going to let the mac and cheese speak for me. It's completely correct."

He waited one beat, scanning her face, as if making sure he was interpreting her comment correctly. Then he stood up, his tall, powerful body unfurling to his full height. He wasn't wearing a shirt, since he'd given his only extra one to her. Muscles rippled up and down his abdomen, flexing under the firm skin, pale where the sun didn't touch it. She licked her lips in anticipation. Sweet Lord in heaven, he was a yummy man.

He offered his hand and pulled her to her feet. The intensity of his gray-eyed gaze set off a flutter of nerves inside her.

When she got nervous, she got pedantic. "By the way, I have to correct you on one thing. Plenty of black folks love mac and cheese. And it has more than two ingredients, because it's best if you mix milk and butter in with the cheese."

"I know how to make mac and cheese. It was all Aiden would eat for about a year."

The reminder that Will had raised his little brother made her want him even more. He was such a good man, a solid, loyal, rock-of-the-ages kind of man. He pulled her against him, so her bare legs tangled with his. Sparks exploded between them. It wouldn't have surprised Merry if literal fireworks were lighting up the room.

Instead, it was just the two of them. No shirt for him, no pants for her. And that was still too much clothing. He lifted her up so her legs wrapped around his hips. His hands firmly supported her ass, the long fingers settling close to the place between her legs that throbbed and howled for his touch. She felt the rise of his erection against her flesh. She groaned with want.

"Will, I know this is probably a bad idea, but I don't even care anymore."

"Maybe it is, maybe it isn't. You have me so spun around I can't think logically. All I know is I want you. As much of yourself as you're willing to give, I'll take."

He moved his fingers closer to the tender center of her desire.

"That feels so good," she moaned. "Take me to bed, Will. Please, before I lose my mind."

"Wouldn't want that," he murmured in her ear. "Your mind is one of the things I love best about you."

If she hadn't been so gone from lust for him, she might have obsessed more about his use of the word "love." But right now, all she wanted was to get their clothes off and get into bed. She ran her hands along the strong muscles of his back, then under the waistband of his sweats. His ass swelled under the fabric, firm muscles flexing as he spun the two of them in the direction of the bed. She reveled in the intoxicating sensation of his glutes clenching and moving with each step.

He dropped her on the edge of the bed, gazing at her with hot eyes. "You have no idea how many times I've pictured something like this. Usually there's some kind of lingerie involved, though. Not my old law school t-shirt."

"Don't like the t-shirt?" She reached for the hem and whipped it off. In nothing but her favorite boy-short Calvin Klein undies, she lifted her chin and let him look his fill. And he did, taking his time the way he did everything. *Deputy Slow-mo strikes again.*

While he drank in her body, she stuck out one foot and hooked it in the waistband of his sweats. She dragged it down, inch by inch, revealing the V-shaped muscle next to his hipbone, the light scattering of hair around his privates, his iron-hard thighs.

He wasn't wearing anything under his clothes either. His erection tented his cotton pants in impressive fashion. She stared at that bulge, desire making her giddy. He was so virile, so sexy.

"You're killing me," he muttered. "These are coming off." He tucked his thumbs into the elastic and peeled the sweatpants down his thighs.

Oh. My. God. Will was definitely packing heat down there. His arousal burst from behind the fabric like a rocket launching. Large and heavy, thick and proud, his erection reared upward at an angle from his thighs.

She swallowed hard, suddenly nervous. He advanced toward her and put one knee on the edge of the bed. "Don't worry about him." He touched himself to show her what he was talking about.

She swallowed. "Why?"

"Because I don't have a condom. Unless you do, we can't have sex."

"No, I don't generally carry condoms around with me." Her disappointment made tears sting her eyes. So stupid, but she'd really gotten her hopes up here.

"I'm a little bit relieved to know that. Condom or not, I intend to make you come until you scream."

She froze, thrills running through her, up and down her skin and around about in her belly. "Oh, really?"

"Oh yes. Really. Lie back."

She did so, scooting toward the headboard to give him more room. As he joined her on the bed, she feasted her eyes on the sight of his naked body, so strong and muscular. When his mouth closed over her nipple, she arched into the sensation, bright pleasure searing her nerve endings.

She clutched at his powerful shoulders as he hunched over her. Living up to his Slow-mo nickname, he painstakingly tasted her body, inch by inch, exploring at a slow, thorough, deliberate, all-consuming pace. He spent so much time on her nipples, drawing out such wild feelings, that she abandoned all shyness—not that she had much of that anyway. She lifted her chest to him, offering herself to his relentless tongue. He curved his hands around her breasts, cupping and squeezing the soft flesh while he moved between them, suckling one nipple then the other.

By the time he moved down her belly, she was moaning like a wild thing, twisting her legs back and forth, seeking relief for the hot bundle of nerves between her legs.

"I know what you want," he murmured as he swirled his tongue across the sensitive skin of her lower belly. "And don't you worry, you're going to get it."

"I want *you*," she moaned. "All of you."

"You want my cock?"

Oh my God. Just him saying the words nearly made her come. "Yes," she said in a smothered voice.

"Then you'll have to see me again," he said smugly. He used his teeth to pull the edge of her panties away from her sex. "I won't leave you unprotected. You know me."

"Mr. Law and Order," she gasped.

"That's right. No glove, no love." He nibbled at the edge of her bush of curls. "God, you are one outstandingly luscious woman. I'm taking these undies off now."

She arched her hips to enable him to remove her panties. She couldn't take her eyes off him as he peeled them down her legs and tossed them on top of the t-shirt she'd already stripped off. Trust Will to keep everything in a nice orderly pile.

"Keeping things tidy, I see," she teased him. "Neat freak."

"Oh, I'm a freak all right. But I don't like everything neat. Some things I like wild." He came back to her, crawling on his knees between her legs. He spread her inner thighs apart with his big hands. She shivered, shudders of anticipation gripping her body. She felt frantic and edgy, as if she might smack him if he didn't give her some release, now.

And when he did, when he lowered that fine brown-haired head to the triangle between her legs and captured her clit with his mouth, she nearly came off the bed, it felt so incredible. She gave a muffled shriek and dug her hands into his hair. Even though he'd gone so slowly before, now he took a whole different approach—rough and relentless, fast and furious. The shift in pace disoriented her. It put her one step behind, her mind trying to catch up with her body.

But her body was too far ahead. It knew things she didn't—that Will was going to blow every other sexual experience away. That she was about to have the most intense orgasm of her life. That he could be trusted to take care of everything she needed, and more.

So she gave up on thinking and abandoned herself to the pure pleasure of *feeling*. Not just the amazing sensations he pulled from her nerve endings. But the freedom that came with them. Freedom to moan and cry out and grind her hips against his mouth and squeeze her own nipples to intensify the sensations.

He growled and murmured to her, words that flowed in one ear and out the other. She understood without the words. She knew what he meant—that he was crazy for her, that he loved the taste of her, that he couldn't get enough, that he wanted her to explode with pleasure.

With his fingers and tongue and mouth and teeth, he urged

her toward a climax that sang toward her like a missile. It was way off on the horizon, a shimmering promise, and then it was right on top of her, roaring like a freight train. She screamed as it hit her. The world burst into bright, shining, sun-struck shards. He stayed with her, licking and rubbing, the warmth and pressure of his touch driving her up, up, higher than she'd ever dreamed possible.

So patient, he was. As if he had all the time in the world to lavish on her. Maybe there was something to that slow-motion approach of his. It made her feel like the center of the world.

Eventually she came spiraling down from that incredible peak. It took a few minutes to catch her breath and get her heart rate back to normal. Every part of her felt languid and happy and complete. She couldn't remember the last time she'd felt this good about life.

She rolled onto her side to face the man who had brought her this incredible experience. Will was leaning on his elbow, a very satisfied, smug smile on his square-jawed face.

"Well look at you, all proud of yourself," she teased. "Bet I can turn that smile into something else."

His smile broadened. "Yeah? How do you intend to do that?"

She reached for the erection still rearing hard and proud between his legs. As soon as she touched it, the grin dropped off his face, replaced with a look of strain.

"Hmm," she murmured as she stroked that rigid flesh. "What's this all about?"

"No condom," he reminded her with a warning glance.

"We'll just have to get creative then. Good thing I'm a specialist with words."

"Words?" He sounded distracted now, which she counted as a triumph.

"Yeah. Personally, I love the feel of a hard cock in my hand." She emphasized the sexier of those words and felt his erection jump in response. "Now that's what I'm talking about." She caressed the satiny skin covering his organ, circling the head, brushing her thumb against the drop of liquid already appearing. "Of course, it's not quite as fun as putting it in my mouth. There's nothing quite as delicious as a thick dick sliding against my tongue; it's better than an ice cream sundae with a cherry on top, better than—" The rest of her words disappeared into a mumble as she pulled his organ into her mouth.

The intimacy was almost shocking. Her connection with him felt so strong, so immediate. She had no idea how long she stroked him like that, but he was already on the edge, so it couldn't have been long. He pulled out, groaned long and hard, his body going rigid as he came into her hand.

Watching him come, his eyes closed, jaw clenched, his powerful body thrusting against her hand—God it was incredible.

When he finally relaxed, he slitted one eye open. "Damn," was all he said. "You sure know your way around some dirty talk." He reached for the nightstand, where he'd left his towel earlier, and snagged it for her. She wiped herself off, then bounced off the bed and skipped into the bathroom. As she washed her hands, joy bubbled through her. She felt light as a feather, as if nothing could ever bother her again. Looking in the mirror, she saw someone relaxed and happy, no hint of deadline pressure or work stress. She barely recognized herself.

When she came back to the bed, he was still flat on his back, one arm covering his eyes, his broad chest rising and falling, his powerful legs sprawled out, his penis curled against his thigh. She paused, wondering if he'd fallen asleep.

But he reached his other hand toward her, beckoning for her to join him. She hopped onto the bed and snuggled against his side, fitting her body perfectly against his. Her head nestled into the notch between his shoulder and his collarbone. His hand made a warm, comforting weight on her hip.

"Your way with words is going to be the death of me," he murmured.

"How about your way with your tongue?" she countered. "You've got skills I didn't know about."

"Hey." He lifted the arm covering his face and stroked the hair away from her face. "I don't know anything. I just follow the moans."

Follow the moans. She liked that phrase. "Sounds like you could write a poem about that. A dirty one."

"I've never written a dirty poem. I'll have to think about that. '*There once was a writer named Merry. She was so freaking smart it was scary.*'" He paused, probably searching for the next line.

"Not bad, but the first two lines are always the easiest," Merry pointed out.

"Is that a challenge?"

"Hells yeah."

"*When she asked for a comment, Will wanted to vomit. So instead he*...um...*licked her like a berry*?"

"Ewww." Merry laughed and swatted him on the side. "I'm a berry now? Let me guess, a *black*berry?"

"Hey, it's the only thing that rhymes!" He caught her hand, laughing. "You're not a blackberry, they're too tart. You're more like a juicy, plump mulberry, sweet and tangy and—"

"Stop!" She clapped her hand over his mouth and tried to force her face into a frown. She was laughing too hard to manage it though. "Comment and vomit do not rhyme, by the way."

"Picky, picky. By the way, have you ever had a mulberry pie? They're my favorite."

"Is that supposed to sound so dirty? Oh my God. Pie!" She sat bolt upright, suddenly remembering the rest of their meal. "I ordered apple pie with whipped cream for dessert."

"Did you have specific plans for that pie? Because I never say no to whipped cream." His voice lowered to a growl. "In bed or out ofbed."

"You have the dirtiest mind, Will Knight. It's just pie. Real pie. Sitting right over there getting soggy. You hungry?"

"Starving." He lifted her from his body in one fell swoop, then rolled off the bed. He strode naked across the room to the desk that still held all the food. He walked like a panther, like a perfectly muscled, well-honed champion athlete.

"Did you ever play any sports?" she asked as she followed him out of bed. She pulled on his t-shirt. She didn't have anything close to a perfect athlete body and had spent zero years in a gym locker room.

"Why, do I have that jock look?"

"You do." She padded across the carpeted floor to the desk, where he was uncovering the pie. "I'm not complaining, by the way. I love your body. I hope that doesn't sound like I'm objectifying you."

"I'm not too worried about it," he said dryly. He unpeeled the plastic wrap from the first slice of pie and used a fork to spread the melting whipped cream over the apples. "I played football in college," he added.

"Quarterback?"

"QB2. Second string. It was a big football school. They didn't miss me when I quit the team."

He handed her the other plate of pie and lowered himself into a chair, propping his feet up on a second one. She took her dessert and wandered over to the window. Pulling aside the drape, she peered into the darkness. Their room faced the steep hillside from which water had been cascading into the swollen creek. Someone's headlights were illuminating the area now, and she could see that the rain had diminished to a light patter and the water was subsiding.

The drama had passed. They could probably head home now. The roads would most likely be fine.

But she didn't want to. She wanted to stay right here with

Will, eating pie next to that huge bed with hours and hours of nakedness awaiting them.

She put down the pie. "Honestly, Will, I doubt that you were ever second-string anything."

He lifted an eyebrow at her over a forkful of apple filling. "Is that a compliment?"

"It was supposed to be."

He pointed his fork at her. "I'm a deputy sheriff, you know. That's second string."

"Yeah, but if you had run for sheriff, you would have won. Everyone says so."

"Damn. And I could have had a big shiny badge." He shrugged. "Oh well."

She came his way and sat on the edge of the bed. "Do you ever regret not completing your law degree?"

He chewed his apple pie thoughtfully. "Maybe. Sometimes. It would come in handy in some situations. But I like being a deputy. I wouldn't want the hassle of running for office. I like being the boots on the ground, the one people come to for answers, the solver of crimes."

"Will Knight, Solver of Crimes." She smiled at him and licked whipped cream off her lips. "Has a certain ring to it."

"That it does. Especially when you say it." He shoved aside his pie and surprised her by scooping her up into his arms. "I have a crazy idea. What if I go from room to room and knock on every door until I find someone with an extra condom?"

She grinned up at him. "I have a better idea. How about if we get a good night's sleep and in the morning, we ask a few discreet questions about Mr. Buckaroo Brown? I interview Nick James about his amazing rescue by a heroic and handsome sheriff's deputy. Then we drive back to Jupiter Point, hitting a convenience store along the way."

He shifted her in his arms. "There's a word for people like you."

"What? Smart?"

"Bossy."

She gasped and pretended to pummel him with her fists. "Oh no, you didn't. You know you're the bossy one. Don't even try to pretend it's me."

"Me, bossy?" He tossed her onto the bed. "You might be right. Take that shirt off. Again."

18

"I'M NOT SURE OUR RELATIONSHIP IS READY FOR SOMETHING LIKE this," said Will the next morning.

"It will require some trust, especially on your part." Merry watched him gravely as she dressed. They hadn't gotten much sleep. Will wasn't quite sure how they'd found the willpower to avoid the condom-requiring part of sex. But they'd gone wild with everything else.

And now...this.

"It's not about trust, it's about experience." He tested his boots, finding them still wet from slogging through the creek.

"How can I get experience if we don't give it a try? You know I can always do it without you." She made a saucy face at him.

Bad girl. It was a good thing they weren't talking about sex.

"Fine. We'll do a little co-investigating. But you have to promise to follow my lead." He put his boots on despite the soggy leather. He couldn't investigate barefoot, could he? Especially while trying to keep Merry out of trouble.

She batted her eyelashes at him. "All you have to do is ask me in your sex voice and I promise to do whatever you want."

"My *sex* voice?"

"Yeah, that growly, bossy voice." She dropped to a lower octave and roughened her tone. "'Take off your shirt...wrap your legs around me...come for me, baby—'"

"Okay, okay." He interrupted before she got too into her imitation of him. Fact was, he was getting turned on by it. He adjusted his jeans, which had suddenly gotten uncomfortably tight again. "Investigation rule number one. I'm not using my sex voice."

"Spoilsport." She pouted as she brushed past him. "Hey, I have an idea about how to find out which room Buckaroo stays in. Try to keep up."

He followed in hot pursuit, one boot still untied. So far, co-investigating with Merry was a lot like doing anything else with Merry. It made him feel alive.

Merry sweet-talked the head of housekeeping into revealing the fact that they kept suite 21 reserved for a big shot from out of town. Will took over from there. He told the front desk clerk that he needed a picture of the spot where the rescue had occurred, and that he'd determined room 21 had the best angle.

Once the clerk gave them the key, they spent half an hour searching every corner of the suite, which had a master bedroom, an expansive living room with a luxurious seating area, and even a kitchenette. It also had a balcony with a sliding glass door that offered easy access to the woods. If Buckaroo wanted to keep visitors off the radar, it would be easy.

He snapped a few pictures of the creek for cover, as well as the woods and the balcony. He'd pass them along to Deputy Jernigan for follow-up. It wasn't really a lead, but worth putting into the file.

After finding no trace of anything suspicious—or really anything at all, since it had been thoroughly cleaned since Buckaroo's last stay—they came across a locked safe in the closet. Unlike most hotel room safes, this one didn't have any instructions about choosing a code to lock it and unlock it.

Merry crouched in front of it, curious as a cat scratching at a closed door. "Do you think we can call the front desk and ask about it?"

"That might be pretty suspicious. 'Hey, I saw this locked safe in a hotel room where I'm taking a photo and just wondered if I can open it.'"

"Hm. I guess that won't work." She pulled her lower lip between her teeth. He was getting to know that gesture. It meant she was concocting some crazy plan. "I'll bet you anything that he's keeping something in there. Maybe you could get a search warrant."

He laughed. "Uh, no. There isn't even a hint of probable cause. I'd be laughed out of the courtroom."

"What if we make up something?" Her eyes brightened. "You know, like I can say I smelled cocaine coming from the direction of the safe. That's probable cause, isn't it?"

"Sure, probable cause to get you charged with falsifying evidence. You can't smell cocaine through a reinforced metal wall."

She pondered for a moment. "Marijuana? That's really smelly. I used to smell it on my stepfather as soon as he walked into our apartment."

He snorted and offered a hand to help her up.

She brushed off the seat of her pants. "That weird noise you just made sounded an awful lot like a 'no comment'."

He slung his arm over her shoulders and guided her out of the closet. "I'll give you points for creativity. Proper investigative procedure, not so much."

"Such a rule-follower," she teased as they stepped back into the bedroom.

"Except where it counts." He stopped and pulled her against him. "In bed."

She closed her eyes and rubbed her firm curves against him. He hardened immediately, blood rushing straight to his cock. All the hot memories from the night before flooded back. The luscious taste of her on his tongue, the perky swell of her nipples under his fingers, the suppleness of her skin, the incredible electricity they generated together.

"Maybe we could investigate *this* together," Merry said, cupping her hand over the bulge in his pants. "Maybe do a sit-down interview sometime."

"No time like the present." He planted his hands under her ass and lifted her up so she could wrap her legs around his hips. This was quickly becoming one of his favorite moves, because of how it kept them face to face, close together, laughing into each other's eyes. He walked her over to the armchair and sank into it. Now she was seated on his lap, her mound pressing into denim covering his swollen cock. "Now this is my kind of sit-down. What did you want to ask?"

He ran his hands lightly up and down her sides. Her hair, with its soft, luscious frizz, glowed in the morning light filtering through the window.

"Hmm..." Her eyes closed halfway, and a sensual smile curved her full lips. "I have a long list of questions. But I already know how you're going to answer. No comment, no comment, no comment. That's all I ever get from Deputy Knight."

"Yeah, well, the deputy just hit a dead-end in this investigation. He clocked out." He tugged at her earlobe with his teeth. "So fire away."

She drew back to look at him in surprise. "Seriously?"

"Yes. We've got that condom-shopping trip coming up. We ought to know more about each other." Besides, he loved having her on his lap like this. He'd submit to an "interview" just to extend the pleasure of that.

"Okay, since you're feeling talkative. Who was your first girlfriend?"

"Mandy Blake, third grade," he said promptly. "She kissed me after I blocked a dodgeball about to knock her glasses off." He ran his tongue along the tendon of her neck, enjoying her shiver of response.

"Always the hero, huh?"

"I do what I can." He nuzzled his nose into the crook of her neck.

"First sex."

"I was sixteen. A neighbor lady whose name I refuse to disclose. Older woman, at least thirty. I used to sneak over there at night."

"You bad boy." She sighed and tilted her head back as he nibbled his way down her throat. "I see what you mean about breaking those rules."

"I only had one rule back then. Have fun. I like to think I've grown up a little since then."

She flexed her hips, tantalizing his erection with the hot mound of her sex. "I think you've grown up in all the right ways," she purred.

This teasing vixen side of Merry might just about kill him. He spread his hands across her lower back, filling them with her curves.

"How about most recent sex?" she asked in a slightly more serious tone.

This was definitely getting into more sketchy territory. Could he get away with a "no—"

"And don't you dare say 'no comment,'" she added.

Figured. "A friend of mine and I have a thing. We get together now and then to blow off steam. It's not serious. Never has been." He didn't want to explain any more than that, because his relationship with Roxy was so different from this new, confusing, mind-blowing thing with Merry.

"You have a fuck-buddy?" She drew back with a frown.

He winced. If only he could have stuck with a "no comment."

"I wouldn't use that term. She's a friend. We've known each other since high school, but neither of us wants a relationship."

She twisted her mouth and squinted one eye, the picture of skepticism. "Uh-huh. You're a hot cop and a good guy. You sure she doesn't want a relationship?"

"Very sure. Sometimes I don't see her for months. I don't know what she does. We don't breathe down each other's necks. If she wants to get together, she calls, and if I'm into it, she comes over. That's about the extent of it."

"What would she think about this? Us? Whatever's going on here?"

He massaged the suddenly tight muscles along her spine. "She wants me to be happy, same as I want for her."

"So if she called you tonight, what would you say?"

He stared at her, finally picking up on the vulnerability lurking behind her eyes. As sassy and verbally adept as Merry was, that confident bravado didn't tell the whole story. Then again, surfaces never did, or he'd be the stick-up-his-ass, law-and-order guy he appeared to be.

"I'd say that I just got involved with someone who has me completely ass over elbows, and that I don't know what exactly is going on or where it's headed, but I can't think about anyone else as long as she's around."

Merry's lips parted, the color rising in her cheeks, painting her beautiful bronze skin a rosier shade. He brushed his thumbs across her cheekbones, giving her time to process how serious he was.

"That's a really nice thing to say."

"You know me. I don't comment unless I have something accurate to report."

A smile quirked up the corners of her mouth. "Indeed I do know you. And it only took three years of frustration."

He let out a slow breath, relieved that they'd navigated that issue okay. "So what about you? Let's turn this around. Same questions back at you. First sex, last sex. Go."

"I thought *I* was conducting this interview?"

"Nope. It's my turn. I've got you in the interrogation room. Picture ugly fluorescent overheads and a very uncomfortable chair."

She flexed her hips against his thighs with a sexy purr. "I'm not sure my imagination is that good."

"Don't distract the interrogator," he said sternly, stilling her movements by planting his hands on her ass. "Now answer the question."

"Fine. First time I had sex, I was in college. Late bloomer."

"No one snapped you up in high school?"

She shook her head with a wry expression. "I told you I went to a private school. The kids there thought I was ghetto, and the kids in my neighborhood thought I was a snob. I never felt totally right in either place."

Her wistful look tugged at his heart. "Sounds tough."

She shrugged. "Sometimes. I used to come home and cry to my mother because some kid made fun of my hair. She'd kind of cuff me upside the head and tell me whatever it was, flip it around. Pretend it was the *best* thing about me, that all those straight-haired kids wished they had hair like mine."

He tangled his fingers in the rich profusion of curls. "Wouldn't be surprised if they did."

"It doesn't even matter." She shrugged impatiently. "Her point was, if it feels like a vulnerability, flip it into a strength. I was always on the outside, always observing. That helped make me a good journalist. Anyway," she blew a breath upwards, rolling her eyes. "That was a long-ass answer to a simple question. First time I had sex, I was a sophomore in college and the guy was a member of the baseball team who needed a little tutoring. He returned the favor." She gave him a naughty wink.

"Tutoring, huh?" God help him, he was jealous of some guy back in college. "Was he black or white?"

She started, maybe because of the starkness of his question. He didn't really think of Merry in those terms—black or white

—but maybe she did. He had to find a way to talk about it honestly.

"Neither. He was Dominican." She watched him warily.

"My family is mostly Scottish. We have that clannish "laird" thing going on. Our family name Knight comes from a Norman knight who kept one of my ancestors as an indentured servant. Several generations back, my ancestors came here to get out from under his thumb. We're like weeds, we grow anywhere."

She stared at him levelly. "Why are we talking about this?"

"Because I want it out on the table. People think in terms of black and white, but most of the time, the closer you look at a person, the more individual details you see. And it's the specifics that count. That's what helps you solve a crime. Or write a good article. Or understand a human being."

"I hope you're not saying there's no difference between someone growing up black and someone growing up white. 'Cuz I've seen both."

"Of course not. I'm saying when I look at you, I see a complex person I want to know inside and out. I see someone who lights me up. Someone brilliant and beautiful. A little irritating, a lot sassy."

"And mixed. Don't leave that out."

"I don't want to leave anything out. I want to know it all."

She tilted her forehead against his and closed her eyes. A long moment passed while she digested his words. He practically held his breath until she spoke again. "How is it you keep pulling these surprises out of your sleeve?"

"Trying to keep you guessing." He twined a finger in her hair and tugged lightly. She purred deep in her chest. "And you still haven't answered the other question. Most recent sex."

"Well, it's a little embarrassing. His name is Vibe. I met him in Los Angeles, while I was shopping."

Another hot wave of jealousy hit him. "Vibe? Jesus, what kind of name is that? *Vibe.* Christ. What is he, some kind of hippie? Or some lamebrain hip-hop star?" He hated the guy and everything about him.

She laughed at him. "Look at you, all jealous. I'll have to introduce you to him. You might like him. He's a real go-getter. Doesn't say much, but that's okay. Sometimes words aren't needed."

He ground his teeth together. "I don't know anyone around here named Vibe. Does he stick to LA?"

"No, he generally hangs out in Jupiter Point, in my apartment. Next to my bed, as a matter of fact. His full name is Vibe E. Rator, but you probably won't find him in the phone book."

He stared at her for a stunned moment, then burst out laughing. "You're going to pay for that one. You got me good. So you're saying the last time you had sex was with a vibrator. And before that?"

"It was four years ago," she said. "A professor at Columbia who dumped me right afterward. I felt like such a fool after that, I didn't want to take a chance with a real-live man. Vibe has been my one and only since then."

He cupped his hands tenderly around her face, then tilted her chin up so their eyes met. Even though she was making light of her sex life, he didn't miss the significance of what she'd told him. "After four years, you're willing to take a chance on me?"

"I already did." She held his gaze steadily. Then she echoed a message she'd sent to him after their first meeting at the observatory. "And I don't regret a thing."

At the trust in her eyes, his heart clenched. Merry was taking a chance by putting her faith in him. Since the tragedy that had destroyed his family, he hadn't let any woman get that close. His brothers and his job got his devotion. Women got what was left.

But with Merry looking at him like that, with belief and promise and adventure in her eyes, everything felt different.

The sound of a key at the door made her fly off his lap. She would have tumbled onto the floor if he hadn't caught her arm.

The door opened and a hotel maid took a step inside, pulling a cleaning cart behind her. She jumped at the sight of him. "This room's supposed to be empty."

"Sorry, we were taking some photos of the creek," Will said smoothly. "We didn't mess anything up, promise."

She nodded and pushed the cart aside to let them pass.

Will waited until they were in the lobby of the lodge before he whispered in Merry's ear. "Did you see that?"

"You mean the way she looked toward the closet right away, soon as she saw us? Of course I did."

They exchanged a tight smile. It was a lead. A real lead. One they'd discovered together, in between exchanging sex stories.

So maybe co-investigating with Merry wasn't the *worst* way to go.

19

Before they left the lodge, Merry did a quick interview with Nick, the rescued boy, and his family. She took some photos of Will and Nick, and of the creek, which was still higher than normal. The storm clouds had cleared away and sunshine struck sparkles in the sodden pine and birch trees surrounding the lodge. The fresh mountain air tasted like pure champagne; or maybe that was the buzz of Will's presence. Hard to tell.

He drove her to her car and gave her a jump, then followed her back to Jupiter Point to make sure she had no trouble. Since he'd gotten paged to help with the aftermath of the storm, he left her at the newspaper. He called in a favor to get his favorite mechanic to pay a house call to her Corolla. Then he left, with a secret scorching look.

He also muttered something about a convenience store.

Merry stumbled through the rest of her day in a state of unbearable anticipation. She wrote up the article about Nick's rescue. She had to work hard not to let her feelings for Will show in the piece. Did he come off as too heroic, too amazing?

Douglas still wanted to see all of her copy before it got

printed, so she emailed him the draft. Right away, he pinged her to come to his office.

If anyone could rain on her afterglow, it would be Douglas.

But for the first time, he had nothing but praise to offer. "You're finally getting it, Merry. You made it big and dramatic. Lots of vivid detail. Nice work. Keep this up and I'll start believing the hype about you. Did you get some photos too?"

"They're on my phone." She handed over her phone and he scanned through them.

"Good stuff." He yelled out his office door. "Chase Merriweather! Someone get Chase in here." He turned back to Merry. "We can play this up on social media."

Chase appeared in the doorway. "You need me?"

"I want this photo to go viral." He swiped between two photos. "The kid and this one of the deputy. Facebook, Instagram, wherever."

She'd taken the photos right after the rescue, before leaving the truck. The first showed Nick rushing into the arms of his parents. The other showed a completely drenched Will about to slump to the ground. Water streamed off his body and his clothes might as well not be there, they were so completely saturated. The light in the shot came from the headlights of someone's car, and managed to delineate every ridge of the muscles rippling in his abdomen. With his legs braced apart, thighs bunching, and his wide shoulders slumped with fatigue, he looked like some kind of weary warrior at the end of a battle in the rain.

"This could go into a calendar. You know the kind, like the firefighters do," said Douglas.

Chase scrutinized the photo. "Hey, isn't that Will Knight, from the flight tours? What were you doing out there with him?"

She frowned at him, hoping he'd get the hint and not blurt out anything inappropriate. "I had car trouble and Deputy Knight helped me out. We took shelter at the lodge to wait out the storm, and happened to see Nick stranded across the creek. Right place, right time."

He gave her a wounded look. "You could have called me. I would have come and helped you."

"That's nice of you, Chase the Intern." She focused on her phone. "I'll send you the photos so you can put them on Facebook or wherever."

"There's something else," said Douglas. "Chase, go ahead and get the ball rolling. Merry, stay here."

As soon as Chase was gone, the door safely shut behind him, Douglas sat on his desk and looked at her sternly.

"Opioids. Talk to me. Got a rough draft yet?"

She scrambled for a good answer. So far, she had plenty of smoke, but no smoking gun. She could speculate that Buckaroo was using the Rootin' Rooster as a central clearinghouse, with various drop-off points in local campgrounds. But she couldn't state that as fact. More importantly, couldn't break her promise to Will.

"It's a big story, Douglas. And I mean *big.* It's going to take time to put it together right."

He gave an impatient gesture. "Doesn't matter. We're dropping it."

"*What?* You can't do that. This story is *important*. Not just big. It matters to people around here."

"I got a call from the sheriff's department. They said you've been moonlighting at some sleazy bar to get the story."

Merry gaped at him. No one at the department knew she was working on the story except Will. Had Will—he wouldn't. *Would he?*

"You can visit some treatment centers, talk to families of addicts, write up a piece about the toll of opioids in small-town America. Etcetera, etcetera. But I'm asking you to stay away from the Rootin' Rooster and anything related to the investigation. And

I can't believe the words 'Rootin' Rooster' just came out of my mouth."

"Douglas." She stepped closer to the desk to make her point. "The story's not ready yet anyway. Why can't I keep working it? Why would the sheriff care about that?"

"Because the investigation has expanded. The DEA has undercover agents on it now. It's huge. And they don't need you in the middle of it."

"But think, Douglas. You just said this was huge. How can we ignore it? We're a *newspaper*. I'm a reporter. So are you. Does it really sit right to pass on the biggest story around here in *years*? That's like, that's like...journalistic negligence."

Disbelief echoed in her voice. His expression tightened. "Watch yourself."

She bit the inside of her mouth to keep any more furious words at bay.

"You don't have the experience to handle a story like this."

"I do," she said hotly. So much for keeping her resentment to herself. "I've *been* working it. I think I know who the kingpin is. I think I know how the distribution network is set up. I'm all over this story, and I need to stay on it. You wanted big? This will be the biggest story of the year!"

He was shaking his head at her, as if she were a child. "I get your enthusiasm. But you're in over your head. If you want this story, you have to prove you're a good soldier. A good team player."

"What are you talking about? I'm a great team player. I've never even taken a sick day. I work all the time. I write more stories than any other reporter, I work weekends, nights—"

"Cold case."

"Excuse me?"

Douglas turned his computer monitor to face her. A newspaper photo of a stern-looking middle-aged man who looked a lot like Will filled the screen. "Jupiter Point's only unsolved murder. The Robert Knight case. *That's* a big story. You already know the family, since you did the Knight and Day story. Prove yourself to me. If you get me that story, maybe we can talk opioids again."

~

MERRY TRIED to work off her stress with a run along Stargazer Beach. She went right from there to a yoga class, but left in mid-downward dog because she was just too antsy. She drove out to the community college for her weekly office hours, but could barely concentrate on her students' complaints about their grades.

Couldn't they tell she was *in crisis*? She couldn't talk about it with any of her Jupiter Point friends—too much was confidential. Carolyn was at her other college gig. Mama was in Japan. Gah! How was she supposed to sort through all these confusing choices?

She could refuse the Knight murder story. But if she did, her new boss would lose his last remaining shreds of patience with her. She could tell him that she and Will were....something. But what, exactly? And how would that affect Douglas' opinion of her? If she did the story about Will's father, would he hate her? If she secretly kept working the opioids story, would she lose her job?

All her choices sucked.

By the time Will knocked on the door of her apartment, Merry felt like one of those bouncing balls made of hundreds of rubber bands. In other words, a nervous wreck. She still didn't know what to do about Douglas's challenge.

But she did know one thing—ratting her out to the sheriff so she'd pull the plug on the Buckaroo story was sheer crap.

She flung the door open to greet him, ready to tear into him.

When she found herself facing a gigantic bouquet of lilies, from tiger to peace to stargazer, she momentarily forgot her fury.

She buried her face in the flowers and inhaled the heavenly fragrance.

Then pollen got up her nose, she sneezed, and all her anger came rushing back.

"Did you go behind my back, Will?" she demanded as he strode into her apartment and looked around. Strangely, Will looked instantly right at home in her space. Maybe her taste was too masculine, she mused, making a mental note to change everything to pink just to spite him.

"For the flowers and condoms?" He whipped out a strip of condoms from his pocket. "Were we supposed to do that together? You need to fill me in on these things, babe."

"Don't you call me babe." She took the bouquet from his hands and marched into the kitchen for a vase. "You know I'm not talking about the flowers, and as for the condoms, I hope you kept your receipt."

She ran water into the bamboo vase, which also happened to drown out his response. When she'd settled the flowers into a pretty display, she set the vase on her kitchen table and turned to face him. For the first time since he'd walked in, she allowed herself to look at him. She didn't want to give in to her attraction before she'd spoken her mind.

He was watching her with an expression somewhere between amusement and bewilderment. Since they'd parted ways, he'd showered, shaved, and changed into black slacks and a taupe button-down shirt. His gray eyes took on a clear, almost sage-green tone from the shirt. With his scruff gone, the planes of his face looked clean and strong.

He looked beautiful. Damn him.

"What's going on?" he asked.

"My boss ordered me off the opioids investigation. He got a call from the sheriff's department." She was watching him closely, so she noticed the expression of relief that flitted across his face. Even though it was quickly followed by one of sympathy, the point had been made. "You agree with him!"

"Yes, I agree. I'm sorry because I know how much you've put into it, but I do agree."

"Then why did I have to find out from my boss? Why didn't you warn me?"

His face turned to stone, and suddenly she knew what it must be like to face him as a criminal suspect. "You think *I* told on you? That I went behind your back...what, sometime after last night? What the hell, Merry?"

"Who else even knows I was working at the Rooster? It had to be you!"

The storm brewing behind his eyes sent a quick thrill through her. "You seriously think I'd do something like that? Stab you in the back, then waltz in here with flowers and condoms, hoping to get lucky?"

She stared at him as the first hint of doubt set in. "It wasn't you?"

"Of course it wasn't me. Jesus, Merry. I've always been straight with you. The DEA has someone undercover at the Rooster. They must have recognized you. If I was going to do that, why wouldn't I have done it earlier, when I first saw you there? Why now?"

Her quick, hot anger was draining away, as it so often did. "But you asked me to drop it."

"And you did. I haven't seen anything in the paper. So why would I do anything more?"

Ugh, he was right. She was wrong. Of all the conflicts they'd had over the years, none of them had involved Will being a liar or a backstabber or a manipulator. He was none of those things, and she knew it.

"I might have jumped to conclusions," she admitted.

"Yeah, you did."

She winced and took a step back. Her butt hit the edge of the table. Will charged forward to catch the vase before it crashed onto the floor. Instead of setting it back in place, he held it in his arms. The tiger lilies brushed his chin. Now he looked furious *and* adorable.

And all her misguided anger was officially gone.

"You're right," she said in a low voice. "Here's the thing. It's hard for me to trust people, especially men. I have reasons for that, but it's not your fault. I shouldn't have thought the worst right away. I'm sorry."

He looked down at her, over the top of the orange-spangled petals, and even though the flowers were beautiful, his eyes captured all her attention. They were so intent, so stormy, so filled with heat. "Did you just say you're sorry?"

"Yes. I'm sorry." She lifted her chin. She didn't particularly enjoy apologizing, and with the quick way her mind worked, occasionally she jumped to the wrong conclusion and had to backtrack. "I am capable of apologizing if I make a mistake. It's a sign of maturity, you know."

"Very true."

"And I'm keeping those flowers," she added in a completely *immature* tone. "You gave them to me, and if you take them back, that's like stealing. You can't steal because you're sworn to uphold the law."

A smile ghosted across his lips. Then it turned into a full-fledged belly laugh. She smiled too, so relieved that she hadn't offended him to the point that he wanted to walk away.

A quick flash of insight told her that would never happen. She couldn't offend him that much. Will wouldn't walk away, he'd stick it out. Work it out.

But she could certainly hurt him. How could she even consider doing the story Douglas wanted her to do?

The story that might mean the difference between losing her job and keeping her job.

Or losing and keeping Will.

She couldn't. Sorry, Douglas. Not happening.

Her gaze dropped to his lips, which still curved in that delighted smile. She forgot all those other worries and remembered how his mouth had felt as he suckled her to orgasm. Her face went hot. Desire shimmered through her. How she wanted this man, with his inner strength, his sense of humor, his thoughtful gestures. His patience.

"The flowers belong to you." He put the vase back on the table. "The more important question is whether I should keep the condoms." He raised a wicked eyebrow at her, and suddenly every bit of the tension between them transformed into something sexual instead.

She pretended to think about the question seriously, tapping her finger on her chin. "Hm. I sincerely doubt you can return them. Besides, it would be such a loser move, wouldn't it?"

"I'd never live it down," he agreed. "It would be all over town in minutes. 'Did you hear Will Knight struck out so hard he had to return his condoms?'"

She giggled. "You might get the sympathy vote from some of the ladies in town. Get some pity pussy."

"*Pity pussy*?"

"Phrase from the hood. A girl feels sorry for you, she might throw you a bone, you know?"

He advanced toward her. "Let me break it down for you. A, I don't need anyone feeling sorry for me. B, I only want one pussy. Yours. So if you don't want to use these damn condoms, they're either going back or they're going in the trash. Because it's you or no one. And I think it should be you." He reached her and cupped his hands behind her neck. "You and me. There's something here, something special and real and I know you feel it too. Tell me you don't."

She thought about denying it—or making a joke, teasing him, something Merry Warren the wisecracking reporter would do. But right now, she had no interest in her reporter side. Her heart reached for Will, longed for him. "I feel it," she said softly. "You know I do."

His eyes darkened. "Then what are we still doing out here in your cleaner-than-I-expected living room?"

"Cleaner than you expected?" She laughed at him. "You're asking for it, Deputy."

"Oh, I am. I'm definitely asking for it. I might even beg for it."

"Now that I gotta see."

He ran his thumb across her lower lip, the touch as light as a butterfly wing. The rough surface of his thumb felt so good it made her blood sizzle. "Merriweather Gabriela Oliveira Warren. I am completely and thoroughly enthralled by you. Will you please take me to your bedroom so we can fuck the way we both are dying to?"

"You looked up my full name." Hardly anyone knew her entire name. She loved hearing it on his lips.

"Yup."

She blinked at him innocently. "How about 'enthralled'? Did you look that up in a thesaurus?"

"That's it." He lifted her up and slung her over his shoulder caveman-style. "Challenging my vocabulary, that's pushing me too far. Brace yourself, woman."

Between her laughter and the excitement rampaging through her, she couldn't even think about bracing herself. All she could do was hang on for the ride as he carried her into her bedroom.

20

Will felt like a new person with Merry laughing in his arms. He felt alive in a way he hadn't for so many years; alive and on fire. He wanted her with a feverish intensity that maybe should have scared him—but didn't.

When he reached her bedroom, which wasn't hard to find in the tiny apartment, he set her down on her feet. The caveman act only went so far. Even though his palms tingled with the need to touch her, he had to make sure they were on the same page with this.

Her bed held a comforter the color of cabernet and a profusion of silk pillows. A yoga mat was propped in the corner with some free weights littered around it. An empty wine glass sat near a pile of books on the nightstand, precariously close to the edge.

He reached out and nudged it to a safer spot.

"Are you trying to tidy up my place?" Merry's brilliant eyes flung sparks at him.

"I wouldn't dare. Besides, I'd rather mess it up some more." He ran his hands lightly up her arms, from wrists to shoulders, bare under her tight, sleeveless top. Electricity hummed between them.

"Checking in one more time. I'm in if you are." He pulled the strip of condoms from his pocket and dangled it between them.

"I let you carry me into the bedroom like a sack of potatoes," she said dryly. "Pretty sure I'm in."

"Merry." He drew her close and lightly brushed his lips against hers. "Not everything needs to be a joke. Sometimes you can just say what you want. What you feel."

"Want to know what I feel?"

He read the caution in her eyes, saw it fighting against the attraction that pulled them together. He hated that she felt so wary. If there was something he could do to fix it, he'd do it. But he didn't have a road map for that. All he had was a burning desire to get Merry into bed and be everything she needed.

She grabbed his ass with both of her hands. "Here's what I feel. I want you, Will Knight. And Imma gonna have you. Mistake or not, I don't even care."

She toppled them both onto her bed—right where he wanted to be. The relief that burned through him was almost savage. This was going to happen. It really was.

Kneeling, they faced each other. Feverishly, he maneuvered her top off her body while she did the same to his shirt. Then they tackled his pants and her leggings, until they were both down to their underwear, tousled and grinning crazily at each other. She reached inside his boxers and touched his erection. He closed his eyes to savor the sensation. Being with Merry brought out the best in him, pieces that he'd tossed in a dust pile and left for dead. She was such a bright star, so effervescent and alive, like a firefly trapped in womanform.

The soft touch of her hand on his chest brought him back to the present. She was drawing it down his chest, tangling her fingers in the swirls of hair there. When he opened his eyes, he saw that she'd taken off her bra. The sight of her deep brown nipples against her glowing skin nearly made him come. He'd been fantasizing about this moment, about getting her naked again, ever since last night. And here she was, even more beautiful than he remembered.

"You are truly a goddess," he breathed. He bent down and licked her nipples, one by one, giving each the dedicated focus it deserved. They pebbled under his tongue, which made him even madder with desire. He touched her thighs, satin skin over firm muscles. Slid his hand under her panties to uncover the moisture already gathering.

She groaned and parted her legs even farther. "I love how you touch me."

"I could do it forever," he said sincerely. "You're exquisite—and no, I didn't look that up in a thesaurus."

She smiled against his lips, because now they were slipping into a kiss, the way a swimmer disappears into a lake. The waters closed over them, shutting out everything but their vibrant need for each other. He drank her kiss like an elixir, as if he needed nothing else in the world, forever more. And still he touched her, gliding his fingers through the sleek, tender folds sheltering her clit.

He grazed the tight little bud with his thumb, making her jolt. He circled it, feeling his way through her responses, noting the exact degree of pressure and friction that had her grinding against his hand.

"Will," she groaned. "God, I can barely stand it." Her hand tightened on his cock and a long sigh came from her lips.

He ground his teeth together. "Hang on." He reached past her for the condoms on the nightstand. It seemed to take forever to rip one free. In the meantime, she never let go of his cock. The way she stroked him, good God, he was harder than steel from her caresses. If he didn't get inside her soon, he might burst. Or cry like a baby.

Finally, he managed to grab a condom. He took a moment to get his boxers off, then sat back on his heels to sheath himself. As she watched, her brown eyes gleaming, he slid the latex over his pounding, swollen erection.

"Will Knight, I gotta say, I had no idea you had all this going on under that uniform." She waved at his groin, or maybe his thigh muscles, he wasn't sure exactly what.

"All you had to do was ask," he told her. "I would have stripped it all off in a flash. Right in the middle of a press briefing."

She laughed and stretched her body luxuriously, elongating the curve of her waist and arching her upper spine in a way that highlighted the magnificence of her breasts. Teasingly, she lifted her bottom and shimmied off her panties. He rose onto his knees and came toward her, feasting his eyes on every secret bit of her. When he was close enough, he braced himself over her, elbows on either side of her. She arched her chest up to brush her nipples against him, then wrapped her legs around the back of his thighs.

"I want you inside me so much it literally hurts," she murmured. "Will you please stop talking and start doing? Feels like we've been talking forever."

"It was all foreplay. All three years of it." He positioned himself at her soft entrance, where heat radiated like the sun. He reached down a hand and dragged it through her curls, finding her wet and slippery and more than ready. With one hand on her inner thigh, he pushed into her, just the tip, just to feel the divine joy of entering her body.

He had to stop there because an orgasm threatened to burst upon him before he'd barely done anything. Let alone given her the experience she deserved.

She gave a gasp and dropped her head back. "Stop fucking around," she ordered in a hoarse voice. "You're making me nuts."

He gritted his teeth hard against the pleasure and thrust deeper. Between the extreme state of his erection and the condom, he needed to take it slow. Inch by agonizing, amazing inch, he seated his cock deep within her, until it felt as if he was touching her deepest core. Impaling her on the proud rod of his erection. Joining them together in wet, slippery, glorious union.

And then her hips moved, and it felt so goddamn good that he couldn't hold back anymore. He flexed his hips to grind deeper, then harder. Then faster. Then more of whatever she wanted, as he tuned into her moans and cries and fingernail scrapes down his back.

She moved with him perfectly. He felt so connected to her, as if he could feel exactly what she was experiencing. The sight of her nude and writhing body was riveting, but he was afraid it would set him off too soon. So he closed his eyes and lost himself in the glorious pleasure of her body wrapped around his.

He gripped her ass so he could move her at will. When that seemed to excite her even more, he picked up the pace and force of his thrusts. Three years of verbal friction made for explosive hunger for each other. Grinding, desperate, sweaty, ecstatic. All his attention focused on her thrusts and responses until they were completely in sync. Down-and-dirty, nitty-gritty, balls-to-the-walls, hot, mind-blowing sex with a woman he respected just as much as he desired.

And maybe even more.

Her movements picked up speed, and he knew her orgasm wasn't far off. *Hang on, just a little longer,* even though he was about to explode. He flexed his hips to drag across her clit and she arched back with a sharp cry as the orgasm hit her. Tight flutters clenched his cock, sending fierce pleasure straight into his bloodstream.

He gave himself a moment to soak in the sight of her spasming body and blissed-out face, but he couldn't hang on to his control. Over the top he went, down into the ferocious convulsions of a climax that shook him like an earthquake.

He swore fiercely as he pumped into her. He couldn't help it; the words just came out, hot, dangerous words like, *Fuck, you're incredible, I want to fuck you all night, you're a goddess, I love this, I love your body, the way you move, it kills me, fuck, you're hot*...and other crazy shit he'd never say if he wasn't under the influence. Her influence.

After he emptied himself, words and all, into her, he let out a guttural groan and collapsed alongside her. Pleasure traveled through him in thick waves. His cock still pulsed, even though he had nothing left. Every bit of him felt drugged with ecstasy, as if sex with Merry had saturated his being on a cellular level.

She lay on her back, eyes half-closed, one hand resting on her stomach, her chest rising and falling. A sheen of sweat made her skin glow.

"Jesus, Merry," he whispered as he peeled off his condom. "What *was* that?"

She let out a soft, dreamy sigh, a very un-Merry-like sound. "I don't even have words. Which hardly ever happens."

After he disposed of the condom, his eyes drifted shut and he must have dozed off, because the next thing he knew, Merry was chuckling softly to herself.

He dragged his eyes open. "What's funny?"

"I think I figured it out."

"Figured what out?"

"Your question about what that was. Have you ever heard the term sexual soul mates?"

He frowned. "I guess. Sure. Why?"

"That must be what we are. Why it was so good. I mean, not to imply you aren't good all on your own, because of course you are. But us together—we must be sexual soul mates. Which is some kind of cosmic joke, because on paper, we shouldn't even get along."

"Hmm." Well, that sure took his after-sex high down a notch. Why did she have to put everything into a category with a neat little label? He didn't like being put in a box. "As long as you have it all figured out."

Her eyebrows drew together. "Are you offended?"

"Not offended. Maybe irritated. Can't it just be whatever it is, without slapping a label on it?"

She rolled onto her side, her curves gleaming in the light from her bedside lamp. She studied him for a moment. "Everyone puts labels on things. Without labels, everything would be a big jumble."

"Maybe a jumble is a good thing now and then."

Her mouth quirked. "I know you mean tumble, so I'm just going to fix that for you. A tumble is definitely a good thing now and then."

He laughed and turned over, resting his head on his biceps. "I had to fall for a writer. I just had to."

Laughter still quivered at the corners of her mouth. He felt as if a hundred years could pass, and he still wouldn't have enough of her wit and spirit.

"It's better than falling for a cop." She made an impish face at him. "Pretty much the last thing I ever thought would happen."

"You have something against deputy sheriffs?"

"Yeah, can't you tell? Just look at me," she said wryly, running her hand over his thigh. "I just mean, I'm usually the last person you police officers want to see, with my little tape recorder and my annoying questions."

"Don't be so sure about that. I never minded. I just acted like I did so you couldn't tell how attracted I was." He nuzzled the gentle curve of her neck.

She relaxed under his touch and tilted her head to give him better access. "You know, I might have been a little prickly for the same reason."

He laughed softly. "Maybe we're not that different. Except where it counts." Curving his hand over her smooth hip, he stroked her skin. "I'm not in your league, in terms of brains, but I must be a little smart because I fell for you."

After a long pause, during which he wondered if he'd

offended her or gotten something wrong, she slid her hand down his chest. "Okay, now you're just trying to get laid again, aren't you? Playing the sweet-guy card. Nice move."

"Yeah? You like that?"

"Yeah, I like it. Especially when it's combined with all *this.*" Her hand traveled down the trail of hair that led to his privates. Just from that touch, his cock was stirring again. It rose to greet her palm, like an eager puppy looking for some love. Embarrassing, that's what it was. He needed to have a talk with that thing.

Later. Because right now, his cock had enough to do.

21

During the next week or so, they worked on proving or disproving Merry's "sexual soul mate" theory. All signs pointed to it being one hundred percent true. They both liked a little edginess in bed, just enough to sharpen the experience. But Merry always needed to feel like she had a say, that she could call a stop to something at any moment. Her description of herself as "prickly" fit. But the benefit of her prickliness was that she told him straight up when she didn't like something.

For instance, she didn't like having her hair touched in the midst of sex. She claimed it made her worry about how she'd have to fix it afterward. She also didn't like having her arms pinned to the bed. At all times, she needed to feel that she had an "out." That she could push him away or jump out of bed. Free herself.

Of course, Will took breaks from thinking about Merry to do his job. Sheriff Perez left on his honeymoon and put him in charge. He temporarily moved into Perez's office, which still smelled like coffee and Altoids, both of which Perez had vowed to quit while he was on his honeymoon.

Catching up with the duties and paperwork involved in the

top job took a lot of attention. For the first time, he had access to the full scope of the fentanyl investigation—and it was impressively big.

Deputy Jernigan arrested a low-level operator and brought him in for questioning. Even though Will wanted to interview the suspect himself, he was released before he got a chance. Paperwork glitch, explained a frustrated Jernigan.

"I don't know what happened. I came in for round two and he was gone. Paperwork's all legit. Maybe it was a computer error."

"Can we get him back in here?"

The big deputy shrugged. "I can try, but chances are he's long gone."

Will did get to interview the potential suspects from Heavenly Hardbodies. Two had clear alibis for the campground fires, and the third, a fisherman named Johnny Diaz, was out at sea for the week.

So he worked on another question that puzzled him.

Who had called the *Mercury News-Gazette* to get Merry pulled off the story? It wasn't Sheriff Perez. As much as he searched his files, he found no notes about it. He asked Cindy, but she knew nothing about that. Neither did Jernigan. It worried him. Something wasn't right with this investigation. Paperwork glitch? Mystery phone call? So few arrests after all this time?

Worst of all, someone knew about Merry's involvement, and that made him nervous.

He decided to keep a close eye on her. Which shouldn't be hard now that he was spending all his free time in bed with her, testing out that sexual soul mate theory.

ON A TYPICAL PRE-WILL EVENING, Merry had worked late or taken an evening yoga class, had drinks with her friends, taught at the community college, or volunteered at her favorite charity, the

Star Bright Shelter for Teens. Sometimes all of the above in a single night because she liked to keep busy.

Post-Will, all of those things were getting neglected. All she wanted to do was race home, pick up some takeout—because they'd need fuel—and spend the entire evening in bed with the phenomenally talented and hellaciously hot Deputy Slow-mo. And yes, she finally saw the advantage of Will's thorough and meticulous attention to detail.

For the first time in her life, she didn't want to be at work. At the paper, she was banned from working on the story she wanted to work on. And she hated the story Douglas had assigned her.

When she told him she didn't want to work the Robert Knight cold case story, he threatened to assign it to Fiona, the "community affairs"—code for gossip—reporter. Fiona had zero scruples and hated the Knight brothers because Ben had dumped her in high school.

So Merry kept the story, but turned herself into Reporter Slow-mo. She dragged her feet on it in every creative way she could think of. She found other news items to turn into big, BIG stories. She unearthed piles of archived material, and told Douglas she needed to read all of it to do the story justice.

She'd scanned a few articles when she'd first heard about Will's father, but delving deeper revealed so many more details, and they were riveting.

A respected local man was found dead in his home on Saturday. Robert Knight was found in a pool of blood on his kitchen floor. His throat had been slashed. Police say they are looking at a number of angles but have no solid suspects yet.

It was a shocking end for a man who had spent much of his career in the Army. After retiring, he married Janine, a much younger woman, and started a family in Jupiter Point. Robert Knight was known as a stern father, a doting husband, a frequent voice in local politics, and a lover of dogs. Neighbors were used to the sight of him jogging with his three Irish setters, his posture always militarily correct. He was a churchgoer, generous with his donations. He leaves behind five children who range in ages from twenty-two to eight. No one from the family would comment for this story. A memorial is planned for this weekend.

Then, later in the investigation...

Local police say they're frustrated by the lack of clues in the Robert Knight murder investigation. At a hastily called town meeting, the police and sheriff's departments tried to reassure Jupiter Point residents, anxious because no suspect has been named.

"We're stepping up patrols, and advise all residents to keep their doors locked and take other reasonable precautions," Police Chief Maddox told the Mercury News-Gazette. *"At this point we have no reason to suspect that whoever killed Robert Knight is still in Jupiter Point. We hope to have more information soon, but until we do, we urge people not to panic. Just keep an eye out for anything unusual."*

There were a few more stories along the same lines. Another update was published when Janine Knight left town. Then another when Will became a deputy sheriff. But generally, the *Mercury News-Gazette* had done a great job keeping the coverage respectful and not sensational.

If she was going to do this story, she intended to do the same. Which meant that she had to request an interview with the Knight brothers.

Which she would do. As soon as she could figure out how to bring up such a sensitive topic. Will *never* talked about his father or the murder. Evie and the others were right. It was like the third rail of the Knight family.

In the meantime, she did her best to back burner the story and for the first time in her life, stopped making work her primary focus. Instead, she abandoned herself to the heady pleasure of hanging out with Will. The sex was mind-blowing, but not just in the usual way of orgasms that made her scream with ecstasy. Will had a way of peering inside her head and finding the things that made her tick.

It was as if his detective's mind was methodically cataloguing all the information he was gleaning about her likes and dislikes, her joys and traumas. Usually, as a reporter, she was the one in that role. But at the same time that Will was "learning" her, he kept throwing up smokescreens about himself. As if he didn't want to delve into painful topics—like his father's murder.

In her mind, she was involved with two men—Will, her amazing lover, and Will, the living embodiment of "no comment."

It would have been more frustrating if he hadn't made up for it with a steady supply of those fantastic orgasms.

"Will," she murmured one evening after he'd fingered her to a screaming climax against the wall in the kitchen. "Will you be my man?"

His broad chest shook in a laugh. "You mean, like your boyfriend?"

"Yeah, except that word sounds so teenybopper. *Boyfriend*." She sang a tune—"'My boyfriend's back and there's gonna be trouble.'"

"I see what you mean. So...you're doing a rewrite? Replacing *boyfriend* with *man*? I just had to fall for a writer. I just had to."

She pulled back and glared up at him. "You're laughing at me. If that's a no, you can take your hands off my ass right now."

"It's not a no, silly." He tightened his grip on her rear, sending pleasure tingles through the rest of her. "Of course I'll be your man. I already have been, in case you're just tuning in. Just going out on a limb here, but that means you're my woman, right?"

"Yes, and you're lucky because I'd be a lousy girlfriend."

"What's the difference?" He smoothed his hands in sensual circles on her ass.

"Well, girlfriends do things like bake cookies for their guys and dress up pretty for dates, whereas I'm more likely to order takeout so we can save time and get right to the good stuff."

She smiled up at him. She loved the feel of Will's hands on her, and the press of his hard body against hers.

In fact, they were pressed so close together that she felt the gurgling of his stomach. "You hungry?"

"Hell yes. How am I supposed to perform as your man on an empty stomach?"

"Well, as your woman, the least I can do is feed you." She whipped out her cell phone. "I have every delivery service in Jupiter Point on speed dial. Pizza, Mexican or healthy California salad?"

"Pizza. No question."

"See what I mean? Soul mates."

She was in the midst of dialing when a knock sounded at her front door. "Damn, that was some fast delivery." He laughed. "Can you get that, while I finish the order?"

"You sure? Won't that let the cat out of the bag?"

"Nah. Unless it's Mrs. Murphy at the door. Last I heard, she doesn't do home book deliveries."

But it wasn't Mrs. Murphy. When she came into the living room, she stopped dead at the shocking sight of a very drunk Chase. The tails of his shirt hung out of his khaki shorts, and he was swaying back and forth.

He was in a stare-down with Will, who looked every inch the law enforcement professional, legs braced apart, all power and authority. Chase gestured wildly at Merry as she came closer.

"So I was right," Chase accused. "You *are* sleeping with him."

Will practically growled as he loomed over Chase. "That's none of your business."

Chase swayed back and forth. "But he's white!"

"So?" Merry put her hands on her hips.

"I thought you didn't like me cuz I'm white!"

"Oh for heaven's sake. I never said I don't like you, Chase. Certainly not because you're white. It's a lot more complicated than that, and you're completely wasted. We can talk about it tomorrow."

"Oh, like we can have lunch next week, and then we never do."

"Come on, I'm taking you home," Will told him, taking a step toward him.

Chase backed away, took a karate-type stance, then staggered. "No."

"It's okay, Will. You don't have to play guard dog." Even though Will didn't relax more than a millimeter, she turned to Chase. "What are you doing here, anyway?"

"I came to talk to you. Privately." He shot a disgruntled glance at Will. "She's my sister, you know, even though she doesn't want to admit it. I'm not going to hurt her."

"Chase, you're drunk. You shouldn't even be here."

"That's all you ever say! You shouldn't be here, I don't want to know you, leave me alone. How do you think that feels? Huh?"

She exchanged an alarmed glance with Will. "Look, I'm sorry. I've been a little busy. We'll definitely talk tomorrow, after you've slept it off. Did you drive here? In that slick BMW?"

He pointed a finger at her and rotated it in a tight circle. "You're jealous. Because I have the car and the nice house and the parents and the money. That's why you don't want to see me."

She pressed her lips together to hold back the angry words that wanted to come out. "You really want to do this now?"

"I came here to tell you something! Something to help you!" He threw up his hands in a defensive gesture, nearly toppling over backwards. Will caught him by the elbow, but he shrugged off the help.

"Okay, shoot. I'm listening."

"I have to speak to you in private. Not him." He waved at Will. "It's confidential. I could get in trouble."

Something occurred to Merry. "Is this about work? Something at the paper?"

He nodded and put a finger to his lips. "Secret."

With bloodshot eyes, he held Merry's gaze, and suddenly she knew what he must be referring to. He had information about the opioids story, the one she wasn't supposed to be covering anymore. Whatever it was, he didn't want Will to hear it.

As always, her reporter's curiosity got the best of her.

"Will, could you give us a minute?"

Will turned his stony cop face toward her. He did not look happy about that decision. He grabbed the jacket he'd hung on the pegboard next to her door. "I'll keep my cell on. Call if you need me."

"Where are you going?"

"I have some work to catch up on. And you." Practically chest to chest with Chase, he fixed him with that penetrating gray gaze of his. "My brothers told me you came by the airstrip again. Do that one more time and we'll charge you with trespassing."

"It's a p...public business. That's not trespassing."

"A, we're not open yet. B, what were you doing there? C, there is no secret stash of money or goods or anything else on that property."

Chase's smile slipped. "You don't understand, I wasn't—"

Will kept talking, brushing off his explanation. "Save it. You're Merry's brother so I'm going to stick with a warning here. But put one toe on that property again and we *will* bring charges."

Will brushed past him into the hallway. With a muffled "good night, Merry," he was gone.

22

CHASE WAVERED BACK AND FORTH ON UNSTEADY FEET. "ALONE AT last," he proclaimed with a sweep of his arm. "Hey, your apartment's nice."

He took a step forward but she held up a hand. "Stop right there and make it quick. What is it you want to tell me?"

"Is Will your boyfriend now? Hey, maybe he'll be my brother-in-law. Half-brother-in-law. If you have kids I'll be an uncle. Half-uncle? Is that a thing?" He gave her that quirky grin that kind of reminded her of her own.

She tried hard not to roll her eyes. "Get on with it, Chase."

"It's big, Merry. A big secret. I'm kind of risking my internship to tell you." He sniffed the air. "Do you have any food? I haven't eaten all day."

She marched into the kitchen and grabbed some cartons of leftover Chinese food from her refrigerator. She found a grocery bag and shoved the little white boxes inside. She carried it out to Chase, who was now surveying her apartment as if he belonged there. She thrust the bag at his chest.

"There you go. Takeout. As in, take it out of my apartment after you tell me what you've got."

He sniffed the bag appreciatively. "I love Chinese food. That's another thing we have in common, wow. So. I found out something you're not going to like."

"*What?* You're driving me crazy here."

"It's about the op...op...opioids investigation."

"I'm not on that story anymore."

"I know that. Everyone's talking about how Douglas doesn't think you can do it. But don't worry, I *know* you can."

An uneasy sensation stole over her, as if her power was leaching out of her. She'd worked so hard to earn respect at the *Gazette*. And she had—until Douglas came along. "It's hard starting over with a new boss," she said in a weak voice.

"Uh-huh. Well, Douglas is going to publish a big exposé about the opioids. He's using all your research. He asked me to set up some social media stuff in advance, that's how I know."

"*What?* When?"

"I don't know exactly when. Probably soon."

She stared at the floor, the nubby texture of her rug blurring. Could Douglas do that? Would she have any recourse? And what did he have against her, anyway—other than the obvious. Female, biracial, somewhat insubordinate—could be any of the above. Or something else entirely.

"I did good, right? Us Merriweathers have to stick together," said Chase. "Can I stay and eat?" He looked hopefully at her couch.

She considered him for a long moment. As drunk as he was, she hated to send him back to the street.

"Fine, you can stay and eat. I'll make you some coffee. Then you need to go home."

"Home? What home?"

"The Goodnight Moon. That's where you're staying, aren't you?"

He screwed up his face. "Not anymore. I'm out of money."

"What?" That didn't even make sense. Chase was the only child of a multi-millionaire. "What are you talking about?"

"They cut me off. Dad didn't want me to come to Jupiter Point to find you. Now they want me to go back to New York, and they cut off my credit cards until I do. They try to control everything. But they can't control me wanting a sister."

A shaft of hurt slammed through her. She barely heard anything he said after the part about "Dad" not wanting him to find her. Her own father was so adamantly against her that he cut Chase off? "Why?" she whispered.

Still holding the bag of takeout, he tilted his head. "Why what?"

"Why don't they want you to know me?"

"I guess they're embarrassed. I don't know. It's stupid, because you're great. I keep telling them that." Those eager puppy dog eyes blinked at her. "But they don't care what I think. They just want me to go back."

She swallowed hard, the pain rippling through her in waves. "You *should* go back."

"What? But we've barely even talked. This is like the first time. That's not fair."

"Fair? What does fair have to do with anything?" All the resentment from her childhood boiled over. "Don't even *talk* to me about fair."

"Okay, okay, don't be mad. I'm kind of drunk, okay?"

"Oh, that's just great. So it's all okay because you're drunk? Look, do you know why I didn't want to see you?"

"No. I'm nice. I'm not like my parents."

"Oh my God. Just shut up and listen. It's not about you. I knew this moment would come, when I'd feel all that horrible rejection all over again. Like I'm nothing. And I know you don't mean it. I know you're not the one who didn't want me. Maybe you're different from your father. My father. But *it still hurts.* Can you get that?"

He stared at her, scrunching his forehead into creases of confusion. "Yes? Maybe?"

"How would you know what it feels like to be rejected for something you can't do anything about? I am what I am." She spread her arms apart, indicating her skin, her body, her entire self.

"He doesn't even know you. Me, he knows. And he doesn't like me. At all. Says I have no amp—ambition." Chase shoved his hands in his pockets, looking utterly miserable. "I'm a loser to him. Too nice, he always says."

"Oh." Well damn, now she felt bad for him. Maybe growing up with everything wasn't all it was cracked up to be. "There's nothing wrong with nice."

He blinked owlishly and swayed back and forth again. "Wait, are you being nice now?"

She threw up her hands. "What am I going to do with you now? You're drunk as a skunk, I can't let you drive. You can't stay here. You ruined my date with Will."

"I can sleep in my car. That's what I've been doing." He staggered a bit. "Food is good though. Thanks for the food."

Oh hell. She surveyed him dubiously. "You've really been sleeping in your car?"

"My *BMW.*"

She heaved a sigh. "Why is it that as soon as I start to feel bad for you, you say something that pisses me off?"

"Maybe because I'm your little brother?" he asked hopefully.

She laughed. "Nice try, but I don't think that's it. You can sleep on my couch tonight. But *just* for tonight. And just because I'm being nice. It doesn't mean we're best friends all of a sudden. And then you need to go back to New York."

"Why?"

"Because that's where you belong."

He wiped the back of his wrist across his forehead. "That money was for you. At the airstrip. I wanted to find it for you."

"Excuse me?"

"So you wouldn't hate me. I wanted a finder's fee, for you."

Torn between bemusement and unwilling affection, she shook her head at him. "I don't need money from you, Chase. You're such a goofball."

"I learned a poem for you, too. Can't remember it now though." He yawned so hugely that he staggered.

"Oh geez." With a roll of her eyes, she took his arm and guided him toward the couch. "Come sit down, and tomorrow we'll look into getting you a ticket home."

"But why?" he said again, as he plopped onto the cushions.

Exasperated, she snapped, "Because I'm your big sister and I'm telling you to." Then she smiled and ruffled his hair.

He grinned up at her. "I heard you! You said it! You're my sister!"

The doorbell rang, reminding her of the pizza she'd ordered. "We're about to find out how deep the family resemblance goes. How do you feel about pizza?"

23

Merry texted Will that she was letting Chase stay on her couch. Will didn't like the idea, but he'd done thorough checks of the kid and found nothing remotely suspicious. Besides, he knew Merry had a limited tolerance for his protective — aka "bossy" — side. So he simply texted her 'good night' and slept in his own bed for the first time in a week.

It was lonely as fuck and he hated it.

The next day, he finally got to question an actual suspect in the fentanyl investigation. Johnny Diaz sat across from Will in the interrogation room, a scared-looking Hispanic guy in an over-sized hockey jersey. His lawyer exuded competence in his tailored business suit. Someone else was paying his legal fees, no doubt about it.

"The smart money says you're being set up," Will told Johnny. "I keep telling my superiors that, but they just want to put some numbers on the board. They want to look good in the papers. They want to hold a news conference and tell the world what rock stars they are because they arrested a major criminal kingpin right here in tiny little Jupiter Point."

Johnny gazed at him blankly.

"Do you know what a kingpin is?"

The suspect shook his head. Will felt a "Grandpa moment" coming on. Good Lord, didn't anyone get an education anymore?

"The kingpin holds it all together. Without the kingpin, it's like a house of cards that'll come crashing down. When I say 'crashing,' read 'going to jail.' Everyone's headed there, it's just a matter of time. So I look at you, and I think, shit, you're young, you need to make a living, plus it's fun to be bad. It's fun to live on the edge. Am I right?"

Johnny nodded, a little less wary now.

"But no party lasts forever. Someone's got to pick up the tab. I'm thinking it shouldn't be you. But maybe I just have a soft spot for a guy who still babysits his kid sister." That tidbit of information had dropped into his lap while he'd researched Johnny. Right away he knew it would be helpful. "Be a shame if you couldn't do that anymore."

Finally, he'd found the crack in Johnny's front. The suspect shot a look at his lawyer, who'd been watching attentively.

The lawyer leaned forward. "Johnny would like to make a deal. But there's a problem. Something you need to know about." He flicked a glance in the direction of the camera in the corner. "Can we talk separately? You're filling in for Sheriff Perez, right?"

Will hid his surprise. This was an unexpected twist for a routine interview.

After Johnny had been taken back to lockup, Will met the lawyer in his office. And that was where the man dropped his bombshell.

Will was still processing it as he drove to the airport to pick up Aiden. Aiden was coming back for a long weekend, and the brothers had decided to hold the Knight and Day Flight Tours Grand Opening while he was home.

Except now Will had *this* to deal with.

According to Johnny Diaz, the drug gang had an agent *inside* the sheriff's department. He didn't know the person's name. But Buckaroo Brown assured all his crew that anyone who got picked up in county territory could count on being released.

Which was exactly what had happened with the suspect Jernigan had brought in.

Will immediately ordered an extra guard to stand watch at the lockup, with strict orders not to release anyone unless he personally signed off on it.

As he drove, thoughts whirling, Will kept putting more pieces together.

That was why the drug ring didn't operate within the city limits of Jupiter Point, because they might get picked up by JPPD instead of a sheriff's deputy. That was why the investigation was getting nowhere. Someone was sabotaging it from the inside. But who?

This couldn't be the sheriff's doing. Why would he leave on his honeymoon when he had something like this going on? Why would he leave Will in charge? No, it had to be someone else.

It blew his mind. If this was true, someone he knew, probably someone he knew well, was assisting Buckaroo Brown in bringing the powerful drugs to Will's hometown. The department only had five deputies and a small civilian support staff. He trusted all of them completely.

But now, he couldn't trust any of them until he knew more.

He suddenly remembered the call to the *Gazette,* the one pressuring Merry off the story. What if that had been the work of the mole? What if she'd gotten too close and they'd decided to take action?

He shuddered at the thought. But if he could find out who had called, he might have a clue on his hands.

He picked up his cell phone to call Merry, then hesitated. A big part of him didn't want to bring her any further into this mess.

But that was his protective boyfriend—or not-boyfriend—

side talking. Merry was a grown woman, smart and good at her job. He should respect that.

He clicked her number. When she answered, the sound of her voice sent an almost violent thrill through him. Her vibrant spirit traveled right through the phone.

"Got a quick question for you, Merry. Any idea who called your editor to pull you off that story?" Even though he tried to ask the question as casually as possible, he could sense her reporter's curiosity perking up.

"Why?"

"I can't say right now. I'd just like to know."

Would she trust him enough to leave it at that? A short silence followed. "I assumed it was the sheriff himself, but I don't think Douglas actually specified. I can try to find out, though."

"I don't think it was Perez. It was someone else. Can you find out without setting off any alarms?"

"What am I, an amateur?"

He laughed, already feeling lighter just from this one short conversation.

"Will you tell me what this is all about when you can?"

"*When* I can, yes. I promise. Thanks, Merry." He softened as he pictured her the way she looked in bed after sex, sprawled across her bed, hair an extravagant fluff against the the silk pillowcase she loved. "See you later?"

"I'm teaching tonight. I'll text you when I'm done."

Being Merry's man was the best gig in town, if you asked him.

MERRY'S OPPORTUNITY TO dig up the information Will wanted came the next day. Every Friday night, after putting to bed the Sunday edition, the staff of the *News-Gazette* always gathered at the Seaview Inn for a round of drinks. Douglas didn't usually join the crew. No one really wanted him to.

But this time, when Douglas announced that he was coming with them, Merry secretly rejoiced. People got chattier when they'd had a drink or two. Maybe she could slide the question into cocktail conversation without him noticing.

The staff members all sat out on the Seaview's flagstone terrace, with its lush view of the hills surrounding Jupiter Point and the ocean glistening in the distance. The setting sun made Merry think of her date with Will at the observatory. The happy memory warmed her as she settled in with her club soda and lime.

The others might be here to drink, but she was still working.

Douglas's presence made everyone feel awkward and, forty-five minutes later, people started to leave. Chase was one of the first to take off, probably because she kept asking him if he'd called his parents yet to schedule his return.

When the sports reporter vacated his seat next to Douglas, she slipped into it.

"I've been wanting to tell you that I like the way you've handled community relations since you arrived." She used her best flattery-will-get-you-everywhere voice. "Especially the sheriff's department."

He frowned at her over his glass of Chardonnay. "How do you mean?"

"I was upset at first, about dropping that story. But it was the right thing to do. Maintaining a good relationship with our law enforcement agencies is a good idea. I did think it was odd, though..." She trailed off, as if she didn't want to say any more.

"What?"

"Well, the sheriff told me about a new arrest. Almost as if he didn't know I'd been pulled off."

"Maybe he didn't. He isn't the one who called me. It was someone else. One of the deputies. Jernigan, I think."

"Ah. That makes more sense then. Jernigan's the deputy handling the opioids investigation."

She paused. Douglas checked his watch, clearly getting ready to leave. She'd gotten the information Will wanted. She should wrap it up and get out of there.

But she didn't. Because she was a journalist and it went against her nature.

"How's that going, by the way?" she said casually. The last two reporters were saying their goodbyes, so she took a moment to wave to them. But no way was she letting Douglas leave before she got in a couple more questions. "The opioids story, I mean."

"How's the Robert Knight story coming?" he shot back.

Damn it. Not the Knight story. That thing was an albatross around her neck. "It's a sensitive story, you know. I want to do it justice. The family gets a lot of respect around here."

He had a funny expression, as if he didn't believe her. "What if I told you I need something for the next edition?"

"I'd say that's ridiculous. You can't just throw together a story like that. You have to do it right."

"So that's a no?"

"Of course it's a no." She dragged the conversation back to the opioids. "But listen, about the investigation, we really shouldn't lose momentum on that one. I hope someone is still on it. Someone with more *experience*."

"Don't worry about it, Merry. Do your job. I assigned you a story that you haven't even touched. Sometimes I wonder how you ever got this job."

White-hot fury flashed through her. She could read between those lines. He was implying that because she was a woman, or a woman of color, or pretty—she'd heard all three—that she hadn't earned her place. "I got this job because I'm good at it."

"Sure."

He pulled out his wallet to pay for his drink. Her time was running out, so she went right to the point. "Are you publishing my investigation without me? Are you planning to use my research without giving me credit?"

He slapped down a twenty and fixed her with a cold stare. "Your work product belongs to the paper, of which I'm in charge. I can do whatever I want, including publish the story that's going on the front page of this weekend's edition."

"*What*? But the sheriff's department asked us to—"

"This has nothing to do with the opioids. This is about the story you should have turned in last week. The one I had to assign to someone else because you refused to do your job."

Her heart turned over in her chest. "What are you talking about?"

"The Robert Knight cold case story is going on the front page this Sunday."

"No. You can't do that."

"Of course I can. It's already done. Fiona made it nice and big."

Her blood froze. "Cancel it. Please, I beg you. We can find a different story. That family deserves so much better than a Fiona hit job."

He smirked and got to his feet. He was such a weenie, with his little bow-tie and that self-righteous smugness he always exuded.

"Douglas, you're being an utter asshole!" she snapped. "If you don't do the right thing, I'll...I'll quit."

Snorting, he glanced down at her. "Don't bother. I've had enough. You're fired."

24

"Where's your new girlfriend?" Aiden asked as he and Will lingered by the drinks table at the Knight and Day Grand Opening the next day.

Suzanne had planned the party and had done a magnificent job. Bunting hung from every corner of the hangar, which was filled with banquet tables and chatting guests. A big cake in the shape of a knight chess piece took up an entire table. Balloons shaped like airplanes floated above the real planes, which sparkled outside in the thin October sunshine.

Aiden looked good, his hair in a spiky bedhead cut. He wore cargo shorts and a t-shirt with dancing tacos on it—an item he hadn't owned when he'd left Jupiter Point. Aiden had always been a sweet-natured kid. After the trauma of the murder, he'd gotten quieter for a time, less bubbly, but he still had an innocence about him that Will would die to protect.

"She's not my 'girlfriend.' What am I, a teenybopper?" He grinned at his youngest brother, who squinted at him.

"You look...uh...different."

"I shaved extra close for the party. Cut my hair."

"No, it's not any of that. You look...happy. Must be thanks to your new girlfriend."

Will rolled his eyes and gave in. He didn't want to deny that he was head over heels for Merry. Last night, she'd texted him the information about Jernigan making that call to the newspaper, then told him she was tired and going to bed early. Another lonely night without her. "Just don't use that word around her. She's particular about words, being a writer and all."

"I can't believe you're dating a writer. Wasn't your last girlfriend a tattoo artist?"

"I support the arts," Will said dryly.

Aiden snorted and sipped from his beer bottle. Will still wasn't used to the sight of him drinking, and technically, nineteen wasn't legal, but try telling a Knight brother that. The older brothers had all been sneaking into bars by the time they were sixteen.

"What about you? Any girlfriends in the works?

A self-conscious expression stole across the kid's face. "Sort of. Not exactly."

Will didn't have time to work out the meaning of that answer. Suzanne was alighting before them like a sunny blond stork.

"Everything looks great," he told her. "Like the real deal."

"You bet it's the real deal. I'm so excited about your flight tours I can hardly stand it! I've started mentioning them in my pitches to honeymooners and people are going crazy for them. You're going to be booked to the gills."

"Not me," he reminded her. "I'm going to be busy arresting bad guys."

Suzanne glanced at Aiden. "Hi there, Aiden, I almost didn't recognize you. So grown up! How's school?"

"It's good. Real good. I like it."

"Awesome. Hey, have you guys seen Merry? I thought she was going to be covering this event for the paper. But then that maniac Fiona started asking me questions."

Will shook his head. "I thought she was coming, but I haven't seen her."

"I'm sure she'll be here any minute." Suzanne gave them both a hug, then moved on to deal with a punch crisis.

Will pulled out his phone and checked his text messages. He hadn't received anything from Merry since last night's text about Jernigan. She hadn't called either. He shot off a quick text to her. *Party is starting. You coming?*

She didn't answer right away, so he turned back to Aiden. "Back to that 'sort of, not exactly' answer. Anything you want to add to that?"

"No," Aiden said forcefully. "And it's going to stay that way."

Will stared in shock at his brother, who was usually the most mellow kid in the world. "Ooookay."

"And don't push me."

"Uh-huh."

"Or argue. I'm not changing my mind. Just give me some space for once."

Whoa. Something was definitely up with Aiden. Will held up his hands in an I'm-not-armed gesture. "Stand down, kiddo. It's your life. Just here to help. And repeat the condom lecture if necessary."

Finn Abrams, one of the Jupiter Point Hotshots, and his fiancée, Lisa Peretti, strolled up, arms wrapped around each other. "Just in time for the condom lecture," said Finn, laughing. "This ought to be good."

Will had gotten to know Finn and Lisa pretty well during the search for Lisa's attacker earlier that year. They'd fallen in love during the drama, and both of them had been radiating happiness and joy ever since. If he didn't like them both so much, it would have been annoying.

"I'm going to go talk to Ben," Aiden said. "He better not mention condoms." And he slouched away toward their two brothers.

"Thanks for coming." Will shook Finn's hand, while Lisa gave him a little hug.

"Congratulations," said Finn. "Great party, great project. As soon as we both have a break in our schedules, we're booking a flight. I want to show Lisa what the wilderness looks like from ten thousand feet."

"Talk to my brothers. They're in charge around here. I'm still in the crime-fighting biz."

"For which we're very grateful," said Lisa.

A few more of the Jupiter Point hotshots joined them—Sean Marcus, Josh Marshall, Rollo Wareham. They all looked rugged, sun-browned, and exhausted from the long fire season.

Since he was next to the drinks table, he handed out beer bottles to the weary firefighters. "Run out of wildfires?" he asked them mildly.

"Mandatory two day rest," Sean told him. "We've been working our asses off."

"We should be asleep right now," Josh agreed, "but we wanted to check out your chopper. That's a sweet piece of machinery there. Can't wait to see that bad boy in action. I mean, hopefully we won't need it," he added quickly. "Not hoping for disaster, just —shit, I'm tired."

The biggest hotshot, Rollo, gave Josh's shoulder a comforting squeeze. Rollo had recently left the hotshots to help out his family's banking empire. Will wondered if he knew the Merriweathers.

Then he wondered if all thoughts led back to Merry.

Josh was moaning slightly. "Rollo, you ought to moonlight as a masseuse. Swear to God. You'd make a killing."

"Those hands are mine, all mine." Brianna popped up next to Rollo and wrapped her arms around his waist. He lit up like a Christmas tree and dropped a kiss on her vivid red hair. "Great party, Will. Hey, have you seen Merry?"

"No." Will was starting to wonder why everyone was asking *him*. "I guess the paper sent someone else."

"Boo. I loved that other story she wrote about you guys."

"She did a good job. She's always does." He heard the pride in his voice. Everyone else did too. They all stared at him, and he felt himself turn a little red. "Uh, I mean, hey, she's a good reporter, that's not news."

Josh gave him a knowing grin. Sean winked one weary green eye at him. Rollo lifted his eyes to the ceiling, whistling innocently.

Will's phone beeped, thank God. He grabbed it from his pocket and saw a text from Merry.

I'll be at the party a bit late. I have to tell you something. You and your brothers. Are you all there?

Instantly he forgot about everyone else in the place, the hotshots, the party guests, everyone except Merry. *Yes*, he texted back. *Is everything okay?*

See you soon, was her only answer.

When he looked up, the hotshots were observing him with worried looks. "Something wrong?" asked Sean.

He looked at Merry's text again. It sounded so serious, so unlike her. Most of her texts had emojis and lots of exclamation points.

He cleared his throat. "Look, go ahead and enjoy the party. Have you tried the Knightini? It was Suzanne's idea. It's a martini with...something..." He trailed off, unable to think about a cocktail when something was clearly going on with Merry.

The group of hotshots and their significant others exchanged glances.

Finn squeezed his shoulder. "Okay, man. Let us know if you need anything." He jerked his head toward the others, and they all trooped away, with Lisa giving him one last worried smile over her shoulder.

Will took a moment to collect himself, then strode toward his brothers. Tobias and Ben were working the Jupiter Point crowd like pros, showing off the planes, telling stories from their military days, talking up the business.

When he reached his brothers, he waited for a break in their conversation with a small knot of women in cocktail dresses. They were all drinking Knightinis, which had little party sticks with mini airplanes instead of umbrellas.

Knight and Day Flight Tours was going to be a huge success; he could feel it. And he was truly happy for them, for the Knight family, or what was left of it. Things were changing so fast. Aiden in college, Tobias and Ben starting a business. Meanwhile, he was the same old sheriff's deputy. An empty-nester at the age of thirty-two. Stuck in place, right where he'd been since the murder.

Finally, they left. Ben stuck his hands in his pockets and squinted at Will. "This is supposed to be a party. What's with the sad face?"

"Merry's on her way and she needs to talk to us. I don't know what it's about but I have a bad feeling."

Tobias, who had crammed his broad chest into a suit jacket for the party, nearly ripped a seam when he shrugged. "Don't worry, bro. Four Knight brothers, all in one place. If we don't kill each other, we can deal with it."

"And I get to meet the new girlfriend," grinned Aiden.

BUT NO ONE was smiling when Merry delivered her news. By the time she arrived, the party was winding down. She'd dressed for it anyway, in a little black dress with a patent leather belt. She looked gorgeous, but barely managed a smile when he introduced her to Aiden. They gathered in a corner of the hangar for privacy.

"I came here to warn you all. I don't know how to say it, besides just spitting it out. The newspaper is running a story about your father and the murder case. I've been told it'll be in the Sunday edition. Tomorrow," she clarified, wincing. "I'm so sorry."

Will experienced a surreal flash of dislocation, as if everything was shifting around him. He couldn't speak. Couldn't react. He felt frozen.

"Why?" asked Tobias. That forbidding scowl would have scared off most women. "Why now?"

"No real reason, except the new editor in chief wants it. It's Jupiter Point's only unsolved murder, and he thinks that's a story. I'm really sorry. I tried to stop it."

"You knew?" The words came out of Will like a whiplash, without him planning to speak.

She glanced at him, then down at the fuel-stained floor of the hangar. "He assigned the story to me. I was dragging my feet on it. I—I screwed up. I wanted to interview you all, if you were willing. I just—never figured out how to ask. He gave the story to someone else and it's already written and done."

"The hell it is," said Ben sharply. "We'll sue. We'll hit back. They have no right to dig up our family history for what...sales? Ratings or whatever?"

"We can't *sue*." Will cut him off in a savage tone. "It's not illegal to write a story about us. It's public knowledge. What is it, some kind of cold-case thing?"

Merry nodded. He could tell she was miserable, but right now, he had no sympathy. She'd known it was coming and never said a word to him. That was the part he couldn't believe. "Why didn't you tell me before?"

"I...I wanted to. But you never talk about what happened, and I kept hoping I could back-burner it, and...I'm sorry, Will!" She took a step backwards, her eyes wide and shiny with tears. "I'm so sorry, all of you. I have no idea what the story says, but I thought you should know it's coming. That's all."

She whirled around and fled out of the hangar. Will stared at the empty space where she had been standing. He should go after her. Tell her not to beat herself up. Tell her it would be okay.

But he still couldn't move.

"Damn it," Tobias swore. "Right when we're opening the business, they pull this? That's fucked up."

Ben paced around in a tight circle, his boots clipping the concrete. "There has to be something we can do."

"There isn't," said Will tightly. "I'm familiar with the laws. They're probably just rehashing what was published at the time, since it's such a rush job. Merry would have done it better." He couldn't keep the bitterness from his voice.

"It's not her fault, bro," said Ben.

Will flung up a hand to stop him. He didn't want to hear that right now. Maybe it wasn't her fault. But she should have fucking told him.

"Who's the new editor?" asked Tobias. "Maybe we need to pay him a visit."

Will shook his head grimly. "I'm the acting sheriff, that can't happen."

"Upholding the law is one thing, but this is our *family*," Tobias growled. "And this is bullshit."

"Guys," said Aiden in a small voice. Everyone ignored him, each brother too caught up in the point they were trying to make.

"You think we wouldn't be back on the front page if we did something stupid?" said Will hotly. "You can't trust reporters."

"Guys," Aiden said. Again, no one paid attention.

"Oh, that's rich. Aren't you sleeping with one?" Ben laughed with no hint of humor.

"So?" Will barked.

"So she came here to warn us. I think we can trust her."

"*Guys*," Aiden shouted. "Stop it! I have something to say."

Shocked, they all snapped their mouths shut and stared at Aiden. He looked nervous now that he had everyone's attention, but he squared his shoulders and carried on. "Maybe this is a good thing."

"*What?*" The chorus of whats made him fall back a step.

"How could this be good?" Will asked, trying his best to stay calm. "Do you remember what it was like when we were in the papers before? It finally feels like people have forgotten and now they want to dig it up again."

"Maybe I don't want to forget!" Aiden burst out. "We never talk about it. We might as well not have had a father. Yeah, someone murdered him. But isn't forgetting as bad as murdering?"

Will's throat closed up, preventing so much as a grunt from coming through. Silence fell across the hangar. Outside, he heard the clink of caterers cleaning up the remains of the party and voices calling goodbye.

"The first class I signed up for at college was Psych 101. Because I always knew it wasn't right to never talk about him. Or Mom and Cassie."

"But that's how we roll," said Tobias. "We eat like savages, we fight like wildebeests, we ignore problems until they give up and go away." Obviously, he was trying a little humor, but all it earned was a disgusted shake of Aiden's sun-streaked head.

"That's stupid. Problems don't just go away. I'll give you my notes from Psych 101."

Tobias shook *his* head, looking appalled at the very thought.

"Maybe this newspaper story will actually make us talk about them. Talk about Mom and Dad and Cassie. Maybe it's a good thing."

The wistful pain in Aiden's voice made Will's stomach twist. All this time, Aiden had been holding on to this need? And keeping quiet about it? He stepped closer to his brother and touched his shoulder. "You never said anything."

"Because it's like the no-man zone. You just don't go there. Like Merry said. No wonder she didn't tell you until now."

Will thought of the stricken expression on Merry's face when she'd fled the hangar. And he hadn't done anything—he'd just stood there and let her go.

"Listen, I need to go after Merry. What do you all say we call a family meeting about this?"

"A *family meeting*?" Tobias snorted. "The Knight brothers don't do family meetings."

"Why not? We're a family, aren't we?" Sternly, he looked from brother to brother. Tobias and Ben could mock if they chose to. But if Aiden wanted to talk, goddamn it, they were going to talk.

No one objected beyond a skeptical raised eyebrow from Tobias.

"Family meeting it is. We'll have a Sunday barbecue tomorrow. We good?" He looked at Aiden. The hope in the kid's face made his heart burn.

"Better go find Merry," Ben reminded him. "If you fuck things up with her, I might disown you."

25

Fired. *Fired.* The thought was so shocking that the words kept repeating in the back of Merry's brain. Even while she took care of business—cleared her stuff from the *News-Gazette* office, met with Human Resources, dressed for the party, made her confession to Will and his brothers—the impossible reality mocked her in an endless loop. Fired. You're fired. Fired.

The only thing that broke the fog was the expression on Will's face as he lashed her with that question. *You knew?*

Why hadn't she said something earlier? Maybe she could have stopped this disaster. She could have protected those four brothers. Even though they were all big, strong warrior types—except maybe Aiden—a father's murder cut to the core. And now they'd have to relive the entire thing.

And she could have stopped it. Now, she could do nothing but watch it happen. Because she was *fired.*

Literally, she didn't know what to do with herself. Without her work, what was she? Maybe she should have taken a vacation sometime in the past eleven years. It would have been practice for unemployment.

When she got back from Knight and Day, she wriggled out of her party dress and pulled on her comfiest yoga pants.

Yoga. She'd have lots of time for yoga now. She could become an expert yoga person.

Except she got bored halfway through class.

And she couldn't afford to stay unemployed. She still owed for her student loans and had maybe two months' rent in the bank. Maybe the community college would hire her full time. Or maybe she should look for a job at another paper. Leave Jupiter Point. Leave Will.

She gave a sob and plopped onto her couch, surveying the apartment she barely spent time in. Would Will care if she left?

You knew?

He probably felt betrayed. He probably thought she'd chosen her job over him.

But she hadn't. She'd refused to do that story, and that's what had gotten her fired. Maybe she could have handled the situation better—been more open with him—but did he have to look at her *like that?*

Her phone beeped. Text from Chase.

I heard. Don't worry, sis. I'll talk to Dad and make a deal. I'll go home IF he helps you out with some $$.

She gave a mirthless laugh and pinched the bridge of her nose, then texted back. *Don't you dare. That's sweet, but I'm not that pathetic.*

I want to help! U need me!

No. Plz don't. Not kidding. Why are you still here?

A rap on the door made her jump to her feet. Ugh, what if it was Chase in the flesh? She didn't want him to witness her failure. She didn't want to see any of her friends, either. They'd all be too freaking sympathetic and she'd probably just cry all over them. She didn't want to see anyone, actually.

Well...maybe Will, she realized as she peeked through the peephole and saw his tall form in the hallway. Yes, definitely Will.

And if he was going to yell at her, she was more than ready to yell back.

She opened the door for him. He was still wearing his nice clothes from the party—a heather-plaid dress shirt and gray trousers. The plaid had a thread of green that gave his eyes a hint of sage. He was beautiful.

"What's wrong?" he asked as soon as he stepped in.

She touched her cheek and realized she still had traces of tears on her face.

That pissed her off. Merriweather Warren wasn't a crybaby. She was tough. Resourceful. Independent. "I'm very sorry about the story, Will. I already told you I was. Do you need more apologies?"

He frowned, looking taken aback by her feistiness. "No. That's not why I'm here." He looked as if he wanted to elaborate, but didn't. The tension built between them.

She turned away, exasperated, and flung herself onto the couch. "An explanation, then? Pretty simple. I wanted to keep my job. Douglas hates me. He already yanked me off one story, then he told me if I did the one about your father, I could get the opioids investigation back. I wasn't sure what to do."

"It never occurred to you to tell me?"

"Jesus, Will. Of course it did! But how? When? You've barely said two words about your father. Remember the last time the subject came up? You said, and I quote, 'I see you've heard about that' in a very tense tone of voice. Obviously, it's a sensitive topic, and I thought I had more time. I was stalling."

She dragged a hand across her eyes. She felt exhausted. Utterly drained. No personal power left in her. However Will wanted to punish her, he ought to just get on with it. "I feel bad enough about it all on my own, but if you want me to feel worse, go ahead. Take your best shot."

Will was standing over her, that frown still creasing his forehead. "You look tired."

"Yes."

He crouched in front of her and took one of her hands in his. The gentleness of the gesture made her breath catch in her throat. "Something else happened. You're too upset. There's something more."

She stared at him. She hadn't told anyone yet that she was fired. Like a coward, she'd waited until the party was almost over to show up at Knight and Day. She hadn't wanted to see anyone, to explain. With any luck, Mrs. Murphy would handle the spreading of the news throughout Jupiter Point.

But the way Will was looking at her, so patient, so concerned, even after she'd dropped her bombshell about the story...

"I got fired," she said, her voice wobbling. "Douglas fired me."

Will's eyes darkened and his hand tightened on hers. "Why? Because of the story?"

"Sort of. Partly. Also because I challenged him. I wasn't doing what he wanted. He's never liked me." Tears leaked from her eyes. She dashed one away and another followed right after it. "He wants everything big and dramatic. The only story of mine he liked was the one with you rescuing that boy." She gave up on trying to stop her tears and let them flow.

The pain wrenched through her being. She'd lost her job. All of the hard work and passion she'd poured into it, gone. As if it never existed. As if it didn't matter. As if she was nothing.

"Aw, honey," Will was murmuring. He picked up her hand and plastered it with kisses. "Don't worry. It'll be okay."

She barely heard him as she sobbed. She thought about how sad her mother would be, how disappointed her favorite journalism professor. All these people who saw her as the dynamo reporter, what would they see now?

She felt like a ghost. A powerless, insignificant ghost.

Will let her cry for a while, keeping her hand intertwined with his. He didn't say much, just let her sob it out. When her tears finally slowed, Will lifted her off the couch and settled her into his arms. She didn't even really know what was happening as he carried her into the bedroom. Still holding her, he used one hand to pull the covers down. He tucked her in, then sat next to her. She hiccupped, one last tear spilling out of her.

"We'll figure this out," he said firmly. "You get some sleep."

She collapsed against her pillow, exhaustion dragging at her like a lead blanket. "So bossy," she murmured.

"No arguing."

"See?" And she fell asleep.

THAT NIGHT, she had one of her extra-vivid dreams, like the ones she used to tell StarLord about. She was racing down Stargazer Beach barefoot, so fast she was practically flying. When she reached the water's edge, her speed was so great that she was able to skim across the surface of the water. It was an amazing feeling to move so fast and to feel the ocean supporting her steps. But a voice called to her from the shore—Will's voice. Her concentration snapped when she looked back, and she splashed into the water.

When she woke up, the uneasy feeling from the dream still clung to her. Will stood by the window, his dress shirt open over his bare chest, a powerful silhouette against the morning light pouring in through her curtains. With one hand braced on the window frame, he parted the curtains and stared outside. He was thinking about something serious, that was for sure.

She stretched, hitting the headboard with her hand, and he turned to face her. "Good morning."

"Good morning. What time is it?" For a moment she panicked, thinking she might be late for work, but then she remembered she was unemployed. "Never mind. Unless you're late? Do you have to get to work?"

"It's Sunday."

"Right. Of course." Sunday...when the front-page article about Will's father's murder was going to come out. Maybe she should stay in bed the whole day. "Thanks for coming over last night. I was afraid you hated me because I didn't—"

"We should get married."

"*Excuse* me?" Her jaw dropped. She clutched the sheets against her chest, then added a pillow, as if barricading herself with the familiar. "What are you talking about?"

"You don't have to worry about getting another job right away. You won't have to leave Jupiter Point. I'll take care of you. "

"You'll take *care* of me?"

She flashed on Chase's text last night, the way he'd right away offered his father's—their father's—money. And just like that, she felt even lower than before. Why did everyone think she couldn't handle this?

"Yeah," Will said, his face still somber. "I care about you. You must know that I...I love you."

It should have been the best moment of her life. Will was telling her that he loved her and wanted to marry her. But it felt all wrong. Her stomach twisted in a sick knot. He was looking at her in that same weird, distant way as last night. If he really loved her, she never would have known from his expression. Where was the passion? The joy?

Something still hung between them, heavy and hard.

"What about the story about your father? I should have told you earlier and I didn't."

His jaw tightened. "I'm willing to overlook that. It's a...it's a tough thing."

She frowned and pushed the covers away, then swung her legs over the side of the bed. "You're right. It's tough. The kind of thing you might want to share with someone you marry. Are you sure you trust me?"

"What are you talking about? I trust you. Didn't I just ask you to marry me?"

"Yes, because you're willing to 'overlook' a few things." Her heart felt like a ball of lead in her chest. She stalked to her dresser and pulled out a new pair of underwear. "But you aren't willing to talk to me."

"That's not true."

"It is. I know how full of flaws I am. I lose my temper too easily. I jump to conclusions. Sometimes I can be bitchy. The kind word is prickly, but it's a thin line sometimes." She yanked off her yoga pants. Aware of his eyes on her, she refused to show any shame or modesty. This was her apartment. Her turf. And damn it, she wanted her power back. "I was trying so hard to respect your boundaries that I screwed up and didn't mention the story. But you put those boundaries there. You're the one with the big 'Keep Out' sign."

He didn't answer, which was fine because she was on a roll now.

"And if you think I'd marry someone so they can *take care* of me, you don't know me at all. I take care of myself."

He finally opened his mouth but she steamrolled over him. "Okay, I got fired. I'm down but I'm not out. If Douglas doesn't respect me, screw him. As long as I respect myself, I can get through. But if I marry you because you feel sorry for me, I'd never respect myself again."

She stormed toward the bathroom completely naked and marched into her shower. As she stood under the pounding water, her fierce surge of fury drained away. Was she crazy, yelling at a man who'd just proposed to her? Yelling at *Will*, who'd come into her life and changed everything?

When she came out, dripping water on her carpet, Will was gone.

26

NOTHING KICKED A GUY IN THE TEETH LIKE A MARRIAGE PROPOSAL rejection.

After leaving Merry's apartment, Will took the long way home, not yet ready to face the big family meeting. He drove the beach road, which required four-wheel drive and really good struts.

Had he really misread Merry that badly? When he was with her, everything made sense, as if she was a light illuminating his little corner of the world. *If you think I'd marry you so you can take care of me, you don't know me at all.*

Of course he didn't think that. Or did he? He thought about all the times he'd tried to protect Merry. The time she'd been tranq-ed. When he'd discovered her working at the Rootin' Rooster. Merry tended to get into trouble, and naturally he wanted to get her out. Because he was an officer of the law, because he was a man, because he loved her.

Had he done the wrong thing, rescuing her? Was that what she was saying? He didn't think so, but also, he'd just been kicked in the teeth so his brain wasn't really functioning right.

When he got home, he found his brothers at the grill behind

the house. It wasn't a "yard" so much as a weed-covered slope that extended for a few hundred yards until it hit a grove of pine trees. They kept enough space mowed to accommodate a basketball hoop, a picnic table, coolers and a gas grill. Whenever Will saw an outdoor chair at a yard sale, he grabbed it. Their motley collection included an old-school barber's chair, a sleek chaise lounge, and some dainty white-wicker chairs straight out of a garden party.

The scent of roasting meat made his mouth water. As he rounded the corner, a beer came flying through the air toward him. He snagged it and cracked it open as he claimed a lawn chair and sank into it with a sigh.

Ben, with a goofy-looking terrycloth headband holding back his hair, patrolled the grill like a tennis champ braced for a return of service. Aiden held a plate of cooked burgers so charred they looked like extra-black hockey pucks.

"Where's Tobias?"

Neither took their eyes off the grill. "Grabbing condiments," Aiden told him. He waved a buzzing fly away from his face. "You're out of relish. This is what happens when I leave."

"Whole place goes to hell," Will agreed. "No argument here."

He offered Aiden a one-sided smile, which was the most he could manage. He didn't need to bring his personal shit into this situation. This family meeting was important to Aiden, and he had to give it his all.

Tobias stepped out the back door cradling an armful of containers ranging from ketchup to mayonnaise. He held them awkwardly, as if he was more used to carrying live grenades than condiments, but he managed to get them onto the picnic table, where he set them next to a paper plate piled high with buns. He sat on the barber's chair, which seemed appropriate considering his shaved head.

"Dearly beloved," he said, toasting them all with a beer. "I've called you here to discuss this thing called Aiden's life."

Aiden rolled his eyes. "This meeting is not about me." He tried to grab the spatula from Ben, who fended him off. "Dude, you're burning them. Some of us don't like eating meat-flavored charcoal."

"Watch and learn from the master," Ben intoned. "Only a few can attain the Zen of burnt animal flesh. Only a few are worthy of the great legacy of burgers past."

Aiden went around him and snagged the barbecue fork to rescue one burger from the grill and plop it on the plate. He carried it to the picnic table, then hopped onto the cedar-planked table top. He always sat on the table, never on the bench. "So anyway, like I was about to say before Ben burned my burger—"

"Say that five times fast," interjected Ben.

Aiden ignored him and continued. "This is an intervention. I learned about them at school."

Will glanced at the bottle in his hand, wondering if beer was off-limits during this meeting.

"Not that kind of intervention," said Aiden. "An intervention for our family. Because our family is *fucked. Up*."

Will cringed. He thought he'd done pretty well, considering. But apparently, Aiden wasn't too impressed. "Hey, we did the best we could."

"I'm not blaming anyone. I know we did the best we could. When Dad was killed, and Mom took Cassie, we were left behind. It's like we all went into our separate corners and dealt with it our own way. And we never talked about it."

Will exchanged glances with Tobias, who focused on a frayed thread in his sleeve. Ben scowled at the remaining burgers on the grill, his spatula poised over the meat.

Aiden shifted to reach into his back pocket. He pulled out a rolled- up copy of the *Mercury News-Gazette*.

"I read today's article. I brought it in case you guys want to see it."

The sight of Merry's newspaper sent a piercing pain straight to Will's heart. He remembered all the times—before they hooked up, even before StarLord and AnonyMs—when he'd searched for her byline, grumbling something like, "What's that girl up to now?"

"Give us the CliffsNotes version," he said.

"Really? No one wants to read it?" Aiden glanced around at them all. "Would you rather shoot it or arrest it or something?"

Ben snorted and turned off the grill, piling the last burgers onto a plate. "That would be more our comfort zone. Good thing we have a college student among us. Go ahead. Lay it on us."

Aiden scratched at a mosquito bite on his knee. He looked so young compared to the rest of their battle-hardened crew. But yet—he was the only one wading into this mess. Will felt a strange sense of pride stealing over him.

"It laid out the basics. Dad was murdered in our kitchen. Someone slashed his throat while the rest of us were sleeping. The murder weapon was never found, but it wasn't one of our knives. Mom was a suspect for a while, but nothing really pointed to her. No fingerprints were found, no footprints or any other clues like that. In the end, they speculated that it was related to something from his Army days. But they never determined what. That would have taken a lot of resources to investigate, and Jupiter Point doesn't have that kind of budget. So the case is still open. Unsolved."

An uneasy silence settled over them.

Ben scowled at the burger he was assembling. Will put down his beer, stomach roiling.

"And no one's working on it," said Aiden. "Just like it never happened."

"What are we supposed to do about that?" Tobias demanded. "The police worked the case. They never even had a good lead."

"So that's it? End of story?" Aiden plopped his plate onto the picnic table. "Cuz that sounds like crap to me."

"The fu—" Tobias began.

"What do you want to do, Aiden?" Will intervened before things got heated. "If the police didn't get anywhere when the crime was fresh, they have even less chance now."

"Not the police. They're useless. Except you," he added hastily. "I didn't mean you."

Will shrugged off the insult; he'd heard much worse during his surrogate parenting years. "Then who?"

"Well, I was thinking we could hire a private detective." Aiden fiddled with his beer bottle, though he had yet to take a drink. "But that's not even the main point. It's not about solving the crime. It's just...our mother is out there somewhere, she left us, she left *me*, and she took Cassie with her, and every once in a while we get a postcard that says they're alive and what—that's *normal*? That's not normal. Does that sound normal to anyone here?"

Will kicked at a clump of grass that needed mowing. What did "normal" have to do with anything? It wasn't normal for your father to be murdered in his own kitchen. It wasn't normal to raise your eight-year-old brother. It wasn't normal to fall for a feisty reporter who had spent the previous three years feuding with you.

And it wasn't normal to keep so much locked inside.

"I looked for Mom after Ben and Tobias left," he said so softly that maybe his brothers wouldn't hear.

But they did. All eyes swiveled to him. Now he knew exactly how suspects in the interrogation room felt. He cleared his throat.

"I was panicking about being a fill-in father. I wanted her to come back and be a damn parent. I investigated for months. And I found her. She and Cassie were in New Mexico. I went to see her while you were at soccer camp, Aiden."

Aiden's mouth fell open, his face flushed.

"They were living in a commune-type place there. When Mom saw me, she had a complete meltdown and started screaming and crying. Cassie came running out. She calmed

Mom down and got her inside. I think she was seventeen by then. She begged me to stay away. She told me that any mention of us made her freak out because it reminded her of Dad and the trauma of the murder."

"Jesus," breathed Ben. "Why didn't you get Cassie out of there?"

"Or get Mom some help?" asked Tobias.

"I said the same thing to Cassie. I wanted her to come back with me. But she insisted that Mom was fine as long as she didn't have to talk about her old life, or Dad, or us. She said she takes her to support groups and therapists. I didn't like it, but in the end, she convinced me to let things continue as they were. So I left them some money and agreed to let them be, as long as Cassie kept sending updates."

"You mean postcards."

"Yeah. Postcards. One came on Saturday, but I didn't get a chance to show you guys before the party."

Will dug in his pocket and took out Cassie's latest card. He passed it around so they could all take in the photo of Graceland and the writing on the back.

He'd memorized it, so he mentally followed along as Aiden read it.

Remember peanut butter and banana sandwiches washed down with Gatorade? Mmmmm. We were rock stars just like Elvis. Just passing through his turf, then on to a job in Georgia. Did I tell you I got my mechanic's license? Hot diggity! Mom's doing great. The other day she actually mentioned that it was Ben's birthday. I mean, it wasn't his birthday, but the fact that she spoke his name means a lot. I'm working up to telling her about Knight and Day. I'm really excited for you guys. I wish I was there, and maybe I will be someday. Give Tobias and Ben and Aiden hugs from me. Or wedgies. Or both. I love you. Cassie.

Aiden finished, then passed the card to Ben. "I miss Cassie. I miss how she used to tease me. Remember when she told me that the Easter Bunny was living in the treehouse?"

Will chuckled. Every single member of the Knight family had a wild streak, but Cassie, the only girl, put her own special twist on it.

"I have all her postcards memorized," Tobias admitted. "I used to recite them to myself when I had to keep myself awake when I was on watch."

"She might have been the biggest rebel of us all," Ben said as he passed the postcard to Tobias. "She was fearless."

Tobias read silently, then looked up. An intense scowl dented his forehead. He flipped the card back to Will and aimed a laser glare at him. "Fuck. Why'd you never tell us you saw them?"

"You guys were gone, Aiden was finally getting into a normal routine. Cassie begged me to keep it quiet. She didn't want anyone else showing up out of the blue. I don't know, fuck. Maybe I should have."

"Damn right you should have." That came from Ben, which cut Will even closer to the bone. Ben was gentler than Tobias, slower to anger. "It's our family too."

"I wanted you guys to have a life," he shot back.

"What, like you didn't? Because of me?" Aiden looked about ready to throw his burger at Will.

Stunned, Will surged to his feet. "Don't put words in my mouth. I didn't say that. Yeah, it might have been tough sometimes. I wished Mom was around. I did the best I could, but I know you needed more and—" He broke off before his voice could crack. He clenched his jaw so hard his molars hurt.

He didn't do this kind of thing. He didn't lose his cool and get all emotional. That just wasn't him.

His throat worked as he stared at the ground. A trail of ants led from the picnic table to a pile of dirt. He fixed his gaze on their busy, heedless highway. Tension gripped the four of them like a fist squeezing tight.

"Look, bro. You've been the anchor all along. You kept our shit together." Tobias's deep voice broke the silence. "No one blames you."

Everyone murmured agreement.

"No." Will shook his head, still watching those ants, because it was easier than seeing the expressions on his brothers' faces. "I was trying to keep a lid on things. Keep control, somehow. Because everything was so nuts."

Ben came closer, leaning on the picnic table next to Aiden. "Sometimes things are like that. They go FUBAR. All you can do is hang on and hope the crash landing works out. You don't have to do it all yourself, you know."

"Huh?"

"You're carrying the whole world on your shoulders. All of us. Aiden. Mom and Cassie. All of Jupiter Point County. Maybe you should give it a rest, Will. Lighten the load, maybe take a vacation."

Finally, Will looked up at the tight circle of his brothers. They were all watching him with similar expressions, something he couldn't identify. It made him uneasy, as if they knew something he didn't.

"A *vacation*? What are you talking about? I don't need a vacation."

"When's the last time you had a break?" Tobias asked, balancing a beer on his thigh.

The last time Will had taken any time off was when he'd gone to see Mom and Cassie. For a moment, he indulged in a fantasy of him and Merry on a remote beach in Mexico. Possibly clothing optional. A hotel room nearby where they could make love all night.

Except that Merry had just thrown his proposal back in his face. Had she dumped him? Was it over? How did you go forward after that?

He shook it off. "Let's get back to the main topic here. This so-called intervention isn't about me. Right, Aiden?" He turned to his youngest brother for help.

"Not really, but this is fun." The little traitor grinned at him. "Merry's cool. You should take her on vacation."

"I'm not going on vacation," he ground out. "Definitely not with Merry."

"Dude, you're not still pissed about the article, are you?" Ben asked. "Sounds like it wasn't so bad. Just a rehash. Nothing that hasn't been all over town before."

Tobias grunted in agreement, and bit into his burger. Aiden licked mustard off the side of his bun. Will blinked at them. They all seemed to agree. No biggie, said their body language. All their anger over the article, Merry getting fired, him getting upset with her...all for what?

"You probably owe Merry an apology," said Aiden, flicking a sesame seed off his bun. "I actually have an idea about that."

"Look, it doesn't matter." Will set aside his beer bottle, having barely taken a sip. "She doesn't need an apology. She doesn't even work there anymore."

"What do you mean?" Ben picked up the paper from the picnic table. "I just saw her name on a story about the new roundabouts."

"It just happened. She got fired."

"Because of this?" Tobias grabbed the paper from Ben and glared at it, as if he actually might open fire on it. "That's not right. That's bullshit."

"It's not our business. I tried to help out, but she kicked me to the curb. Merry's her own woman. She doesn't want or need..." His throat clenched tight. "Me."

Aware of the gaze of his brothers, he fought for control. He put a hand over his eyes and battled his vocal cords, which wanted to seize up instead of working. The moment dragged on. He felt a hand on his back, another on his head—his brothers reaching out. He felt their love and sympathy flowing toward him, into him, surrounding him.

But this was his problem. His mess. His brothers couldn't help him win back Merry's heart. And without it, his future held no joy.

"Is this family meeting over yet?" he finally managed. "This thing is going to kill me."

All his brothers laughed...and that did help.

27

Merry couldn't seem to get motivated to get out of bed. When she missed her usual morning latte at the Venus and Mars, word got back to Suzanne. Suzanne called her immediately. Merry didn't have the will to withstand her worried questioning. As soon as Merry told her what had happened at the newspaper, her party-planner friend took action.

Suzanne was basically the border collie of friends, the one who got everyone in one place and made it a party. Calls were made. Lisa was sent to pick Merry up. Merry called Carolyn, who was around for fall break. Late that afternoon, they all gathered at the Orbit for emergency margaritas.

Packed into a booth with Evie, Brianna, Suzanne, Lisa, and Carolyn, Merry related the story of her firing. Which meant she had to explain about the Knight murder story in the Sunday paper, and exactly why she'd slow-mo-ed it, dooming her job.

"So it's true. You and Will," said Suzanne triumphantly. "I knew it!"

"Was Will the online mystery man?" Brianna wriggled with excitement. "I never would have pegged him for a secret sensitive guy."

"I would," Evie said. "I always thought he had hidden depths. He's helped my mom out a few times."

Lisa was smiling widely. "Will is a great guy. He really is. And I think you're perfect for each other. This is fantastic news. Does it make up a little bit for losing your job?"

"Who's Will?" Carolyn asked in confusion.

"Will Knight," Suzanne explained. "He's a Jupiter Point sheriff's deputy."

Carolyn frowned thoughtfully. "I know that name from somewhere."

"He's an excellent deputy," said Suzanne. "Not to mention all-around good guy and the ultimate hot cop."

Merry couldn't take it anymore. "We broke up last night. Or at least I think we did."

They all froze in shock, some in mid-Margarita swallow, others with tortilla chips halfway to their mouths.

Lisa carefully put down her drink. "What do you mean, you 'think' you did?"

Merry told that story too. It had definitely been a busy few days.

"One of the notoriously single Knight brothers asked you to marry him?" Evie asked in surprise.

"Yes, but he didn't really mean it. He was being protective."

"I don't know," Suzanne said dubiously. "From what I know of Will, he doesn't do things unless he really means them."

"Yes, but—" She swallowed, because all of this talk of Will was making her heart ache even more.

"There are more Knight brothers?" Carolyn asked. She still wore a distracted look as she toyed with the orange slice that came with her drink.

"Four of them. Each one hunkier than the next," Brianna explained. "All single, including Will...now, I guess..." She trailed off. Trust Brianna to stumble onto something tactless to say.

Merry gripped the vinyl seat of the booth with both hands. "Can we change the subject?"

The other women exchanged glances. "Sure," said Lisa. "Good idea. Um...have you thought about your next move?"

"A little bit. I've been working nonstop since the age of fifteen. I was thinking maybe I should take a vacation." She heard the doubt dripping from her own voice. Vacation? What would she do all alone on a vacation?

"I can set you up with something fun," Suzanne said promptly. "Honeymooners aren't the only ones who need getaways."

Merry made a little face, because that just sounded sad. "That's a sweet thought, but—"

"You could spend some time in the Breton lookout tower," Lisa suggested. "It's a great place to collect your thoughts."

Alone in a tower in the wilderness? That sounded like a horror movie to Merry. The last time she'd been out in those woods, she'd gotten attacked by a gunman.

But maybe she should open her mind. "Is there Internet?"

"It's a little sketchy, but—"

"Nope, that's out. Thanks anyway, you guys. Look, we've been talking about me this whole time. I'm unemployed and single, blah blah, waah waah. Please, let's move on. Seen any good movies lately? Read any good books? Has anyone met the new observatory director yet? Suzanne, how's Faith doing? Is she walking yet?"

"She's...uh, only seven months old."

"Well, is that too early for walking? What do I know?" She picked up her margarita and slurped up a big mouthful. But the sweet, tangy slush didn't make her feel better. It loosened something inside her, something that had been trying to flow out ever since Will left her apartment. "It's not like I'm ever going to have kids."

"Oh Merry, you don't know that." Carolyn put an arm around her shoulder.

"I do know that," she said fiercely. "Because I'll never meet a man better than Will and I'm going to be alone forever. I know I kept saying that's what I wanted, that I can only rely on myself, but I *miss him.*"

To her own shock and amazement, she burst into tears.

The other women rushed to reassure her, to pat her shoulder, her hand or whatever they could reach. But their soothing "it'll be okays" did nothing for her.

"It *won't* be okay. You should have seen the look on his face when I turned him down. I know he comes off as a stern law-officer type, but he has a completely different side to him too. And I really hurt him. And why? Just for my own pride?"

Next to her, Lisa was rubbing her arm. "You told him how you felt. He's a grown man, a mature man. He can handle it."

"Think of everything else he's been through," added Evie. "He held his family together after the murder. He has a lot of inner strength."

That just made Merry sob harder. "I know he does. This is on me. I'm afraid of being weak. Of people not respecting me. But Will *does* respect me. He loves me. I know he does. Being with him won't take my personal power. And what use is power anyway if it's afraid of love? Huh? Can anyone answer that?"

From across the table, Carolyn kept feeding her Kleenex. Merry plucked another one from the box as her friend spoke. "If he loves you, and you love him, you can fix this. Maybe this is just a bump in the road."

"I bet every single one of us had a moment when we totally screwed up with the guy we wanted. I know I did," said Lisa. "I flew back to Houston, letting Finn think I didn't love him."

"And I snuck away from Manhattan without telling Rollo, just because I made a fool of myself in front of a bunch of rich people," Brianna added.

"I got trapped on top of a burning house," said Suzanne.

"And I nearly got caught in a wildfire," Evie chimed in.

Carolyn held up the box of tissues again. Merry snagged another and blew her nose.

Brianna offered her the empty plastic basket that had contained their tortilla chips. She'd cleared everything out of it except the greasy liner. Merry dropped the used Kleenex into it.

Not to be outdone in the help-offering category, Suzanne snatched up Merry's margarita and held it up for her.

Merry looked around at her friends—Brianna with the basket, Carolyn with the tissues, Suzanne with the margarita, Evie with the words of comfort, Lisa with an arm around her shoulders.

And she began sobbing again. "You guys are being so nice to me, and I'm such a prickly porcupine."

"No, you're not!" Brianna bonked her on the arm with the basket. "You're always here for us. You have the biggest heart in the world. You care about people and you're wicked smart and you're funny too."

Suzanne was nodding in agreement, still holding up the margarita for her. "You were totally there for me when I was trying to figure out what to do about the baby. You were the first person I told because I knew I could trust you and that you'd give me great advice. You're not prickly, you're just smart. And every single one of us is lucky to have you as a friend."

"There is no one I'd rather have in my corner," said Lisa. "You always have our backs."

"But I didn't even tell you I have a brother!"

Everyone froze and stared at her in shock. "A *what*?" said Brianna.

"A half-brother. He's white, so you probably didn't put it together—"

"The intern from the newspaper!" Evie exclaimed. "The one tagging along after you like a puppy."

"Yes. And I've been a total bitch to him when all he wants is to get to know me." She snatched another tissue from the box.

"You had your reasons," Carolyn said firmly. "Good ones."

"No. Don't be nice to me." She blew her nose. "I told Will he had a big 'keep out' sign, but who am I to talk? I've said nothing but 'keep out' to Chase." She blew her nose. "And I was a lot meaner about it too. I've screwed everything up with everyone."

She balled up the Kleenex and tossed it in the basket.

"Not with us," said Lisa firmly. "We're here for you. What do you want us to do? Find Will? Send you both to a tropical island where you can work things out?"

"We can make that happen," Suzanne said confidently. "I know some guys with planes."

Merry produced a loud, wet, embarrassing sob. This was ridiculous. She was the cynical one, the self-sufficient, fast-talking, take-no-crap one. What was she doing crying her eyes out like a sentimental fool?

The answer was blindingly obvious.

She was in love with Will.

Funny how she could help everyone else with their problems, but have such a massive blind spot about her own heart.

She loved Will. She loved him in a way that was completely new to her. It was nothing like what she'd felt for any previous boyfriend. Will wasn't about a fun, wild surface. He was about the strength and caring that existed underneath. Strong, thoughtful, patient, smart, wry Will.

And her feelings for him went deep. They'd taken root in her heart, and every beat made them grow stronger. So unless she intended to rip the entire thing out once and for all, she'd better face it.

She loved Will Knight.

With sudden determination, she wiped the tears off her face. "You guys are right. I need to find Will." She rose to her feet, and Lisa scooted over to let her out. She looked around the little circle of concerned faces. "This might sound unusual coming from the jaded one of the crew, but I seriously love you all. With all my heart."

"We love you, too, Merry," said Suzanne, stepping up as spokesperson. "But where are you going? Didn't you drive with Brianna?"

"I can walk home from here. I just want to clear my head. I need to come up with the right words to say. I am a writer, after all. I gotta get this right."

~

OUTSIDE THE ORBIT, night had fallen. The wrought iron street-lamps gave the downtown streets a cozy glow. Honeymooners wandered hand in hand down Constellation Way, peering into the storefronts and kissing at random moments.

Her phone buzzed. Her wild hope that it might be Will disappeared when she saw the text from Chase.

Big news! I have a present for you! You're going to love this. It's something big about your drug story. Where R U? Anywhere near the Gazette?

Oh no. She'd told Chase to go home, not investigate a news story. *Are you crazy? Stay out of it. And I don't work there anymore.*

I know something about that too. You might get your job back. I'm like Santa right now with so much good news. I'm your inside man, sis!

Merry sucked in a breath. Get her job back ... now that got her attention. *Tell me more.*

I'm leaving the Gazette now, let's meet.

The *Mercury News-Gazette* building was only a few blocks from the Orbit; she was already heading that direction. It wouldn't do any harm to hear what Chase meant about getting her job back. And she could lecture him about going home at the same time. *Heading that way now from the Orbit*, she texted. Then she added, *I'm sorry for how I've acted.*

It's ok. You're going to love me for this.

Their paths crossed outside the Venus and Mars, which was shuttered for the night. Chase bounded toward her, his sneakers slapping against the pavement. "I know you told me to go home," he said quickly. "I couldn't leave yet, not until I did something for you."

She shook her head at him, but this time it was more affectionate than scolding. "I told you I don't need anything like that."

"But this is different. This is about your job, and I know you care about that."

Her heart twisted at the wistful tone of his voice. "Chase—"

He threw up a hand. "Let me just do my thing, okay? Give me a chance here." When she nodded, he continued. "Guess who called Douglas today? The Knight family. All the brothers. They said that article left out a big part of the story—them. They want to give a group interview to talk about how the murder affected them, their lives since then. That sort of thing."

Wow. She absorbed that information with a sense of bittersweet sadness. That kind of interview was exactly what she'd had in mind—if she'd ever had the nerve to suggest it. "That'll make a great story."

"Yup. They want to do it after the sheriff gets back from his honeymoon."

A young couple locked in an embrace strolled past them. Merry couldn't see their faces in the darkness, but no doubt they were honeymooners too. Everyone was in love, while she just drove people away. And for what? A job she no longer had.

"I still don't see why this would get my job back."

"Because they say they'll only talk to you. They said you're the best reporter there and the only one they trust to do the story right. Douglas threw a fit."

"Whoa. Seriously?" A sense of warmth expanded inside her heart. "That's...amazing. I wish I could have seen his face."

Chase grinned. "People said he threw things. I heard he broke a chair. He's going to call you tomorrow. Sweet, huh?"

She couldn't get over it. The Knight brothers were coming to her rescue, but not in a weird way. In a legitimate way.

"Thanks, Chase. Thanks for telling me. I really appreciate it, and I'm sorry I've been so standoffish. You're a good guy, but I still think—"

"Wait, that's not even the best part! This is the craziest thing. I sort of snuck into Douglas' office to get some information for you. I got a phone number from the file, I think it's one of the top bad guys. I called it just to make sure it was real, but I hung up right away. I figured you could decide what to do. But then someone called me back! I said I was calling from the *Mercury News-Gazette* and he actually said he wanted to talk to a reporter. He even mentioned you by name. Isn't that amazing? Everyone knows you, Merry. You're like the best reporter in California, and you're my sister. How cool is that? I told him I'd set it up. His number's in my phone."

He beamed at her and presented her with his phone. She looked at it blankly. He'd called one of Buckaroo's gang members? "Did you tell him your name?"

"I...no...maybe. I don't remember exactly. Does that matter?"

She didn't know, but the idea of Buckaroo knowing anything about either her or Chase gave her chills. "You're saying he called you back? What else did he say? Did he give his name?"

Chase blinked rapidly. "Did I mess up? I thought I was helping."

"I don't know. I'm going to call Will."

She took her own phone out of her bag and searched for Will's name. "Send me that number, Chase, and any other info you have. I'll take it from here," she said, scrolling quickly through her favorites for Will's number.

A muffled sound made her look up. Before she could process what she was witnessing—Chase in a headlock—someone slammed into her back.

She rammed her elbow backwards and heard a grunt as she

connected, started to whirl around, but then something came over her head—something scratchy and woolen and sound-muffling—and everything went dark.

Her arms were pinned to her sides. The man—had to be, he was so big—lifted her off her feet and dumped her into the back-seat of a car.

28

With no Merry waiting to light up his night, Will stayed late at the office. Her message that Deputy Jernigan had made that call to the newspaper sent him sifting through Jernigan's files with a microscope. Why had Jernigan lied to him about that? If he was working for Buckaroo right under their noses, Will couldn't find evidence for it. He had to talk to him face to face, see if he could catch him out.

He intended it to be a low-key conversation, but as soon as he saw Jernigan walk into the break room, he got furious.

Shocking his fellow officer, he shoved him against the wall, spilling his coffee down his shirt. "Why'd you call the paper about the fentanyl story and then lie about it?"

"The fuck are you talking about?" Jernigan was a burly African-American deputy, a solid, unflappable dude.

"You asked them to take Merry off the story. To dump it. Why?"

"I didn't. Thought you and Perez had that handled."

Will released him. God, that made sense. Perez had asked him to talk to Merry after the press conference. "You didn't call the new editor over there? Douglas Wentworth?"

"No. That'd be up to the sheriff, not me." Jernigan brushed at the coffee on his uniform shirt. "What's gotten into you? This isn't like you."

"Damn, I'm sorry, Jernigan. Maybe someone called using your name." Will tore off a handful of paper towels for him. Could he trust Jernigan? Should he tell him about the possible mole in the department? "Have you noticed anything off about this investigation? Anything set off alarms?"

"Well, we got skunked with that first arrest, with the faulty paperwork. Other than that, no. Well, and this. I don't usually get attacked in the break room."

Will rubbed his forehead with the heel of his hand. "Sorry, man. Really sorry."

"We still got that Johnny Diaz guy in lockup. Let's go talk to him," Jernigan suggested.

"Ahem." In the doorway, Cindy cleared her throat. "Will, there's a phone call for you. Seemed important, but then again, this does too."

"Take a message."

"I tried. They said they have to talk to you and only you. They also said something really weird. They said 'Christmas is coming early.'"

"What?" Will frowned at the office assistant, who shrugged.

"Told you it was weird. I have some paperwork to process, so I'll let you two get back to your brawl. He's on hold on line two. If Christmas is coming early, I need to get my shopping done. Merry Christmas!"

Merry Christmas. *Merry*.

He ran out of the break room into the sheriff's office and grabbed the phone. A deep growling voice answered.

"Deputy Will Knight, we have your girlfriend. You must do exactly what I say."

His blood turned to ice, but somehow he knew exactly what to do. *Keep him talking. Stall.*

"I don't have a girlfriend." He grabbed his cell, activated the voice recorder and held it up to the phone. He didn't have a way to trace the call—the Jupiter Point Sheriff's Department wasn't exactly the FBI—but at least he could record it.

A pause, then the voice came back. "She says she's your woman. Doesn't like the term 'girlfriend'."

Oh God, they really had her. He wanted to yell. He wanted to tear this creature apart. But he kept his voice calm. "Let me talk to her."

"In a minute. If you agree to my demands, you can talk to her."

"What do you want?"

"You have a suspect in custody. Johnny Diaz. You need to release him. Then we'll release Merry."

"Listen, this is a stupid move, whoever you are. Merry is a reporter. You're kidnapping a respected member of the community. You're impeding a police investigation. Johnny's small potatoes, he's not worth the risk you're taking. Just let Merry go."

But even as he spoke, he realized the problem. Johnny had a good lawyer and he was about to blow the whistle on someone. Buckaroo wanted him out of there before he could do so.

"We'll let her go. As soon as Johnny is released. And it's got to be soon. You have one hour."

Jesus. One hour? They really wanted to spring Johnny. The guy would probably be dead if he let him out. "That's impossible."

"You're the acting sheriff. You can make it happen."

Play along. Make him think he's won. "Fuck, I don't care if some lowlife walks free, it happens all the time. I'll do it, I just have to pull a few strings. Now let me talk to Merry so I can make sure she's okay."

Another short pause, and then Merry's voice came on the line, shaky and breathless. "Will?"

His heart clenched. Sweat sprang to his palms, making his hand slip on the phone. This was really happening. Jesus Christ. "Merry, are you okay?"

"So far, yes. I'm safe for now." There was something funny in the way she said that, but he couldn't quite put his finger on it. Maybe it was because she was terrified. "I love you. I just wanted to say that in case I don't get another chance. All that stuff I said the other night, I left out the most important thing. I love you so much. Just do what they say, okay? Please stay safe. I couldn't bear it if I lost you. Promise?"

"Of course, my love. I love you too."

Then the deep-voiced man was back. "That's enough. One hour."

Will hung up the phone, his mind whirring. Merry had been trying to tell him something, he'd bet his life on it. But what?

He clicked the replay button on his phone and listened to her again. And again.

The third time, it hit him. She'd used the word "safe" twice.

Safe.

Merry was being held in the Sweet Mountain Lodge, in the room with the locked safe.

Of course, knowing that and figuring out what to do about it without tipping anyone off—in one hour—were two different things.

His first impulse, of course, was to go in with guns blazing and bust her out of there. He'd need backup for that, which meant bringing in someone from the department. But he still didn't know who was working with Buckaroo. Jernigan *probably* wasn't. But maybe the guy had just put on a really smooth act. Right now, Sheriff Perez was the only one he was sure about.

He could reach out to the DEA, but he didn't know those guys. He hadn't been working with them. And he had one hour. Too little time to mount a full-scale rescue operation with unknown elements. *Tick tick tick...*

He had only one good option. Too bad it would get him fired.

He grabbed everything he needed—weapons, handcuffs—

and swung out of the office. He loped past Cindy's desk. "You should go home, Cindy. We're done for the night."

"Wait! Really? I figured you were working late on something important and might need my always-cheerful and productive help."

He turned, impatient at the delay. "I'm good. I'm headed out."

She nodded. "Sure, temporary boss." She adjusted her cute cat-eye glasses. "Anything else before I go?"

"Nope. Have a good night." With a wave, he brushed her off and hurried out to his car. One hour. *Tick tick tick...*

Obeying the speed limits, the drive to Sweet Mountain Lodge took about forty-five minutes. But this was not the time to be law-and-order Will. This moment called for wild, rule-breaking Will Knight.

And the other Knight brothers.

As he drove, he called Tobias and Ben and filled them in. "I can't trust anyone else. This is completely against policy and I will get fired for pulling you guys in. I'll try to take all the blame but I can't guarantee anything. But I could sure use the backup. Just another set of eyes or two, and someone to call for reinforcements if shit goes haywire."

Tobias asked exactly one question. "Where do you need us?"

Ben didn't ask any questions, just said, "Text me directions, I'm there."

Oh yeah. The Knight brothers were back in action. Skirting the law just like the old days. And he had absolutely no regrets.

It was only as he hurtled down the highway that something occurred to him.

Was it a little odd that Cindy was working so late? Of all the people in the office, she was the most on top of things. She knew there was nothing urgent happening tonight. Unless...she was expecting a change in plans.

Cindy. *Cindy*?

Mind officially blown, he stepped on the accelerator and zoomed toward the lodge. If Cindy was in on this, and if she warned the assholes he was up to something, he had even less than an hour.

29

As places to be held hostage went, a suite at the Sweet Mountain Lodge wasn't too shabby. Merry's hands were bound together with a zip tie and she wore a gag, even though the kidnappers had lowered it so she could talk to Will. Even though she was tied to an armchair, at least it was luxuriously cushioned and comfortable.

In fact, she had good memories of this chair. The last time she'd occupied it, Will's lap had been under her during the best "sit-down" interview ever.

Will.

Hearing his voice on the phone had changed everything. All her panic had vanished. She knew without an iota of doubt that Will would be coming for her.

Chase was in the chair next to hers, also tied up, and he couldn't stop apologizing. When he wasn't beating up on himself, he was yelling at the two men standing guard over them.

"This is all *my* fault! Just let her go! My family has money. Why don't you hold me for ransom? I'll give you their number. Just let Merry go."

They just rolled their eyes at him. "Give it a rest, kid, or we'll put your damn gag back. It's all going to work out as long as everyone does what they're told," said one of them. The guards were tough-looking dudes in camo pants who paid a lot more attention to their cell phones than to Chase's pleas. Obviously, they were low-level operators getting their instructions from someone more important. Buckaroo?

"Save your energy," she advised Chase under her breath. "Right now there's nothing we can do."

"Do you hate me now?" A bruise on his cheekbone was turning the color of an eggplant. "I don't blame you if you do. I suck. I'm really sorry."

"Of course I don't hate you. How could you possibly know *this* would happen?" She glanced around at the suite and nearly laughed at the absurdity. "They're not going to hurt us. We're just bait."

"Do you think he'll do what they say? I bet he does. He loves you."

The confidence in his voice made Merry's heart skip. "I don't know what he'll do." She shot a glance at the guards, who were listening half-heartedly.

Chase didn't seem to notice her warning. "Will Knight seems like the kind of person who would do anything for his girlfriend."

"I'm not his..." Halfway through the sentence, Merry gave up on correcting his terminology. It didn't bother her anymore. She wanted Will to be her boyfriend, man, lover, whatever. Even thinking about him made her feel happy and safe. Even though she was tied up in a hotel suite with two bad guys and her bumbling half-brother, she felt safe because his deep voice kept running through her head—*I love you, Merry.*

She was perfectly safe because Will loved her, and Will's love was an amazing, deep, strong, powerful force of nature. With the strength of his love, he'd saved his family, stood guard over his town, and definitely, without question, won her wary heart.

Besides, he was smart and a good detective and without a

doubt he'd pick up on the clue she'd dropped. He would rescue her, she knew it. He'd rescue them both. She wouldn't let anything to happen to her sweet but clueless half-brother.

She glanced at Chase and noticed that his whole body was trembling. He kept clenching and unclenching his fists. He was probably terrified, because he didn't have the same certainty she did that Will would get them out.

"Listen, Chase. After this is over, I'm going to make you dinner. Do you like black bean chili? It's like the only thing I really know how to make. I like it extra spicy, just to warn you."

"Chili?" He swung his head to gape at her. "You're going to make me chili after I got you kidnapped?"

"Sure! This is a bonding experience. You know something, little brother? We should have gotten kidnapped together ages ago." She wrinkled her nose at him. "It'll make a great post for your Tumblr, right?"

One corner of his mouth twitched, then the other, as the famous Merriweather smile lit up his face. "You're amazing. You're really brave."

"You're pretty brave yourself, defying your parents to come out here and meet me."

"I knew it was the right thing. Definitely worth getting kidnapped."

She laughed and shifted her position so her shoulders didn't ache so much.

"Are you in pain?" Chase asked. She shook her head, since there wasn't anything he could do about it anyway.

"Do you want me to recite that poem I memorized for you? Actually, it's just one line that really made me think of you. We studied it in English Lit. It's by Langston Hughes. It goes," he cleared his throat, "'They'll see how beautiful I am, and be ashamed.' That's my father. Our father. He should be ashamed."

Tears sprang hard to Merry's eyes. She bit her lip to keep from losing it in front of her kidnappers. "That's...that's sweet, Chase.

You're a really good brother and I'm glad you stuck it out here in Jupiter Point. It's a lot more fun to be kidnapped with someone than all alone."

He grinned at her, then they both went quiet at the sound of a knock on the door. The guards jumped to attention, weapons drawn. One guard aimed the gun toward Merry and Chase, while the other came and pulled their gags back into position.

"Hotel security." That tough male voice sounded familiar. It wasn't Will's, but she'd definitely heard it before. "We've had reports of loud voices in this room. Is everything okay?"

"Sorry about that," answered one of the guards. "We'll keep it down."

"Do you mind opening up so I can have a look around?"

The guards shared a glance, looking even more alarmed.

Merry bit her tongue, desperate to call out or say something. For a mouthy person like her, this was torture. Rescue was so close, but so far. Then a soft scratching at the sliding glass door that opened onto the balcony caught her attention.

Crouched next to the door, weapon in hand, was Will. From her position, she was the only one who could see him.

His finger covered his lips in a "quiet" gesture. She nodded, glad for the gag that offered an extra guarantee.

But the door had one of those horizontal sliders that locked. She'd seen them click it into position. She shook her head slightly with a glance at the lock. He scowled at her, shaking his own head.

Trust him.

She turned her attention back to the guards, who were still arguing with the man at the door. Neither of them was looking her way. Maybe she could reach the slider with her foot.

But he'd told her not to. And this was his realm. And those guys had guns. And face it, she was a reporter, not a soldier.

And then everything happened at once.

The hotel security guy pounded on the door, yelling to be let in or he'd call the cops. The balcony door slid open and Will slipped through. Chase looked over at him, eyes popping open. For a terrifying moment, Merry thought he was going to give Will away through sheer cluelessness. But he shut his mouth and said nothing.

Will gestured to them to stay quiet as he prowled toward the door. She went still as a statue and watched with her heart in her mouth as Will padded silently across the floor.

He reached the closest guard and jammed a gun into the back of his neck. "Sheriff's department, drop your weapons."

The first guard did what Will said, but the other one didn't drop his gun. Instead he aimed it at Will—and Merry felt her heart seize in her chest.

No. Please God, no.

Time seemed to freeze as Will and the other guard faced off with each other. She flinched, expecting a bullet, a retort, an explosion.

Instead, came a crash. The door burst open, slamming the other gunman in the face. Will's two brothers stormed in, weapons drawn. Will pushed the guard he'd been holding toward Tobias, who quickly spun him out of the way. Moving so fast he was a blur, Will kicked the door out of the way and jammed the second gunman's arm against the wall. He grabbed the gun out of his hand, then yanked his arm behind his back and pulled out a set of handcuffs.

Within moments, both kidnappers were face down on the carpeted floor while Will read them their rights. "Keep an eye on them, guys," he told Tobias and Ben.

Then, finally, he turned to Merry. The fierce look in his eyes burned through her. He strode to her side and pulled off the gag, then reached behind her to cut through the zip ties. She flexed her wrists. Blood poured back through her constricted veins. It felt as if sharp needles were jabbing her. When he sliced through the ties binding her ankles, she nearly cried from the physical relief.

"Are you all right?" he asked her.

She nodded, too overcome to speak. He cupped her face in his hands and kissed her so deep and hard and true that her heart just about exploded. She surrendered to the overwhelming relief and joy of that kiss, until something tugged at her awareness, and she pulled away.

"Chase," she gasped. "Help him too."

He gave her one last lingering, scorching look, then crossed to free Chase from his bonds. "Trouble just runs in your family, doesn't it?" he asked the kid.

Chase grinned and rubbed his wrists. For a guy who'd just been kidnapped, he looked like he was having the time of his life.

AFTER WILL HAD CALLED dispatch to pick up the perps, he walked Merry out to the parking lot, where Tobias' Land Rover waited. Chase was already inside, gesturing wildly as he told the story to Tobias and Ben. Now that the adrenaline had worn off, her mind was busy putting all the pieces together.

"Did you get their cell phones? I'm pretty sure they were on the phone with Buckaroo the entire time."

Will shot her a look that somehow managed to combine affection and irritation. It felt so blessedly *normal* to see that look on his face. "You don't say."

"I'm not trying to interfere with your investigation," she added hastily. "I'm sure you know what you're doing."

"Well, yes, I did rescue you, after all."

Yes, he *had* rescued her. In so many ways she didn't know where to start. But that didn't mean she couldn't tease him like always. "That's true, but I had something to do with it too. I did provide a pretty crucial piece of information."

"Yes, you did. Very clever, the way you slid "safe" in there. I had to listen twice before I got it. Way to think on your feet. Nice cover."

She frowned and stopped walking, still several yards from the Land Rover. "Wait. Hold up. You think what I said was a cover?"

He cocked his head at her. She noticed that he had a scratch on his neck, probably from the arrest. "Last I heard, you were telling me you didn't need me."

"No. No." Unable to bear the thought that he didn't understand, she gripped his arm. "I meant every word I said on the phone. I love you. I had it all wrong that night. I mean, not completely wrong—I still want to stand on my own two feet. But I do need you. Because I love you."

His forearm tensed under her touch, his muscles bunching in reaction. "But what about everything you said about respecting yourself? I don't want to get in the way."

"You aren't. *I* was getting in the way. I can respect myself just fine *and* be with the man I love. It's all in here, see?" She tapped her chest, over her heart. "It all starts here. And you know something else? I can respect myself without that damn job. Screw Douglas. Screw the paper. I don't need them. I need myself, and I need you. I need *us*. So if I never get another job in journalism, I'm fine with that. If I'm with you, I'll be happy. Maybe I'll switch to some other profession that doesn't require irritating my favorite deputy sheriff."

"Merry..." His eyebrows drew together in a frown, his gray eyes serious. Why was he frowning? Was he about to say 'no, too late, you lose?' Out of sheer terror, she kept on talking. If she kept the words coming, he couldn't break her heart, could he?

"I thought about it, and the reason I love reporting is to speak up for people. I can do that in a lot of different ways. Police work is one way, for instance. Legal work. I could even be a teacher. Journalism just happens to be the career I chose, but now I'm choosing you, and—"

"Merry. Stop it. Don't leave journalism. You're a great reporter, and you've worked too hard to give that up."

"Oh," she whispered, looking down. She couldn't come up with anything else to say. For once in her life, she was at a complete loss for words. She'd laid her heart completely on the line. Offered to give up her profession, and Will, of all people, knew how much that meant. But he didn't want what she was offering. Maybe he didn't want *her.* Maybe she'd ruined everything with her harsh words the other night.

Will swore under his breath, then took hold of her chin and lifted her face, forcing her to meet his eyes. "What I mean is, I love you and I intend to be with you. No matter what our jobs are."

Her heart gave a thump, as if he'd just brought her back to life with emergency verbal CPR. "You do?" She blinked back the mist of tears.

"I do. I love you. You can pester me with questions for the rest of your life and I'll be happy." He blotted a stray tear that rolled onto his thumb. "And I want you to start with my father. I want to share it all with you. No more 'keep out' signs. But as as for our jobs—it's not an issue anymore. This incident is going to get me fired."

And just like that, she forgot all about her own troubles. She forgot everything except the injustice of Will—*Will*, the best deputy in town!—getting fired. "No! That's unacceptable. You rescued us, why should you get fired?"

Ben rolled down the window of the passenger seat and leaned out. "You coming, Merry?"

She barely heard him, focusing completely on Will.

"I didn't follow protocols. I got two civilians to assist in this takedown."

"But it worked. They can't fire you. I'll write an op-ed for the paper, I'll start a petition. Everyone in Jupiter Point knows you're the best."

He threw his head back and laughed. "Listen, Merry. It's not a bad thing at all. As soon as I made the decision, I felt free. Some people have been saying that I've been in a rut."

"Total rut," called Ben. "Good thing you showed up to kick him in the ass."

"He's right," said Will. "Chasing you around is practically a full-time job all on its own. Besides, I have some other things I want to do, and we should talk about them, but not now. I need to get our suspects booked."

She sighed, realizing that the moment for privacy was gone. She rose on tiptoe to kiss him, a sweet, intimate touch that promised heat and passion and devotion. "You know, I just realized something. I always say I want to take care of myself. But today I had three Knights come to my rescue. And I'm not complaining one bit."

Will wrapped his arms around her and lifted her up, so she gazed down into his stern, smiling face. "You're forgetting the fact that you told us where to find you. I wouldn't exactly call you a damsel in distress. More like a damsel in command."

She smiled joyfully down at him. "I'll stick with 'damsel in love.'"

30

WILL DIDN'T GET FIRED; HE RESIGNED. HE DIDN'T WANT TO CREATE a publicity problem for Sheriff Perez, who came back from his honeymoon to a big, complicated mess. The DEA was upset, his own department was upset, and Cindy...Cindy was missing.

Will blamed himself for that.

"I should have seen it," he told Perez. "I went through everyone's background in detail except for hers. If I had, maybe I would have seen the problem."

The sheriff, whose tropical honeymoon glow was quickly fading, scratched his tanned face. "I never saw it coming either. Cindy Tran, Jesus. She's a star employee. We need to find her and get her into custody."

"I don't think it's her fault. I dug a little deeper and found out her family owes Buckaroo money. He probably made her do it in exchange for not calling in the loan."

"Maybe. We won't know unless we find her." Perez longingly eyed the tin of Altoids on his desk. "And now that you're leaving, how's that supposed to happen?"

"I have a suggestion about that, as a matter of fact. Did you know that Jupiter Point doesn't have a single private investigator?"

Perez stared at him, then gave in and grabbed his Altoids. "You have got to be kidding me."

"Nope. I need some free time to pursue a few things. Family stuff."

Perez looked at him as he turned the tin over in his hands. "Your father. The Robert Knight case."

Will had never discussed the topic of his father with the sheriff. It felt strange, but he'd better get used to it. If he was going to start down this path, he'd have to talk about it a lot.

"Yes. In fact, I was hoping that I could take a look at the files once again, while I'm still employed here."

"Sure, but I have one stipulation."

"What's that?"

"Don't do anything stupid or reckless. If you find something, come to me or to Chief Becker. Let us handle it."

Will nodded slowly. He'd done his lone wolf act for Merry's sake. But when it came down to it, he was a law-and-order guy, not some vigilante. "I can live with that. As for Cindy, I'd like to take on that case, no pay necessary. I feel responsible. And I'm worried about her. If she's on the run from Buckaroo, she won't last long. If she's under his control, same thing. Are you okay with that?"

Perez rolled a mint between his fingers. "Do you know how nice it was to just lie on a tropical beach for two weeks with no decisions to make? Nothing except blended or on the rocks? Dancing before dinner or after? Who's turn is it to be on to—"

"Okay, I get the point," Will interrupted hurriedly. "I'll make the decision for you. Let me find Cindy, no charge, and you handle everything once I locate her. Deal?"

"Deal."

They shook hands on it, then Will got to his feet. "One more thing. All this vacation and tropical-island shit—can you tell me a little more about that?"

31

A FEW DAYS LATER, WILL LAY WITH MERRY ON A WOVEN STRAW beach mat. His hand rested on her left thigh, while her left foot rubbed against his. Their dip in the ocean had covered their skin with salt, which was now being baked in by the sun. He kept wiggling around trying to get the most comfortable position for his ass. But every time he shifted, he hit a stone or a seashell or God knew what. He stared up at the sky. Even though he wore sunglasses, it seemed too damn bright.

Beach vacations sucked.

But he refused to utter a word of complaint, because no doubt Merry was loving this. This was their first getaway together. Their first vacation. And the fact that Merry was at his side made up for all the discomfort.

He had no idea why people raved about this beach thing. But he'd lie here in this roasting oven, on this bed of sand, sticky and salty, as long as Merry wanted him to.

"Having fun?" he asked, turning his head toward her. She too wore sunglasses, along with a white head scarf to keep the sand out of her hair. The seaside sun added a rosy depth to the bronze of her skin. She looked glorious and insanely sexy in her tiny orange bikini.

So there was that.

"It's so pretty here," she said in response. "And we have the whole beach to ourselves."

He noticed that she hadn't exactly answered the question. "We can go in the water again."

"No, that's okay," she said quickly. "My hair's had enough salt for one day."

"More ice tea?"

"Sure."

He opened the cooler with one hand and fished out a cold bottle of lemony ice tea. He screwed off the top and handed it to her. "Beachside cabana boy, at your service. Tips accepted."

"In kiss form?"

"Won't argue."

She kissed his shoulder, then his biceps. Her soft lips pressed against his flesh, and just like that, he felt complete. "Any news about the arraignment?" she murmured.

"I thought we weren't going to talk about work out here."

"Right. But this isn't about work so much as about public safety. Those two jerks do work for a convicted drug lord, after all."

"Last I heard, they're singing like birds and things aren't looking good for old Buckaroo."

Merry rolled back onto her side of the mat. "Well isn't that a shame. Chase is writing about it on his Tumblr, too. He picked the wrong intern to kidnap."

"Oh yeah, real tough guy," said Will dryly.

"In his own way, he is. I have to give him credit. Oh, did I tell you my mother's headed back to the States next month? She's coming to Jupiter Point to meet you. She calls you the man who 'captured my heart'."

"I pursued it long enough. It was just a matter of time before I captured it." He brushed a kiss onto her lips, and they took a moment to revel in the bone-deep knowledge of how much they loved each other.

She pulled away to flick a sand flea off her stomach. "What's with all the bugs out here? Is that normal?"

"Probably. We're outdoors, and that's kind of their territory."

"I'm not complaining," she added hastily. "This is great. Vacation. Wow. No wonder people are always raving about vacations."

"Right." He peered at her, but couldn't read her expression behind her dark sunglasses. "Have you decided what to do about the offer from the *Gazette*?"

"I thought we weren't talking about work out here?" She nudged his leg with her toe.

"It's not really a question about work," he countered. "It's about your future. Your passion. Your dreams. Those things all matter to me. I want you to be happy."

"I am happy. I'm with you, and that makes me happy. But you're right, I do have my dreams, and running a new investigative unit at the *Gazette* would be awesome. First, I'd wrap up the Buckaroo story. That should never have been shelved. Next, I'd do your family's story the way it ought to be done. After that, there's this story about pesticides that—"

"So you're going to take it?" he asked, amused.

"Maybe I ought to take it. With a job like that, I can really make things happen. I can choose which stories we follow. I can shake things up. Put our newspaper on the map. A few great investigative pieces, and we could really get some attention. The downside is having to work with Douglas, but I can't let that stop me. The board ordered him to hire me back, so he probably won't mess with me again."

"Congratulations, I'm really proud of you. You're going to do great."

"Well, I haven't decided yet. I told Douglas he'd have to wait until the end of our vacation. Vacation comes first. We both deserve one. Work can wait."

"Uh-huh." He knew his Merry, and her decision had been made. Most likely, she'd made it as soon as Douglas had made the offer. A little crab crawled across his foot. He shook it off. "The local wildlife sure is happy to have us here."

"Yup." She pointed at a seagull flying past. "I swear that same bird has been cruising around up there, just waiting for a chance to peck us."

"It's a seagull, and of course it's not the *same* seagull," he scoffed. "There are tons of them out here."

"Whatever. I don't trust any of them." She lifted her sunglasses to stare balefully up at the soaring bird.

He laughed, finding her delightful as always. He loved her in all her moods, including bird-phobic. As long as none of her moods involved kicking him to the curb again, he could handle them. And since she'd accepted an engagement ring and his second wedding proposal—made on this very beach just an hour ago—he had high hopes that wouldn't happen.

"Speaking of circling vultures..." she said.

He laughed again. He couldn't help it, she just amused him without even trying.

"Have you guys figured out what to do about Aiden?"

Just yesterday, they'd gotten a group email from Aiden. In it, he'd announced that he intended to leave college at the end of the semester. He'd made a vague reference to not going back to Evergreen, but maybe attending classes at the Jupiter Point Community College to finish his degree.

However, he also said that he'd have to fit classes in between pursuing the love of his life, a woman who had burst into his life like a golden Goddess riding a sun chariot.

His exact words.

Oh, and he also wanted access to his share of the life insurance money they kept in trust for him. To say that the other Knight brothers were alarmed would be the understatement of all time.

"Tobias is going to handle it. He's going to head out to Evergreen and find out what's going on. I have too much happening, between finding Cindy and finding Mom and Cassie, and maybe solving my dad's murder, not to mention lavishing love and attention on my woman." He rested a hand on her stomach, so warm from the sun.

"Your *fiancée*."

"Yes, that's the one. My StarLady."

"Oh no. Not going with StarLady. Not happening." She sighed and arched under his caress. "No matter how much I love your hands."

"AnonyMissus?" he asked hopefully.

She laughed, that wholehearted, wonderful laugh that always made his heart burst with joy. "We might have a problem here. Merry Knight's a little awkward too. I don't know, Will. This getting-married thing is going to be complicated."

"No, it isn't," he said firmly. "I love you and you love me and we're together and that's that."

"Yes, officer."

She slid her hand across his swimming briefs to where his erection bulged, already aroused by the mere thought of them together. He closed his eyes, awaiting her touch.

Instead, she shrieked. "What *is* that?"

He sat up to see what she was talking about. A bit of seaweed had gotten tucked into the waistband of his shorts. "It's nothing. Just seaweed."

"It slimed me."

He couldn't help it; he laughed. "Are you sure you're enjoying this whole beach experience?"

"Hell no! Sorry. I mean, I love being with you. But I'd enjoy it a lot more at home. In bed. With my laptop nearby. And no ban on talking about work. But that's okay, I'm fine staying out here. I can ignore the bugs and slime and all that. I want you to have fun. You need this vacation."

"All I need is you. I can skip the crab bites and sunburn. I'm calling it, let's go home."

With an expression of tremendous relief, she clambered to her feet and brushed sand off her sexy legs. "How long will it take Ben to come get us?"

"About ten minutes. He's all fueled up and ready. I just have to radio him." He got to his feet and hunted for the handheld radio Ben had left with them when he dropped them off in the chopper.

"I'm glad I got to see one of these islands out here." Merry tossed their snacks and sunscreen into the tote they'd brought. "Good material for an article. And the best thing about it?"

"It's five miles from Jupiter Point?" he asked dryly, already knowing the answer.

"Yup. But you know what, we had our vacation, we got engaged, I made my decision, we swam and sunbathed and cheated death by seagull. I think I'm good." Then she paused, cocking her head at him. "Except for one thing."

He stopped rolling up the beach mat as he caught her expression, with that special glint in her eye. The one that fired up his lust for her every single time. "What's that brilliant mind of yours thinking now?"

"That I've always wanted to have sex on a deserted island. I had a very explicit dream about it once. In fact, you were part of that dream. So I'm thinking, let's hold off on that radio call just a little while longer." She dropped the tote bag and stepped onto the beach mat, where she pressed her bikini-clad body against him.

Instant, glorious heat roared to life between them. It was always there. All it took was one or the other of them blowing on the flames. With words, a look, a touch, a text message, an email, a call, it didn't matter.

"I do love the way you think," he told her as his arms went around her, and hers around him. And that was right where they belonged.

ABOUT THE AUTHOR

Jennifer Bernard is a USA Today bestselling author of contemporary romance. Her books have been called "an irresistible reading experience" full of "quick wit and sizzling love scenes." A graduate of Harvard and former news promo producer, she left big city life in Los Angeles for true love in Alaska, where she now lives with her husband and stepdaughters. She still hasn't adjusted to the cold, so most often she can be found cuddling with her laptop and a cup of tea. No stranger to book success, she also writes erotic novellas under a naughty secret name that she's happy to share with the curious. You can learn more about Jennifer and her books, and sign up for her newsletter, at JenniferBernard.net.

Connect with Jennifer online:

JenniferBernard.net
Jen@JenniferBernard.net

ALSO BY JENNIFER BERNARD

Jupiter Point Series

Set the Night on Fire ~ Book 1

Burn So Bright ~ Book 2

Into the Flames ~ Book 3

Setting Off Sparks ~ Book 4

Seeing Stars

(Prequel and Hope Falls Kindle World Novella)

The Bachelor Firemen of San Gabriel

The Fireman Who Loved Me

Hot for Fireman

Sex and the Single Fireman

How to Tame a Wild Fireman

Four Weddings and a Fireman

The Night Belongs to Fireman

Novellas

One Fine Fireman

Desperately Seeking Fireman

It's a Wonderful Fireman

Love Between the Bases

All of Me

Caught By You

Getting Wound Up (crossover with Sapphire Falls)

Drive You Wild

Crushing It

Double Play

Made in the USA
San Bernardino, CA
04 September 2017